THE SILVER BRANCH

DAYLE CARNAHAN MCKINNEY

Text and images copyright © 2019 Dayle Carnahan McKinney.

All rights reserved. No part of this book may be used or reproduced by any means, graphic, electronic, or mechanical, including photocopying, recording, taping or by any information storage retrieval system without the written permission of the author except in the case of brief quotations embodied in critical articles and reviews.

Scripture quotations marked (NIV) are taken from the Holy Bible, New International Version®, NIV®. Copyright © 1973, 1978, 1984, 2011 by Biblica, Inc.™ Used by permission of Zondervan. All rights reserved worldwide. www.zondervan.com The "NIV" and "New International Version" are trademarks registered in the United States Patent and Trademark Office by Biblica, Inc.™

This is a work of fiction. All of the characters, names, incidents, organizations, and dialogue in this novel are either the products of the author's imagination or are used fictitiously.

Archway Publishing books may be ordered through booksellers or by contacting:

Archway Publishing
1663 Liberty Drive
Bloomington, IN 47403
www.archwaypublishing.com
1 (888) 242-5904

Because of the dynamic nature of the Internet, any web addresses or links contained in this book may have changed since publication and may no longer be valid. The views expressed in this work are solely those of the author and do not necessarily reflect the views of the publisher, and the publisher hereby disclaims any responsibility for them.

Any people depicted in stock imagery provided by Getty Images are models, and such images are being used for illustrative purposes only. Certain stock imagery © Getty Images.

ISBN: 978-1-4808-7454-1 (sc)
ISBN: 978-1-4808-7456-5 (hc)
ISBN: 978-1-4808-7455-8 (e)

Library of Congress Control Number: 2019901571

Print information available on the last page.

Archway Publishing rev. date: 2/20/2019

Long life to Henry
And may this song ne'er cease!
God grant his children
And his children's children peace,
Till some man comes taking
The moon between his teeth!

French Nursery Rhyme

"Apart from technological advancements and
creature comforts, mankind's true evolution
is a spiritual one, entailing the realization
of who he is and where he came from."

Dr. Susan Martinez

If you are a descendant of:

Poker Bill Armstrong & Lizzie Ebright
or
Joe Carnahan & Amanda "Matt" Young
or
John Whitcanack & Della Doan
or
Oliver McKinney & Rose McEuen

This book is for you!

INTRODUCTION

MY SISTER, SUSAN, and my brother, Shawn, are the characters of Ma Suit and Hazno in the story you are about to read. Susan has grandchildren who call her Ma Suit and Shawn uses Hazno Dinero to sign his remarkable paintings. My brother is a comic much like our father, Brownie. My name in the story is Aria because the fairies who live in the cottonwood forest at the edge of my property told my seer friend, Jim Landers, that I am an aria like in the opera. I had to look it up because Jim and I didn't know what it meant. It said it is an elaborate melody for a single voice. All the other people in the story are referred to by their real names except for my husband, Don, who come to think of it, really is Little Prince Emery!

My dear friend, Tim Hicks, has labeled his wife, Kimi, and I as Cuckoo For Coco Puffs. This particular story will only verify that overarching observation. Yet, it is as a proud card-carrying member of the Cuckoo For Coco Puffs Society (CCPS) that I present this story anyway!

I do not claim to be an author nor do I have any inclination to pursue such an endeavor ever again. My hat is off to all writers of all times now having walked in their moccasins. But I am, as my friend Kimi pointed out, a storyteller and I found a doozy of one to tell when all I was doing was looking up my genealogy. The book presented itself as the only way to record the story while simultaneously unweaving for posterity an amazingly tight knit family tree and at the same time postulating an answer to the age old question of Who Am I and Where Did I Come From?

Twelve percent of Americans think that Noah was married to Joan of Arc. So if this information is not quite perfect, and believe me it can't be, at least I took a stab at eliminating a contrived history, like that of Noah and Joan, in my own family tree. Pretty much all of the information contained in this book can be read for free on the internet. Is it crazy information? You betcha! That's what makes it fun! Is it true? You be the judge.

The story shows up in the dates. Or rather in the lack of them when I threw them all out. In order to tell the story I was attempting to follow six separate genealogical lines back through history so as to put them all into historical context. My observations were non-sensical much of the time. I made scrolls but they didn't match up. The further history receded, the more incomprehensible history itself became when viewed from genealogical records. Then I read about a Mayan woman in Mexico who referred to her ancestors according to the number of generations away from her, so that her great-great grandmother would be the third in a continuous line of grandparents who she then called her third-ago grandmother.

I went back to the scroll, erased all the dates and plugged in generation-ago numbers instead. Voila!, it worked. Grandfathers on my mother's side who had married grandmothers on my dad's (this happens a lot!) ended up on a correct or plausibly correct generation number. A generation averaging thirty-three years to child bearing age gives a one hundred year timespan every three generations so that one thousand years ago my 33rd ago grandparents were alive and walking the earth. And two thousand years ago my 66th ago grandparents would have been alive and walking the earth. And we all know what happened then!

The seed of the idea for this story developed out of my utter surprise to discover not only who my ancestors turned out to be, but stranger still, just exactly when they lived and walked the earth.

The truth hurts.

A Basque proverb

PROLOGUE

The Dream of the Green Diamond

I'M SITTING IN a plane on the tarmac in Shannon, Ireland, waiting to take off for the trip home to California. My heart is racing wildly and my palms are sweating. I'm convinced that everyone on this plane is airport security and watching my every move. I had been approached by an impossibly short man while standing in the bottleneck waiting to pass through the security gate. He shoved something into my hand while I was bent over attaching the luggage tag to my carry-on. He whispered cryptic instructions before disappearing underneath the crowd. My first instruction was to protect the item with my very life, if need be. Under no circumstances was I to allow it to fall into the hands of the authority types who would gladly kill to take it away from me. What I see when I open my hand is a large gleaming green diamond. I probably would have thrown it on the ground to be rid of it but I am more frightened by the strange little man who gave it to me (I think he may be a fairy) than I am of the authority types I am about to pass through. I place the gem in my bra, near my heart and have no idea how I make it past the security people with their x-ray machines. Now I think that getting off the plane in Palm Springs will be more difficult and dangerous so I am anticipating a long terror-filled ride home with the fairy man's final words echoing repeatedly in my fear pounding, panic struck, confused mind… "Find this!"

CHAPTER ONE

"We're all pilgrims on the same journey - but some pilgrims have better road maps."

Nelson DeMille

ONCE UPON A time the queen of Elphame fell asleep and woke up in a world where she had no memory of who she was. She was born with a shock of white hair and her parents named her Aria.

Aria grew up and grew old. Not real old, but getting there. Her blond hair was sprinkled with grey and she didn't climb stairs as fast as she used to. Her life was hard in the way that all lives are hard. And her life was good in the way that all lives are good. What Aria did possess that most others did not was an Eden in which to live.

Aria's Eden was in the same desert where she was born. Desert Edens provide an abundance of fresh air which was a good thing since Aria needed fresh air like some people need city life. Her windows and doors remained open throughout most of the seasons. The five acres of her Eden adjoined an ancient cottonwood grove to which Aria and her dogs started and ended each day. They walked in cold weather. They walked in hot weather. They walked in blast-furnace weather and never tired of it. Aria's small slice of Nature had taught her heart to sing. A singing heart, she learned, could almost drown out the moans of sorrow. And what life is without sorrow?

The trees of the grove and the trees of her five acres were filled with birds. Aria loved the birds. She tossed seed to them each morning after the walk. It was a pastime she had inherited from her grandmother, Irma. The bevy of quail that lived beneath the roots of the desert willow in her yard bore testament to her feeding as they waddled out, fat and happy, to partake of each mornings generous portion.

The birds and the dogs and the walks to the cottonwoods were all a part of Aria's ordinary life. The world outside her Eden was fraught with deceptions, intrigues, and alarming revelations. Far from ordinary, the world often presented itself as dark and growing mysteriously darker. She often pondered why that should be. Why shouldn't the world at large be as kind and ordinary as her Eden? Yet her pondering leaned in the opposite direction as well. Why was her Eden so ordinary? Why, in fact, was Aria so very ordinary? She was neither rich nor famous. She hadn't painted a Mona Lisa or written a symphony or found the cure for cancer. She never started a corporation or wrote a book or even climbed to the top of any mountain. She was just ordinary Aria and she knew that something was missing. She just didn't know what it was and she had become doubtful of ever discovering it. So she fed the birds in the hopes that her singing heart would also drown out her longing.

Then something changed. Something small but tinged with magic. One particular morning something extraordinary crossed the boundary line of ordinary. When the bevy of quail surfaced for their morning repast, one among them was paper white. As plump as his nest mates, Aria watched in stunned disbelief as, white top knot bobbing, he pecked at the seeds she had spread atop the sand. She stood transfixed by the sight of how wonderfully extraordinary he was. Then the phone rang. Aria was being invited by her sister, Ma Suit, to accompany her to the Emerald Isle, to Magical, Mystical Ireland. Now Aria pondered the synchronicity of the Phone Call of Joy with the appearance of the paper white quail. It certainly felt like magic. Unaccustomed to magic, Aria decided that she might just encounter it on their journey in Ireland as well. And since she expected it, it arrived.

Aria and Ma Suit traveled through Ireland with a bevy of women and a learned guide in a paper white coach. At night they dined and slept in castles. If Aria had any problems, and who doesn't?, she forgot all about them. The forgetting, in itself, was a form of magic.

One afternoon, a woman in their group asked of the guide of the coach for a clarification. His response would rock Aria's world.

"What is the difference", the woman asked, "between a Shanty Irishman and a Lace Curtain Irishman?"

"A Shanty Irishman is ordinary and will always be ordinary. A Lace Curtain Irishman is also ordinary but has no plans to stay that way", he replied.

In that moment, Aria realized that she was of the lace curtain variety and her life found new purpose. Later, when Ma Suit questioned her as to what memory gift she would want to take home from Ireland, her reply was immediate. "Irish lace curtains."

The same tour guide who had set Aria on her new course in life was also either thoughtful enough, or perhaps trained, to point out to the women in his charge just which of the trees they passed by on the coach were the famous Fairy Trees of Ireland.

However, it was near the village of Cong that Aria and Ma Suit accidentally found an undiscovered one of their own.

They would be sleeping in their last castle on the last day of their tour, the Castle of Spirits on the Lake of the Man of the Sea. Ignoring the warning of a young woman among them that the castle forest she had just ridden through on horseback was enchanted and perhaps best to be avoided lest the way back become lost, Aria and Ma Suit walked into the woods anyway. Confident in the map they had been issued by the castle staff and the suit of God's armor that Ma Suit wore so humbly, they traipsed unafraid into the Irish woods. And got lost.

Or at least, ridiculously turned around. For instead of the clearly marked path leading to the village of Cong, they found themselves at the garbage dump for the Castle of Spirits. An employee with a forklift was adding to a small mountain of empty liquor bottles glistening in the setting sun. And there it was, the Fairy Tree, just beyond the small glass mountain. It stood out from the ordinary trees around it. So much so that Aria and Ma Suit left the path altogether and walked into the forest to stand in its beauty. It was in this close vicinity that they were able to see the fairy door near its earthen roots. The door was really just a hole in the tree as can be found in many trees. But over the top of the small hole, growing from the tree itself, was a shingled awning. Attached to the tiny awning with proportionately tiny nails was a blue curtain, its laced raw edge torn, not sewn.

Aria was shocked again that magic was showing up in her life. It only served to confuse her since magic did not happen to ordinary people. She had privately resolved to move her way out of ordinariness and use a sigil of a lace curtain to empower her quest. Days later, that very sigil is found hanging from an awning that shouldn't exist in a tree she never should have seen. Even Ma Suit did not know of Aria's inward resolve to leave ordinary behind. But somebody did. Was she being watched?

That last night in the castle Aria dreamed the dream of the Green Diamond.

More years passed. Aria forgot all about the dream. Even the curtain in the Fairy Tree seemed more like a tale oft told but perhaps not completely true. A paper white quail never again found its way to Aria's morning feast. Aria didn't feel compelled to look for magic anymore, resignedly content in the allotment given to her. The little ones in Aria's life were not so jaded. They loved her tales of the paper white quail and the Fairy Tree. One week each year, nephews, grandchildren, little friends, and neighbors pilgrimed to her camp of comfort that she had created for them in her Eden. Her fairy tree story had added a new dimension to camp life. To the old standards of puppet theater productions and scavenger hunts in which to find the same raw potato hundreds of times in a row, new activities arose. Fairy forts had to be built and very wee pancakes had to be cooked daily and left on flat stones by the little doors. Powdered sugar trails throughout the yard had to be monitored for signs of fairy footprints. Little eyes staid open long into the night in hopes of sightings and visitations.

During this one week each year the world operated in homeostasis if only on Aria's five acre Eden. For the other fifty-one weeks the world still seemed to be going to hell in a hand-basket. The cares of the world only seemed to grow heavier with the passing of time. Aria bore it all with as much grace as she could muster but still she wondered constantly at the absurdity of a world that functioned so effortlessly in the negative. She knew that she would never understand any of it and she became okay with that. She figured, due to the magic of the paper white quail and the blue curtain, that she might be a little bit north of ordinary now and she was grateful enough for that small blessing. And since she no longer expected magic, it arrived.

It manifested as falling stars.

Aria had just completed another pretty ordinary day. The sun had gone down and the stars were coming out. She made herself a cup of Constant Comment cinnamon tea like her grandmother used to drink and a slice of her neighbor's homemade dill toast with apple cactus jelly and carried them upstairs to her glass tower room built for her by the lord mayor of her Eden, Little Prince Emery. Or so his siblings called him. He wore the name with pride and built a castle out of cast offs and discards. The glass tower room was his crowning achievement.

The staircase was dark as she climbed to the top but the glass tower room was ablaze with light. When she saw what was causing such brilliance she dropped the toast and spilled the tea. Every star in the sky was falling. It resembled a rain of sparklers. She ran out onto the tower balcony to get a better look and nearly collapsed at the the beauty of it. Only a sight so extraordinary could distract Aria to such a degree that she missed seeing the woman seated on her balcony puffing on a little white pipe.

"It's my favorite memory", the woman said as she rose to her feet. "I thought I would share it with you. It happens in 1833 and is called The Night the Stars Fell."

Then Aria screamed. She hadn't wanted to and was embarrassed that she had but the surprise was too much. The scream was involuntary.

"Na biodh eagla ort", the pretty little woman said.

"That's not English. Now you're not speaking English", Aria rattled in her agitation. "Where are you from and what are you doing on my balcony uninvited?"

"I said to you 'be not afraid' in Gaelic. My name is Mariah Morris and I am the grandmother of your grandfather."

"Any grandmother of my grandfather would be dead by now. You don't look dead so your claim is ridiculous." The light show going on over Aria's head had her feeling way less confident in her own opinion but still it made sense.

Mariah stared silently at the celestial display for a few moments to allow Aria a chance to adjust to the high strangeness that had suddenly entered her ordinary life. "Your perception of what is possible is limited by your beliefs. Are you not the granddaughter of a farmer by the name of John Whitcanack in Cantril, Iowa?"

"That is the name of my grandfather", Aria admitted intrigued.

"John is my grandson."

"Why is this happening to me?", Aria demanded to know.

Mariah blew out a puff of aromatic pipe smoke before answering. "You have strange blood. Strange blood is watched. In watching, it was discovered that you have questions. If you are interested in learning the answers your time has arrived."

"Oh my God!", Aria exclaimed, "you're an angel and I'm about to die, aren't I?"

"I said that your blood was strange, not sick, so no, you are not about to die."

"Then if you are speaking the truth, what are my questions?"

"That is the first one. Shall we continue?"

"Are you serious?", Aria began to whine, "I have no idea what questions I am seeking the answers to. Can't you give me a clue?"

"I will give you your family history as it flows through me and your grandfather, John, as my reply. And I shall do that by telling you about the brother of my grandfather, my great uncle, Robert Morris. Uncle Robert is no ordinary man. He is one among a number of men working to forge a fledgling nation and becomes a signer of the Declaration of Independence. You'll find his signature right next to that of Mr. Hancock. Our Uncle Robert, you see, is a very wealthy man. He bankrolls the Revolutionary War which makes George Washington so grateful that he appoints him as Treasurer of the United States. Uncle Robert turns down the position and offers it instead to Alexander Hamilton. Although Uncle Robert declines the appointment he still uses his own money along with a loan from France to fund the country's first bank. Later in life, Uncle Robert is placed into debtor's prison and eventually he dies a pauper. Seemingly obvious injustices like that which befall Uncle Robert confound you and disturb your peace of mind. You would like to know why people don't just do what they ought to do which is simply the right thing. I am asking you now if you would like to go where you can discover the answer to this."

"Go?" Aria gasped in alarm, "Go where?"

"To the Beginning of Things."

"Do you expect me to travel to a place where time began? I don't think so. I'm not sure I'm even all that interested in these answers. I mean, I can live without them. Besides, I don't think you can even get there from here." Aria laughed in a nervous sort of way that held no mirth whatsoever.

"You'd be surprised where you can get to from here. But you will have no need to travel any further back than to the Beginning of Things. I speak of things as they are in your reality. You may accept or decline this offer as you wish. However if you decline, it is highly improbable that the opportunity will ever be made available to you again."

Aria knew that she would be declining but she didn't quite know how to say it. "I think I may be too afraid to go", she finally admitted.

"That is expected. All I can say is that as your grandmother it is not my desire to put you at risk or place you in jeopardy. Yet, I also cannot promise complete safety as all adventures imply the possibility of danger. Fear is an old friend that keeps you near hearth and home. This friend, however, will never be able to answer your questions."

"Would you be coming along with me?" Aria was feeling the first chink in her armor.

"I'm entrusted with guiding you to the place where your passport is being kept. You cannot make the journey without it."

"How long a journey will it be?"

"It lasts until you arrive."

"You're not going to tell me, are you?"

"I can't. I've never made the journey and I've never known of anyone who has."

"Is that statement supposed to be reassuring? If you came here to talk me into this then you may have just failed. Was this all your idea or did someone send you?"

"The Council."

"What council?", Aria fired back.

"The one appointed by the Watchers."

"And just why should I trust them to care what happens to me?"

"Because they are your grandparents too."

Aria looked up at the spectacle happening in the sky and wondered what to do. She really was too afraid to go but she had always perceived herself as brave and now she was being told that she was being watched as well. Whoever was watching would know whether she was truly brave or not by her thoughts. But what about her actions? If you were afraid but acted brave anyway did that count as actually being brave? So swallowing down the bile she felt rising in her throat, Aria did what she didn't know she was capable of doing and accepted the adventure to go to the Beginning of Things.

Mariah wasted no time. She reached out with her free hand and pulled back the fabric of reality. The star filled sky pulled back like a curtain on a stage revealing an altogether different reality behind it. For there, steps away from the balcony, was the cozy warmth of a private library. Non-falling stars could be seen through its frosted windows. Wonderful old leather bound books lined its shelves and small flames danced in a fireplace beneath. Five people turned in their seats to watch as the two women entered.

Standing now amidst these strangers, Aria could not remember having stepped off her balcony into this room, but the door had closed and her Eden was no longer in sight. Mariah began the introductions before they even sat down.

"These five people and myself as well", Mariah began, "are all from the same approximate time in history. We are all your third-ago grandparents, meaning three generations back from you. As I told you already I am the grandmother of your grandfather, John Whitcanack. Mr. Joseph Doan here is the grandfather of John's wife, your grandmother, Della Doan. Joseph and I are on your mother's side of the family. Ancestors on your father's side are May Brookfield, grandmother of your grandmother, Irma Armstrong. Nancy Sublett, grandmother of your grandfather, Edwin Carnahan and her husband, Newt Young, also Edwin's grandfather. The last gentleman is not your grandfather at all. He is Wilson McEuen and the grandfather of your Emery's grandmother, Rose McEuen. Mr. McEuen is here for two very important reasons, the first being humility. The story that will unfold like a flower before you is not for you and yours alone. The second reason is even more important than the first. You need the passport to travel to where you are going and it has been passed to the ancestors of Emery's clan so is therefore Mr. McEuen's to give or to withhold.

Aria stood staring at the collection of people in the room. There was little doubt that these people were related to her. She recognized her grandmother Irma's face in that of May Brookfield, saw her dad and her brother in Newt Young, and her mother in Mariah. The resemblance between Mr. McEuen and her Emery was uncanny. She shook hands all around and then she and Mariah took seats with them near the comforting fire where Mariah continued as the spokesperson for the group.

"We are chosen by the Council to acquaint you with your American ancestors. Since you are not native American, but rather of European descent, your American heritage does not go back very far in history. However, we will be the starting point for our individual genealogical lines and a reference point for you as you meet our ancestors. The

Council has asked, for this reason, that you think of me as Mariah of the Masons."

"Why?"

"Because I related to you the story of our early ancestor, Uncle Robert Morris, who signs the Declaration of Independence and a large percentage of the signers are Masons."

"Did you know that my dad, my Grandpa Ed, my Uncle Dale, and my cousin, Paula, are all members of the Masonic Order?"

"We do know that. These affiliations are not unexpected by us. Even your grandfather, Newt, is a member of the Odd Fellows, another similar organization. Before you hear the accounts of your American parentage let us replace the toast and tea you were planning to enjoy which is now splayed across your tower room floor."

As if on cue a young man introduced as John entered the library pushing a cart loaded down with an elaborate silver tea set and delicate bone china cups. Warm rolls and muffins filled napkin lined baskets and there were honey pots in three different shades. Aria was surprised that once John the server had completed his task of pouring the tea and passing out the rolls, Mariah insisted that he remain in the library and partake of the tea and orations as well. It seemed to Aria that this was a bit of an intrusion on what sounded like a personal trek through her family history making it feel like a violation and she wished he wasn't there. Uh oh. Humility was one of her lessons and she had failed it right off the bat.

Joseph Doan was the first one to set down his napkin and tell his tale. "Our first well known relative in America is Stephen Hopkins, an adventurer who sails to Jamestown, Virginia in 1609 on the flagship of the London Company called the Sea Venture. Well, the Sea Venture runs afoul and leaves all on board shipwrecked on an island for longer than they want to be there. Mr. Hopkins, who is your eleventh-ago grandfather, convinces the disgruntled crew that it will be better to return to England from whence they had come than to continue on to the colony. But our grandfather is not the captain and the captain is not too pleased when, against his command, return to England they did. He promptly has Grandfather arrested for mutiny. It's quite a famous story and there is even an account of it under the Shakespeare name called The Tempest. Grandfather is Stephano in the story. But Grandfather's arrest for his insubordination is not the end of my tale because before long he is exonerated and heads once again on a ship to America, this one belonging to the New England Company. And this time he has his family with him, a second wife who is pregnant, a teenage daughter, a young son, and even a couple of servant boys who will be given the right, over time, to work off their passage in exchange for the opportunity. Well, wouldn't you know it, that little ship runs into bad weather as well and pushes it off course turning their four week journey into ten. Stephen's newest son, Oceanus, ends up being born at sea."

"What was the name of that ship?"

"The Mayflower."

"What? I had a relative on the Mayflower?"

"Four of them actually. Stephen's daughter, Constance, is also your grandparent and her brothers, Giles, and little Oceanus are your uncles."

"Then that means", Aria said dumbstruck, "that I had two grandparents that lived in Plymouth, Massachussetts!"

"More than that", he added. "It is called Plimouth Plantation then and you probably have a dozen or more grandparents who live there."

"How could there be that many?"

"Marriage. It's a small community. Your grandmother, Constance, from the Mayflower, marries and gives birth in Plimouth to a daughter, also Constance, who grows up and marries another Plimouth born native, Daniel Doan, son of Deacon John Doan, who is our first American ancestor on the Doan line."

"So my grandparents were Pilgrims!", Aria commented in awe.

"Stephen Hopkins is no Pilgrim. The Pilgrims hire the Mayflower to take them to Jamestown. Grandfather is hired by the New England Company to work on their behalf for the Pilgrims. Drifting off course at the wrong time of year leaves them no alternative but to establish a colony where they land. Grandfather works in the colony as a scout and develops a friendship with Squanto and the native Indian community. But he is also an adventurer and is looking to make money so he opens Plimouth's first pub and is known to sell nutmeg at exorbitant prices. The Pilgrim community in the plantation insist that the pub be closed on Sundays so Grandfather simply invites all those in search of a drink over to his house when the tavern is closed. No indeed, Stephen Hopkins is not a Pilgrim."

"But you said that Mr. Doan was a deacon, so he must have been a Pilgrim."

"John Doan does not arrive with the Pilgrims in 1620. Grandfather John arrives in 1630 when he sails over with the first five ships of the Winthrop Fleet. He lists his occupation as tailor but prior to arriving in Massachusetts he is in business with John Shirley who is the London goldsmith serving as the treasurer for the New England Company."

"So then Mr. Doan's children and Mr. Hopkins' children marry each other and I end up with a dozen grandparents in Plimouth?"

"John Doan's sister, Anne, also migrates to the colony and she marries William Twining. Their granddaughter, Mehitible, marries the son of Daniel and Constance Doan."

"I think I see how this goes", Aria commented reluctantly. She contemplated all the health weaknesses in her family and wondered if they originated in Plimouth Plantation.

"It has been suggested", Joseph concluded, "that you remember me as Joseph of the New England Company."

"These are your historic roots on your mother's side of the family", Mariah clarified, "now let us move on to your father's side and begin with Nancy Ann Sublett Young."

"I want to say right in the beginning that I asked if you could remember me as Nancy Ann of the Furs in honor of our famous mountain man uncle, William Sublett. But they want us to go back to our American beginnings so I must relate the history of William Claiborne instead. I am allowed however to give you a brief account of Uncle William Sublett. He is an icon of the American Westward Movement and a co-owner of the Rocky Mountain Fur Company.

He founds Fort William at the mouth of the Yellowstone River that is renamed Fort Laramie. His associate, Jedediah Smith, is the first to cross over into the Mojave Desert in the California of your Eden."

Aria remembered being glued to her television set once a week to watch the western drama called Laramie. An absolute favorite of hers and her best friend, Debbie, with whom after which she had prolonged phone conversations rehashing the episode. Thanks to television, the Old West was only as far away as her childhood. "I guess that wasn't all that long ago, was it? When did the Claiborne ancestor arrive in America?"

"Colonel William Claiborne is his name. The Evil Genius of Virginia they call him. And he arrives in Jamestown in 1621, one year after the Mayflower lands. He is your eleventh-ago grandfather, educated at Cambridge University in England and dispatched to survey and manage both the Maryland and Virginia colonies for the Virginia Company. His arrival in 1621corresponds to the arrival of the Puritans into Plimouth Plantation and although he is a Puritan sympathizer we do know that he isn't a Puritan."

"How can you be so sure that he isn't one as well?"

"Because he comes to the colony from Westmoreland in Northern England. The Puritans come from every county in England except Westmoreland."

"I thought I heard you say that he was a surveyor. Why do you call him Col. Claiborne?"

"He commands the Virginia Militia in the third Anglo-Powhaten War."

"I'm not familiar with that."

"The English versus the Indians", Nancy explained, "the Powhatens are the tribe of Pocahontas. The ultimate result of the wars is the establishment of Indian reservations. Anyway, Col. Claiborne is made the first Secretary of the Treasurer of the Virginia Colony of Jamestown and the Council wants you to remember me as Nancy Ann of the Virginia Company. My husband will be the next to speak", she said looking over at Newt.

"Our furthest ancestor in America", Newt told, "is your thirteenth-ago grandfather, Thomas Dudley, who sails in the same Winthrop fleet of ships as your grandfather, John Doan. Governor Winthrop and grandfather Thomas establish the Massachusetts Bay Colony together. Thomas Dudley is the second most influential person in that organization. He is elected not once but four times as the governor of Massachusetts and is the founder of Cambridge, building the first home there. I believe it is called Newtown at this time. He promotes and signs the charter for Harvard University. His daughter, your aunt, Ann Bradstreet, is America's first published poet. And grandfather Thomas Dudley is a Puritan."

"Is that a good thing or bad?"

"History records him as a persistent heresy hunter."

"I don't know what that is. I don't know what heresy means."

"The word is from the Greek haeresis which simply means choice. It comes to mean the wrong choice. In other words, contrary to orthodox doctrines. And it is our grandfather who figures prominently in the persecution of Anne Hutchinson. He charges her with the slander of male ministers that she has openly criticized, for which she is found guilty, labeled a heretic, and declared an instrument of the devil. You may not know of her but you are probably familiar with the character who portrays her in Nathaniel Hawthorne's book, the Scarlet Letter."

"Hester Prynne!" Aria said. "She was the woman who had to wear the big red A on the bodice of her gowns because she was accused of adultery."

"That's correct. Mr. Hawthorne bases that character on Ann Hutchinson and her treatment by your grandfather at the heresy trial. It is Grandfather's participation in that trial that ends up giving Puritanism such a harsh reputation. The Council wants you to remember me as Newt of the Massachusetts Bay Colony."

Who would have thought that Aria would have so many movers and shakers in her family tree. They all arrived within ten years of each other and worked for big organizations bent on shaping and owning a new nation. And Uncle Robert Morris even signed on the dotted line and used his own funds to bankroll it. But Aria didn't feel as proud as she thought she would. One ancestor was called an evil genius and he corrals the native inhabitants so that his company can take their land. And another one declared what was probably a perfectly sane woman, guilty only of conflicting ideologies, to be an instrument of the devil. What's the punishment for that? And the one ancestor that gives financially from personal coffers ends up living as a pauper in the very country he financed. What tale would this last grandparent have to tell? She turned to look at the thin woman who looked so much like her grandmother, Irma.

May Brookfield began her oration. "The branches of my family tree will vary from the stories you have heard so far. These others are English. The line you will follow from me is Scottish. You have been listening to stories of the English elite ruling class and their influence on the American colonies through the birth of a nation. We are the outlaw class. We are the reivers, or raiders, living on the border between England and Scotland, claiming fealty to neither. I speak of the Armstrongs, the fiercest of all the border reivers. All little boys want to grow up to be a reiver as it is an exalted occupation. The English ride through the borderlands on their way to vanquish the Scots and steal whatever they want as they pass through. The Scots ride through on their way to vanquish the English and steal as much themselves. A reiver goes out and steals it back. And they are good at it. The Armstrongs are the very nemesis of Mary Queen of Scots and Edward I, King of England, so devastating is their might. When they grow too strong to subdue, measures are taken to dismantle them. But by then they have built a cavalry of clans that can be assembled at a moments notice. The rulers take away their fine horses and give them one option…to be farmers. But the Armstrongs, mighty warriors, refuse to till the soil so they leave. First to Northern Ireland. Then to America."

"Then I shall remember you as May of the Reivers?"

"No. My connection will be one of the most significant but it won't come through a famous grandfather. Our original Armstrong grandfather in America has no historical fame but his descendant does. That descendent would be a cousin, I guess."

"What did our cousin do?"

"He is credited with being the first person to walk on the moon."

"Neil Armstrong? One small step for man, one giant leap for mankind…that Neil Armstrong? What ancestor do we have in common?"

"John Armstrong, your seventh-ago grandfather, who immigrated from Northern Ireland. The Council wants you to remember me as May of the Moon Men."

"Would you prefer I remember you as May of the Reivers?"

"I actually prefer the moon connection. Reivers worship the moon. All Scots do."

Mariah cut off the conversation before Aria could inquire as to what May had meant by that bizarre statement. "We must wrap up our meeting", Mariah announced, "so that you can get some rest. Once we conclude our business with Mr. McEuen, then John will show you to your sleeping quarters for tonight. Have you any questions beforehand?"

"Yes", Aria exclaimed, "where exactly am I? I see the frost on these windows so I assume I'm not in my desert anymore since it was seventy-nine degrees when I left there."

To Aria's surprise, it was May who answered and not Mariah. "Inverary Castle, Loch Fyne, Argyll, Scotland."

Aria blurted out her shocked response, "I left my entire continent? Wait a minute!How the heck will I be getting home again?"

"With Mr. McEuen's passport."

"I'm freaking out here", Aria said in great agitation. "Why did you bring me all the way to Scotland to tell me about my American ancestors?"

May responded without a hint of alarm over Aria's emotional state. "This is closer to the Beginning of Things."

"Inverary Castle?"

"Scotland."

"Why wasn't I taken straight to where this beginning place is? Why bring me here to this castle?"

"Your journey is an unfoldment and would be ineffective if you jumped to the end. This is chosen as the starting point due to the connection of so much of your family tree to the Campbells of Argyll. I am a direct descendent of Sir Colin Mor Campbell, first chief of clan Campbell and Inverary Castle is their primary seat. My granddaughter, Irma, marries Edwin Carnahan and the Carnahans are vassals of the Campbells after they are pushed out of their homes in Northern Ireland. Even Mr. McEuen's clan, who also make a home here on Loch Fyne, lose those lands to the Campbells but are taken in by them to serve as their bards."

"Do you mean some sort of servant?"

"No. A bard has the same status and importance as a family attorney but whose primary responsibility is as a genealogist, entrusted with reciting the genealogies at all births, weddings and baptisms. Even your Emery's McKinney clan are at times either enemies or vassals of the Campbell clan. And although Mariah is not of Scots descent, it is the tradition held up by her Morris ancestors that have a continued observance all the way into modern times in a small Scottish village near the English border called Gretna Green."

Then Wilson McEuen stood up and all conversation ceased. He walked over to one of the shelves and picked up a small ancient wooden box adorned with Celtic knot-work designs. He sat back down and placed the box gently on his lap. Aria was sure that everyone in the room was holding their breath in anticipation of Wilson opening the box. The scent was the first thing to escape the old wooden container. It was intoxicating and now no one was holding their breath but rather breathing in great lungfuls of the scented air. Removing the perfumed item, Wilson held it up for all to see. It appeared to be a small branch plucked from a tree and it must have been plucked fairly recently as the scent was emanating from fresh white blossoms which ran the entire length of the branch. Between the buds hung nine tiny red-gold apples and wound between the apples and the flowers was a whisper thin silver ribbon that seemed to shine somehow from within. Holding the branch in front of him at arms length, Wilson gave it a little shake and to Aria's amazement the little apples gave off a tinkling sound like bells and played a bit of a refrain from a melody that Aria recognized but could not place. Tears formed in the corners of her eyes as she both grasped for the memory of the tune which enchanted her and reacted to the realization that what she was seeing was real magic. So this was to be her passport. And her relief was deep and reassuring. If she had come here by magic then certainly it was going to take magic to get her home again.

"It is called the Silver Branch", Wilson explained to Aria, "and it comes into the possession of my ancestor, your Emery's and mine, by the name of Cormac macArt. In Irish history you will hear of this king called Longbeard."

"So then did Longbeard make the same journey that I am on?"

"His circumstances are different. He not only begs for the Branch, he swaps for it."

"Swapped with what?"

"His wife and his son and his daughter."

"Really? Was he glad he made the swap?"

"Not at all. But macLir is kind enough to give his family back to him."

"Who is macLir?"

"Manannan macLir, ruler of the Otherworld."

"What other world?"

"The one beneath your feet. Summerland, it's often called. Summer never ends there. Here in Celtic lands we call it Emain Ablach, the Plain of Apples."

Aria knew now that she could not accept it. "I think that it is too fine a gift to give to the likes of ordinary me. I'm not a king in Ireland and he was willing to give up his family for it so I cannot comprehend its worth but I'm sure that it is more than I deserve."

"The Council thinks otherwise", Wilson said and then chuckled, "and who on earth told you that you are ordinary?" He held out his hand and offered her the branch. "Have Mariah tie it to your waist with the ribbon. Take it off at night when you sleep but be careful not to leave it behind in the morning as there is no time for backtracking to retrieve it."

She thanked Wilson as Mariah tied the branch to her waist. It hung almost weightless at her side. Her trembling caused the miraculously alive apple bells to chime a slightly mournful tune that perfectly matched her mixed emotions about having decided that she was up to this adventure in the first place.

Before she could sit down again, John the tea server, stood up and opened the library door indicating that it was time to go and Aria was quickly ushered out without even saying good night or good bye or nice to have met you. This bothered Aria as the door shut behind her and she watched as John scurried down the long moonlit hallway. For a split second she considered returning to the library to make the appropriate farewells but just then John took a turn down an adjoining corridor and Aria knew that if she didn't run now she was never going to find him. How utterly rude! She and her irritation raced out after John.

"Slow down please!", Aria called after John's continuously disappearing form down the shadowy corridors. But he never altered his pace and she was somewhat breathless when she finally did catch up with him. That only happened because he had ceased running and was holding open her bedroom door for her. She glowered her disapproval as she moved past him into the room.

"We leave at dawn. Be ready."

"Excuse me?", she spat with double insolence. But he was already gone.

Of all the incredible events of this day, it was Aria's anger about her treatment by John, the castle underling, that she kept replaying as she changed into the nightdress that had been laid out for her. She had not failed to notice that there was no such thing as a clock or a telephone in her room so she would have no idea when dawn arrived. What time was dawn anyway? Now she would have to sleep light in order to comply with his directive which made her all the madder because she was completely exhausted from this experience. Well if she wasn't ready by dawn, whenever that was, so be it! She could file a complaint.

Aria finally fell asleep as she wrote and rewrote the complaint in her head.

Photograph taken by the author, March 24, 2004, Cong, Ireland

Newt of the Massachusetts Bay Colony

May of the Moon Men

May of the Moon Men

Wilson of the Silver Branch

Financed Revolutionary War

ROBERT MORRIS JR.
Masons

Signer, Declaration of Independence

Founded 1st U.S. Bank

U.S. Senator 1789-95

Ancestor of May of the Moon Men

Col. William Claiborne
The Virginia Company

Ancestor of Nancy Ann of the Virginia Company

Ancestor of Newt of the Massachusetts Bay Colony

- RECRUITED PASSENGER • PUB OWNER
- MAYFLOWER
- FOUNDING FAMILIES - VIRGINIA
- Plimouth Plantation
- Shakespeare's Stephano in The Tempest

Stephen Hopkins
The New England Company

Ancestor of Joseph of the New England Company

Deacon John Doan
The New England Company

Assistant Governor - Plimouth Plantation

Founder Eastham, Mass. Cape Cod

Ancestor of Joseph of the New England Company

CHAPTER TWO

"The only thing new in the world is
the history you don't know."

33rd U.S. President Harry Solomon Truman
33rd Degree Freemason

ARIA WOKE BEFORE dawn and the prearranged departure. She could smell the heady fragrance of the Silver Branch on the nightstand but when she reached for her clothes in the dark room they seemed to be gone. In a panic she felt her way around the room like a newly blinded person trying to locate the jeans and tee shirt she had been wearing before she went to bed last night. Her fingers at last chanced upon a velvety fabric that felt like a long, perhaps floor length, dress. She quickly pulled the nightgown over her head and slipped into the soft dress. The glow of pre-dawn began to infiltrate the corners of the dark room enabling her to see the amenities that had been set out for her consisting of a hair brush, creams, powders, and even a chamber pot. Alongside these were a delicately embroidered pair of shoes and a fabric cap in matching colors. The anger and irritation she had taken to sleep with her was returning with the force of a freight train for surely these items had not been in the room when she arrived and her own clothes were clearly missing which could only mean that someone had entered her room while she slept and exchanged them. More than likely that someone was John, the castle servant. Trembling now at the thought of his intrusion she still quickly tidied her hair, placed the cap on her head and put on the shoes. Just as the first hint of sunlight brightened the windows of the room there was a knock at the door.

Aria opened the door with a snide remark at the ready but John beat her to it.

"Whoa!", he said and winked in good nature. "Now this is what a lady should look like. Pants are for men to wear, don't you think? Let's not tarry though, time is not our friend."

His observation was evidently Aria's last straw and her voice had an angry, indignant tone when she responded. "I beg your pardon, son! I won't be leaving with you this morning and if you would be so accommodating as to escort me to where my grandparents are I would appreciate it and I will kindly refrain from registering my complaints against you so that you may keep your job."

John stared at her for under a second and then burst out laughing. "Well well. To the manor born, are we?" Struggling to contain his mirth he continued, "Don't worry, Child, I can honor your request this very instant for I am your twelfth-ago grandfather, John Wilson, on the line of Joseph of the New England Company."

Aria was shocked and confused on so many levels. First off, he had just called her "child" while obviously much younger than herself. And he had called her a snob which remarkably turned out to be true. Another painful injection of humility. But still her ego demanded that she save face by putting him on the spot. "Why did you keep your identity a secret from me last night?"

"Your ancestry weaves in and out like a Celtic braid, so tightly in fact, that at times it may even appear tangled. It isn't the Council's intention to deceive you but rather to have your starting point be as simple as possible. Your path here in Europe will run through the genealogical lines of the five grandparents you met last night as well as Mr. McEuen. I am only one of many you shall meet."

"And where does that path end?"

But John didn't hear the question as he quickly turned and headed down the long corridor of her ancestor's castle. She caught up with him as they descended the stairs to the Great Hall. He slowed his pace on the steps enabling her to speak again.

"Are you a Campbell too, John?"

"I'm an Englishman but I move to America."

"With your family?"

"I meet and marry my wife there. She is your twelfth-ago grandmother, Catherine Rudd."

"Was she also English?"

"No. American. She is born in Chuckatuck, Virginia in 1607."

"Oh my gosh", Aria exclaimed, "you married an American Indian?"

"No I didn't", he responded and hit the bottom of the stairs and picked up his speedier pace right across the large room and out the door. Aria was still standing at the bottom of the stairs lost both in the beauty of the room and the struggle she was having with her history dates from grade school. Wasn't Jamestown America's first colony? And wasn't that in 1607? Where the heck was Chuckamuck? Suddenly she realized that Scotland was outside the door so she raced to see it.

It assailed her senses the moment she stepped outside. The grandeur and the beauty was overwhelming and she stood transfixed by the sight. She didn't see John so she decided to wait near the door until he pulled the car around. But then she heard his irritated voice calling to her from further down the driveway. He was standing next to an old fashioned horse and carriage team, both of them inky black in the morning dawn. It was like something you might ride down Main Street in Disneyland. Embarrassed that she had been expecting a car and noticing John's air of impatience, she ran to the carriage and jumped in with him. The carriage took off like a rocket but Aria did not think that she had seen a driver and she wondered what the big hurry was all about. "Why are we on a time schedule?"

"We aren't. You are. My assignment is to escort you to Carrick Castle so that you can have breakfast with the countesses." He noticed the goose bumps on her arms and handed her a soft plaid wool cloak that she was grateful to wrap up in. Mornings in Scotland were a lot nippier than mornings in Southern California this time of year.

"Then why am I on a time schedule? This place is so beautiful. I'd love to spend time here and I'm sort of disappointed that I didn't get to see more of that wonderful castle. Will I be coming back after breakfast?"

"You are missing the magnitude of this event. Tourism is not on the agenda. A door is being held open for you that cannot remain open for very long. You are far more blessed than you currently understand."

"Oh but I do appreciate it!", Aria gushed and yet she realized that she wasn't acting like it or honestly feeling it. So she resolved to blunder on anyway since she had no other options. "Last night I met my third-ago grandparents and you tell me that you and your wife are my twelfth-ago, so are the countesses even further back in history?"

"Good deduction. The countesses are your twenty-second-ago and your twenty- third-ago grandmothers so that puts them about seven hundred years in your past. The Council may hop you around a little in the historical timeline but it will only be to accommodate your ability to meet up with all who have been selected to facilitate your quest."

"Will I spend the night at this new castle tonight?"

"You will dine with the countesses and then must be quickly on your way to Westmoreland."

"The Westmoreland in England that didn't have any Puritans?" Aria felt like patting herself on the back for having remembered that bizarre bit of information.

"That's the one."

"Will I sleep in a castle in Westmoreland tonight?" Suddenly only castles seemed the logical choice for her accommodations.

"Tonight you will be traveling to France."

"France?", her voice squeaked as fresh fear hit her. "But I can't go to France!"

"Why not?"

"Because I don't speak French."

John laughed anew. "You don't speak Old English or the Scots dialect either. How can we communicate with you in languages you don't understand? You hear us in your own vernacular. The babel of language has been removed or this exercise is completely ineffective. Your fears are unwarranted. Na biodh eagla ort."

"I know. Don't be afraid." His words were lost on her. She was already jumping several new fears ahead. Like for instance, how the heck was she getting to France? She was traveling seven hundred years into the past in a horse drawn carriage. What would she be riding to France? A Viking ship? A raft? Would she be warm enough in this gown? Could she keep the warm wool cloak? So much to worry about and so little time. These horses pulling her carriage must be traveling at a full gallop to have the landscape whizzing by so fast. Should she worry about that too? In a desperate attempt to distract herself she turned to John and struck up a conversation about his wife. "So this Chuckamacallit place where your wife was born is the first settlement in the New World?"

"The New World? You're funny, Child! Settlement of America doesn't start in Chuckatuck and it doesn't start in Jamestown in 1607 either. Prince Madog of Wales arrives in 1160 and even the Basque sailors are selling American beaver pelts to the English in the sixteenth century. The Spanish arrive. The pirates arrive. Settlements have been developing for centuries when I arrive."

Aria had to contemplate this for a minute. Something was terribly amiss in her public school education. Once a year pictures were painted of the Nina and the Pinta and the Santa Maria to tack up around the classroom and Chris Columbus in his velvet coat loomed large as the hero of, joy of joys, a day without school! Then only a short month later pictures were painted of Pilgrim men and Pilgrim women and turkeys traced around an open hand print and those got tacked up on the classroom walls as well. To a school child it said that Columbus discovered America and a month later the Pilgrims came over and had turkey with the Indians. She wondered how much she appeared the dim bulb to her grandfather that she had mistaken as castle staff.

"So what made you decide to immigrate to Chuckintuck?"

"I never said I immigrated to Chuckatuck. You assumed that. Do you know that you do that? Make assumptions?"

Aria looked out the window in embarrassment and stopped talking. Finally the silence grew uncomfortable so she asked him another question. "Are you a Puritan, John?"

"Well yes, but one might think otherwise in consideration of my lineage. Big time Church of England, nemesis of the Puritans. Grandfather William Wilson is the Prebendary of the St. George Chapel in Windsor Castle belonging to the Knights of the Garter. William's wife, grandmother Isabell Woodhall, is the great niece of Edmund Grindall, the Archbishop of Canterbury and grandfather William is his chaplain. So, like I said, you would think that I would not be a Puritan. And yet both Grandfather and his friend, Henry Hastings, the earl of Huntingdon, were known to share Puritan views."

"Who are the Knights of the Garter?"

"The highest order of knighthood in the world even into your modern age where it is headed by England's queen, Elizabeth II."

"Your grandfather is one of them?"

"He served their religious needs only. The knighthood is limited to twenty five members at a time."

"The Archbishop of Canterbury is a big deal, right?" Aria pondered her connection to this religious royalty. "It's almost like being related to the Pope!"

"Oh, believe me, you're related to the Pope!", he laughed.

"Seriously? Which one?"

"The first. But that information is left for last."

There was no way Aria could even begin to wrap her mind around the idea of being related to Peter, the apostle, who hung out with Jesus so she quickly changed the subject. "So where in America did you immigrate to if it wasn't Chuckatuck?"

"I am the first minister of Charlestown, right across the Charles River from Boston."

"When was that?"

"I sail with the first five ships of the Winthrop Fleet in 1630."

Aria stared dumbfounded at him. "Is this even possible? You sailed on the same fleet of ships to America as my grandfather John Doan in

Plimouth Plantation and also my grandfather, Thomas Dudley, who was governor of Massachusetts? Did you guys know each other?"

"I know your grandfather, Thomas Dudley well. He and Governor Winthrop and I, along with another gentleman named Issac Johnson, entered into a formal covenant to walk together in the fellowship of the gospel."

"And did you?"

"Not according to Anne Hutchinson. She said I lack the seal of the spirit. Her accusation is the cause of her trial."

"You? You're the male minister that she slandered? And your pal Governor Dudley, the heresy hunter, persecutes her for it?" She was now looking at John with new eyes.

Aria had stepped off her balcony into Scotland. Maybe the world really was that small. Three of her grandfathers, two from her mother's side and one from her dad's were together on the same ships from England almost four hundred years ago. Her mom's relative got slandered so her dad's relative defended his male honor and some poor woman's life was ruined for it. She was done with stories about ancestral exploits in America. "Why am I going to Westmoreland?"

"You will attend the rush bearing at St. Columba's church in Warcop."

"Church?", she blurted out with some disdain before catching herself. She was, after all conversing with her grandfather, the first minister in Charlestown. But still, she wasn't all that comfortable attending strange churches. You could never be sure of the etiquette and you didn't know the songs.

"Na biodh eagla ort. They won't eat you! Now turn around and look your first upon Castle Carrick."

Her head whipped around in astonishment. Castle Carrick already? They had been traveling for only a short time and yet the scenery outside the carriage window had changed and a new castle came into view. The carriage screeched to a stop and the door swung open by itself. Aria got out but John remained in his seat.

"Aren't you coming inside?"

"No."

"But you must. You can't leave me. I don't even know these people."

John laughed at her again as he pulled shut the carriage door. "You didn't know me until last night."

"How will I get to Westmoreland?" Her voice sounded whiney again and even she didn't like it.

"You worry a lot, do you know that?" he called out as the carriage turned back toward Inverary Castle.

"At least tell me how I'm getting to France?", she yelled loudly at the receding carriage. She wasn't sure if she heard his reply properly or even if she heard it at all.

"On the submarine", the voice may have said as it trailed away.

Stunned and overwhelmed, Aria turned around and saw a man in a kilt waiting to greet her. Through no fault of his own she was a bit too curt when she spoke to him, "So you're a grandfather, right?"

"Right you are, Lass. But not yours. I'm the ancestor of Emery of your Eden and Wilson McEuen. I am Ewen of Otter, the last clan chief of clan macEwen and ancestor to all McEuens who come after me. I'm also your guide to Westmoreland and they have us on a pretty tight schedule so we had best step lively." With his introduction done he turned and entered the door with Aria staying close behind so as not to get lost. Yet even as she breathlessly bounded after him up the stairs she had time to notice that he had the same bird legs sticking out from beneath his kilt as her Emery.

The two countesses met them at the door of the room at the top of the stairs which offered a picture-perfect view of Loch Goil and the steep forested land that raced down to meet it. Hot venison sausages, grilled salmon and oat cakes dominated a table set for four. The younger countess took Aria's cloak and placed it near the fireplace to warm during her stay. She introduced herself as Marjorie.

"I am the Countess of Carrick and this is my Aunt Erricka who is also the Countess of Carrick. You are related to both of us on your father's side through May of the Moon Men. Your time is short with us so we should sit down and have our meal now." Aria, feeling suddenly famished, was more than happy to do just that. And to save time she fired off her questions between mouthfuls.

"Are you my Campbell relatives?"

"I am", Erricka responded, "but only by marriage. My husband is Archibald Campbell, Duke of Argyll. However, it is our son, Sir Colin Mor Campbell, who is considered the first great chief of the Campbell clan. Marjorie is my brother's child. It is her son who gives this castle to the Campbells."

"Was your son a duke or a lord or something here in this castle, Marjorie?"

Marjorie smiled and winked at her aunt before answering. "My son is the king."

"The King of Carrick?"

"The King of Scotland. His name is Robert the Bruce. Have you ever heard of him?"

Aria was trying very hard not to look as shocked as she felt. "I am related to the mother of Robert the Bruce? I have heard of him. My fourth grade teacher told us a story about how he was inspired by a little spider to keep trying or some such thing. It's funny, I grew up thinking everyone was told that story and I was surprised that neither my sister, Ma Suit, nor my brother, Hazno, had ever heard it. Interesting that I would end up meeting the mother of the Bruce. Life is full of coincidences!"

"All events are simultaneous." Erricka amended. "You cannot comprehend the concept of universal time as you are trapped in a linear time-bound world. Would you believe me if I said that this excursion you are currently on is known of and prepared for when you are in the fourth grade? Is your teacher a Scots woman?"

Aria's eyebrows flew up and she quickly responded. "Her name was Mrs. Russell and she had red hair!" Her facial expression quickly changed to skeptical. "It still could just be a coincidence that my fourth grade teacher was possibly of Scottish descent. I imagine that a great deal of people are of Scottish descent. Maybe even half the teachers at Cathedral City Elementary School for all I know."

Ewen laughed out loud at her remark. "Highly unlikely, Lass, to find a percentage as high as that outside of Scotland. "During the time that you are living, in the modern era, only one half of one percent of all the human beings living on earth can claim Scottish descent."

"And now here I am visiting the land of my father's ancestors!"

"Your mother's too, child" Marjorie chimed in. "Your mother Helen's own grandmother, Anna Ellicott, is born here in the United Kingdom. The Ellicotts, also called the Elliotts, are fierce border reivers like their comrades in arms, the Armstrongs."

"Hold on a second. I have to digest this and I'm not talking about this delicious salmon and sausage", Aria said. "My great grandpa, Poker Bill Armstrong, on my dad's side and my great grandma, Anna Ellicott, on my mom's side, are both descended from border reivers? And we are only one half of one percent of the world's population? Did the Armstrongs and the Ellicotts know of each other?"

"The Armstrongs and the Elliotts are thick as thieves!" Marjorie blurted out laughing.

"Then what of Mom and Dad? No coincidence that my dad was uprooted from his home and his high school in Los Angeles because his parents took a job near the small Iowa community of Cantril where my mother grew up? No coincidence there?"

The three of them stared at her deadpan. Aria continued, "Okay. I get it. Preordained, right? And what about my meeting Emery? We are both of Scots descent. Was that preordained as well? Scots just automatically hook up with other Scots?" She didn't sound convinced.

"We macEwens aren't actually Scots at the start", Ewen explained.

"Of course you are! You're wearing a kilt and you're a clan chief in Scotland."

"Lots of folk come to Scotland. The macEwen clan is a blend of Irish mercenaries of the Northern Irish O'Neal clan who come to Argyll and marry the daughters of the Vikings who are already living here. Our first ancestor here in Argyll is Anrothan ua Niall who marries the daughter of the Viking serving as king of Cowal. So you see we are a blend of Northern Irish and Norse that are called the Gallowglass and we are as elite a class of mercenary warriors as the Armstrongs and the Elliotts are reivers."

"The Gallowglass establish Galloway in the south where Robert is born." Marjorie added.

Aria couldn't accept that preordination was real and she didn't want to talk about it any more. Emery's clan may not have started out Scottish but certainly they became Scottish so Ewen's point was moot. "What about this moon thing? I'm required to remember May associated with it because a famous but distant cousin walked on the moon. What's that all about?"

"Perhaps preordination!", Erricka said and winked at Marjorie. "Perhaps it is important that a Scotsman, an Armstrong, always be associated with the moon. On Loch Fyne, where Inverary Castle and Castle macEwen stand, it is tradition to bow to the new moon and say "Lady Moon, Lady Moon, I bow to Thee."

"Lady Moon? I thought there was a man in the moon."

"You speck of Endymion, but that tale is for later. Regardless, it is an elf maiden who controls the moon and spins the stars."

Aria looked at Erricka like she was off her rocker. She and Emery had watched the moon landing together as youngsters and had insider information that Erricka obviously lacked. "Well Lady Moon, Man in the Moon, whatever! It all sounds very romantic but I seriously doubt that cousin Neil Armstrong met any elf maidens when he was walking around on the moon."

"No one ever walked on the moon, Lass", Ewen stated.

"Stop! Stop! Stop it right now!" Aria had her hands in the air as if holding off an attacker. "I've heard this blarney before. In my age it's called a conspiracy theory and you'll get laughed out of the room if you adhere to it. Of course we went to the moon. We watched it on TV."

"Do you know what your Moon Men are busy building fifty years after the moon landing, Lass? Well, I'll tell you. It's a special shielded vehicle called the Orion that will enable humans and sensitive equipment to safely pass through the Van Allen Radiation Belts so they can journey to the moon and beyond."

Aria had to digest this information too for just a second before responding. "How did we do it in 1969? This is absurd. NASA knew about the Van Allen Radiation Belts then. They wouldn't have sent Neil and Buzz and company into harm's way. It would have killed them."

"And yet it doesn't, does it?"

"Why such a monstrous lie? It makes no sense. Maybe they had an early prototype of this Orion vehicle back then. How is it working now?"

"Still untested", Ewen answered. "The rocketry necessary to launch it into space is not yet developed in 2018. Either technology devolves over time or you are lied to."

"There has to be another explanation", Aria said but she couldn't think of one.

"You will hear it said that it is easier to fool someone than to convince them they have been fooled."

"Then it's a pretty big lie so there must be a reason."

"Distraction", Marjorie said. "It's a ploy as old as the hills. They have you looking up so you won't be looking down. An inquisitive Byrd has just discovered Hyperborea and there is no lie deemed big enough to hide that secret from you."

"Where is Hyperborea?"

"Beneath your feet. The Lands Beneath. Where summer never ends", Ewen spoke. Do you ever wonder why they call the missions to the moon Apollo? Do you know who Apollo is?"

"I think he's a sun god or something."

"That's right, Lass. It is the name of the sun god in Hyperborea."

"Shouldn't they have used the name of the moon god?"

"Hyperborea has no moon", Marjorie interjected. "This is a perplexing subject and worthy of much pondering but our time together is short this morning so maybe you should ask whatever questions you may still have about Scotland before you leave for Westmoreland."

"I'm embarrassed to admit how little I know about Scotland. I know about your son, Marjorie, because of the spider story and I know about William Wallace because I saw the movie that was made about him not wanting to give up his freedom. And now I know that Scots worship the Lady in the Moon but I don't really know why."

Marjorie was pleased and told her that it was more than they expected She explained to Aria that although she wasn't related to William Wallace, the spider story was about him. Wallace and the Bruce were both fighting against English rule and against King Edward I, Hammer of the Scots, in particular. Edward tortures Wallace on the rack where he dies. And even though Robert and John Comyns are appointed joint guardians after Wallace's death, Robert cannot get beyond being terrified by what Edward did to Wallace and decides to quit before Edward does the same to him."

"So that's when he hides in the cave and sees the spider!", Aria surmises.

"Well that is how the story goes. In actuality Robert is hiding out with the Campbells. They have no idea who he is. They just offer up their barn to a stranger as a place to stay. It's in the barn that Robert sees the spider. Thanks to another Campbell relative, Angus Og macDonald, who commands Robert's forces, he and Robert and the Scots fight one last decisive battle, the Battle of Bannockburn, which they win, granting Scotland the right to remain a free Albigensian culture for another three hundred years."

"What kind of culture?"

"Albigensian", Ewen repeated, "from the word albi. An albi is a female elf."

"A culture of fairies?"

"Oh no! A fairy and an elf are very different folk."

This was said in such earnestness that Aria just knew he was teasing her so she started to laugh but she laughed alone. "You are teasing me, right?"

A somber Erricka replied, "We are not here in this limited capacity to have fun with you, Child."

Aria was both embarrassed by that remark and perturbed by it. One minute they are talking Scottish independence and then, Bam!, it's one giant leap to fairyland. This couldn't possibly be happening. "Well that works out", Aria said, "because I'm not enjoying this conversation. I'm a long way from home and my nerves are on edge and I didn't get enough sleep due to a fear of missing my ride so forgive me if I have difficulty believing in Santa's little helpers."

"Aren't those the same folk who tacked the blue curtain to the little awning over the door in the fairy tree?"

That comment hit Aria hard. What a hypocrite she was. She was the one that had instigated the fairy hunting at Camp Comfort after seeing the little curtain under the awning. She said she believed in fairies but evidently she did not. To a child who believes, no proof is necessary. To an adult who does not, no proof is enough. A sad commentary on the person she perceived herself to be. With deep humility she asked, "What's the difference between an elf and a fairy?"

"The elves are the elite ruling class of the fairies."

"Do any of you personally know an elf?"

Erricka answered but they all looked ready to. "Our granddaughter's husband, Angus Og Mor, is fostered by the dark elves. It's the son of Angus who commands Robert's forces at Bannockburn. But I don't know his foster folks."

"We have an elf by the name of Black Donald in our line", Ewen added, "he is tall and gaunt and always dresses in green but he'll arrive long after my time. Now I can see by the distress on your face that you have had enough talk about the unfamiliar and it's a good thing really because it's time to leave. Grab your cloak warming by the fire and lets head back to the carriage. You have a swan waiting for you and a time schedule to keep."

The two countesses came to life when Ewen made this pronouncement. Marjorie fetched the cloak and wrapped it around Aria's shoulders, smiling all the while. She handed Aria a silver coin and told her to treat herself to an ale. Erricka also foisted coins on her with the same suggestion. They gushed over how much they wished they could join her and she wondered what kind of church elicited such delight and also sold beer. Elf church?

Aria was glad once they were tucked back within the same carriage she had shared with John earlier that day. It was familiar in a very unfamiliar world. The soft cloak retained it's warmth and comforted her also. "I'm here to ask questions, aren't I, Ewen?"

"That's what I was told. Do you have a question, Lass?"

"Am I only spoken to when I have a question?"

"Yes."

"Why?"

"I don't know if you have ever heard about how Sir Galahad's quest to find the Holy Grail eluded him the first time that he nearly had it because he failed to ask a question."

"Oh don't tell me I'm searching for the Holy Grail!"

"Okay. I have no idea what you are searching for. I was just asked to escort you to the transport station."

"Where a giant swan is waiting to carry me to Northern England?"

"That's right. Don't fret. I loved my first ride."

"I can see that smile on your face, Ewen. You're teasing me. You're all teasing me and I'm going to find out why." But that wasn't a question and he didn't reply. "Where is the transport station?"

"Near Loch Lomond."

"Is that where your castle is?"

"Castle macEwen is on Loch Fyne, same as Inverary."

"You served the Campbells as bards because they were your neighbors?"

"One of my descendants loses castle macEwen to the Campbells in a gambling debt. That is when we go to work for them as bards. We're Irish remember. We have a bit of fame where it comes to Gaelic poetry so we're good at being their bards. Evidently we aren't very good at gambling."

"Sorry you lose your castle. Does it make you sad?"

"Children of the Mist, we are called, having no land of our own. Fortunes change. Look at the Armstrongs forced out to Northern Ireland. Fiercest of the border clans but pushed out all the same. Even we macEwens, we Gallowglass, leave for Ireland since we have no land to hold us here in Scotland. But then aren't we Northern Irish in the first place? And aren't we also here at King Robert's Cave already and it's time to catch a swan."

"What? This is either a very small country or these horses can move with unnatural speed. Does the swan move this fast?" Aria's heart began to race.

"Na biodh eagla ort. Try to keep up but be careful not to slip." Ewen jumped out of the carriage and in through the opening of a large wet cave. Aria had to hold up her dress skirt to keep it dry as she hurried in behind him. When he began a descent down a spiral staircase that had been cut into the cave wall she slowed way down. The stone steps were slippery from the moisture they seemed to sweat out and Aria would not break her neck racing down them just to catch a swan she didn't want to ride. Her slow descent in the dim light of the cave only added to her fears. She could not see Ewen who was far ahead of her and she could no longer hear him either. She was alone in an endless spiral and just when panic set in that there was no end, she found it. And there was Ewen. And there was the swan. Aria instantly wore a smile as big as his.

The swan was a boat. An exact replica of the ones she and Ma Suit had seen carrying tourists around the canal in Boston Common. This swan boat also floated in a canal. One filled with glacier colored turquoise water.

Ewen helped Aria into the boat and stepped back. "You aren't coming with me, are you?", she asked.

"No need. It's a quick ride. You'll be there in no time. There will be a sign, Temple Sowerby Station. The boat knows to stop. You'll be met."

The canal entered a tunnel but before the swan floated leisurely into it, Aria looked back upon her Emery's smiling grandfather wearing his plaid kilt over his familiar skinny legs. Although the tunnel was dark, the bright turquoise water gave off it's own illumination and splashed turquoise images across the ceiling of the tunnel as it moved. She intended to use this slow paced vehicle to finally take a deep breath and assess her situation but the water reflection images dancing overhead kept her so distracted by visions of stags leaping, bears lumbering, and dragons soaring that once again she was shocked when the ride ended and the station sign came into view. Now back in a large and better lit chamber, it was easy to see the young woman standing on the platform beneath the sign.

"Welcome to Westmoreland." The woman helped Aria to disembark. "My name is Catherine de Clifford de Greystoke and I am your aunt and not your grandmother. My parents, your grandparents, are awaiting your arrival at St. Columba's church. I have a carriage for us to use up at the surface."

The stairs they took up were wider, drier, brighter, and much safer than the ones she had descended in King Robert's Cave. Also, her aunt Catherine didn't seem to be in a rush like her male guide counterparts so the two of them climbed casually to the top.

"I've heard that name, Greystoke, before. In a book maybe?"

"More than likely. Greystoke is the ancestral home of my husband. Castle Greystoke is very near here in Appleby."

"Appleby? I thought this was Westmoreland and we are in St. Columba."

"Appleby is the seat of the county of Westmoreland. St. Columba's is the church in Warcop which is only three or four miles from Appleby. Father is the Sheriff of Westmoreland and the Lord of Appleby Castle."

"You wouldn't happen to know who the Claibornes are, would you? Evidently I had a grandfather in Virginia who lived in Westmoreland."

"William the American Colonel is descended from the Claibornes who have a village and a hall right here in the Eden Valley."

Aria's heart swelled at the sound of the word Eden. They call this place Eden. Suddenly it felt like home. "My home is called Eden." She couldn't help but smile as she said it.

"Of course it would be, Child. And this place is also called Avalon."

The stairs ended at a door where Catherine stopped and informed Aria that they were not to speak until they had passed through the building on the other side of the door and were fully outside of it where the carriage stood waiting.

"Why can't we talk?"

"Because women are not allowed in Temple Sowerby."

Aria stayed close to Catherine as they walked from one long passageway to another until entering what must have been the sanctuary of the temple. The high vaulted ceiling was painted a bright rich blue and covered with golden stars. Yet knowing that women were not allowed was too unsettling to spend time examining details and Aria was relieved to leave the building altogether. The carriage and its matched team waited patiently in a warm wonderful Northern English day. Aria threw off her cloak and was again reminded of home with its heat. The carriage and the team were both black and white. The white carriage was trimmed with black enamel and the white horses emblazoned with black spots and impossibly long manes and tails.

The ride to Warcop was not at breakneck speed as the driverless team was content to plod along the gorgeous English countryside. Aria came to fall in love with this new Eden at a comfortable pace.

"Why aren't women allowed in Temple Sowerby?"

"The temple belongs to the knights. It's their rule."

"Are you talking about the Knights of the Garter? I'm related to their vicar."

"Temple Sowerby belongs to the Templar Knights."

"And they don't like women, huh?"

"I would hardly say that. Their order is dedicated to women, Mary Magdelene in particular."

"You never said where I might have heard your husband's Greystoke name, did you?"

"His name is not Greystoke. It is the name of the castle. The current Lord of Greystoke in your time is the one for whom the stories are written. He is Lord John Clayton."

"I don't remember ever reading any stories about a John Clayton. Maybe I'm mistaken."

"The stories are about Tarzan. That is Lord Clayton's other name."

"I was right! You guys are teasing me and this proves it! The Tarzan books are probably a hundred years old. Tarzan, even if he were real, would be long dead by my time."

"I believe that Lord Clayton is one hundred thirty years old in your modern age. He lives in quiet seclusion at the castle."

"That seems impossible but I suppose not out of the realm of possibilities. However the Tarzan character is a literary invention more than likely based on Mr. Clayton just as Hester Prynne was based on Anne Hutchinson. Mr. Clayton was certainly not raised by apes."

"Lord Clayton is raised by Aborigines in Gabon after losing his parents."

The carriage entered the outskirts of the village of Warcop and Aria felt the excitement of a country fair as crowds of people filled the street ambling toward what must be the church. The team inched along past throngs of flower bedecked people swigging beer and laughing children chasing around and between the adults in a riot of color, sound, and gaiety. A small girl was lifted up to the carriage window to pass in garlands of miniature roses and wild flowers for Aria and Catherine to place on their heads like crowns.. And Aria's love of this Eden grew deeper.

The Maypole came into view before the church, towering over the festivities like a pastel rainbow of fluttering ribbons. The streamers of colored fabric draped from the top of the pole to the ground where the dancers performed. Bright colored tents surrounded the little church where ales and breads and spice scented cakes were being sold.

"I feel silly", Aria said. "I was under the impression this was a church event. I didn't realize that only the church grounds are being used to stage this lovely fair."

"It is a church event. It's called a rush bearing. Do you see those carts over there with the irises in them, the rushes? Well this is the day when the old rushes on the floor of St. Columba's are removed and new ones installed. England is known for its rain and the rushes soak up mud off the feet of the parishioners."

"Is this a regular Christian church? Because in America there isn't quite so much drunkenness at church events."

Catherine pointed up to where a cross would have been visible on a regular church and yet was missing here. In its place was an open ring containing what looked like a plus sign. Or a pie chart cut into quarters. She explained the anomaly to Aria. "We call that symbol the Creator's Cross or the ball and cross. It is the logo of the sacred tribes. And yet this is, as you call it, a regular church. The Anglican church of England embraces these beliefs and sanctions these Whitson Ale traditions to continue even into your modern age. At least here in Westmoreland, they do."

"What is a Whitson Ale?"

"Its a fundraiser for the community. Money is raised for the needy by selling cakes and ales. To the folks in the community, who rarely ever drink spirits, it's a great excuse to get drunk. And there are different types of events. For instance a Bride Ale is to raise money for the newly betrothed. It's where you get the modern word bridal."

The music out on the lawn swelled and drowned out conversation. A new set of dancers ran to the Maypole and each grabbed the end of a colored ribbon. They wound and unwound them as the music played while the silver bells dangling from leather thongs tied around their knees jingled and jangled in choreographed delight. Aria was thrilled at the sight.

"This is a lot of celebration just to change the sawdust on the floor." Aria remarked. "Where does a Maypole come in?"

"It's May. The changing of the season. May is the time of the Morris Men. These traditions are much older than the Anglican church. They intertwine and will persist."

"Who are the Morris Men?"

"Morris Men dance in the seasons. In old traditions there are only two seasons. They begin on the first of May and the first of November. The dance is an ancient rite of the Elder Faith."

"How much elder?"

"Not elder as in older. But elder as in the tree. The elder tree."

"This is a tree hugger church?" Oh boy, Aria thought, open mouth, insert foot. Why did she have to speak without thinking? She braced for the retort for surely she had just insulted all these people.

"I guess a reverence for nature is discomforting in the modern age. Do you comprehend the source of Lord Clayton's fame?"

"I thought it was for surviving his childhood raised by monkeys but I realize that I may be wrong."

"He is remembered for his affinity with the animal kingdom. He loves the animals.

They love him too. He doesn't make a religion out of them, nor does Columba of the trees. Have you never felt a reverence for a tree, Child?"

Aria touched the unbelievable apple branch at her side and marveled to think from where it might have come. She also thought of the shingled awning with the little blue curtain over the fairy door. Once she had stood beneath the Angel Oak, the oldest oak on the east coast of America. Once she had stood beneath the oldest oak on the western side of America in a small town called Tehachupi. She felt reverence in their presence. She had also felt reverence standing at the foot of the tallest trees in the world, the giant redwoods of Northern California and she remembered feeling moved to give one an affectionate hug when her wise friend, Bonnie, hugged it first. She herself, as it turned out, was a tree hugger. And a hypocrite evidently.

The trip to Warcop ended under an apple tree. It was so large that it was being utilized as shade for the picnic laid out beneath it. Set apart from the throng of revelers, the setting provided both shelter from the bright sunshine along with some privacy. This picnic was of a different variety from that of the other parishioners for here a heavy oak table sat beneath the tree and was set with the finest of delicate china and shining cutlery. Serving staff stood by the four people seated at the table who all looked up when the carriage arrived and Catherine and Aria got out.

A man and three women stood to greet them. Catherine introduced the man as her father, Roger de Clifford, Aria's eighteenth-ago grandfather and the Lord of Appleby Castle, and one of the three women as her mother, Maud de Beauchamp. She and her parents, she said, were on the line of Joseph of the New England Company. The remaining two women were on her father's side through May of the Moon Men and Nancy Ann of the Virginia Company. Margaret Strickland, her eighteenth-ago grandmother, was also a resident of Westmoreland whereas the other woman, Elizabeth Dispenser, her twenty-second-ago grandmother lived later and elsewhere. She was, however, the great granddaughter of King Edward I, Hammer of the Scots who was the torturer and murderer of William Wallace.

Before Aunt Catherine had disappeared from view in yet another carriage, Aria was already asking Margaret Strickland if she knew the de Cliffords, Maud and Roger, in her lifetime since they all lived in Westmoreland and they were all her eighteenth-ago grandparents.

"Of course, Child. Roger is our constable here. He and Maud live at Appleby Castle and my husband, Robert Lowther, and I live at Sizergh Castle. This little village of Warcop is my inheritance but I give it to Roger. It's only a few miles from his home."

Overhearing her remark, Roger interjected, "Speaking of our little village, would you be so kind as to take this purse of coins and distribute them to the sellers in the tents. Margaret can show you around and I'll wager a cold ale that there will be places of honor for the heiress and her guest reserved for viewing the dancers if you wish. Then when you are ready you can return here where the four of us will join you in a meal before you have to go." Turning now to Margaret he said, "If you see any of those golden cakes with the honeyed nuts, could you bring me two this year?"

Aria and Margaret walked to the tents surrounding the church. The local children knew the heiress by sight and a line resembling little ducklings formed behind the two women as they entered each tent. Margaret purchased treats and each child left with enough for both hands and additional sweets tucked into pockets for later. She bought golden cakes for Roger and each of his guests and had them sent over to the table under the apple tree. With their last coins, the women purchased a frothy ale for themselves and made their way to their seats in front of the Maypole.

"Why do the dancers paint their faces black?"

"Because the Morris Men accompany the Coal Black Man. They enter and exit through the chimney."

"Like Santa!", Aria said as she watched the conversing dancers adjusting their knee bells while the musicians were taking their ale break.. "I doubt there is any connection but it was my third-ago grandmother, Mariah Morris, who talked me into coming here."

"The connections are always present. The Morris clan is ancient and your grandmother, Mariah, is a descendent of this line. There are tales that associate the Morris Men with Merry the Gypsy, where you hear them called Merry's Men."

"The Morris clan is Egyptian?"

"No. Merry the Gypsy is mentioned in the bible where she is called St. Mary Jacobs. She is a Nazarine priestess and a companion of Mary Magdelene when she relocates to Septimania in France. Her name is spelled with an E and not an A which indicates her connection to the sea. Mer is sea. She is a sea maid. Or a mermaid."

"I never read that Mary Magdelene traveled with a mermaid", Aria pointed out with certainty.

"You probably never read that she moved to France either, did you? Perhaps there is a great deal about Mary Magdelene that you don't know."

"I'm sure you're right about that. But I can definitely say that I never ever heard of anyone called Merry the Gypsy."

"Your lack of knowledge about her is by design. St. Mary Jacobs is greatly revered in her lifetime and beyond. So much so that Emperor Constantine has her veneration banned along with her greenwood marriages. Her oath of wedlock is called 'to marry'."

"What is a greenwood marriage?"

"It is a marriage that is only binding for a year and a day. If, after this time, a couple discovers they are infertile, it enables them the freedom to find another mate who might not be. It is known as a hand fasting and is still being performed in a Scottish village a little north of here called Gretna Green up until your twentieth century."

"Why there?"

"Gretna Green marks the center of the Dal Riata kingdom. The Dal Riata are the Albigens of Western Scotland and adhere to the same belief systems. The Albigens of Eastern Scotland are called the Picts and St. Colomba is their apostle. The Romans occupy Britain and bring their high universal church with them. When Columba steps out of bounds and crowns Aedan macGabran as Uther Pendragon he officially establishes the Dal Riata kingdom in Britain upsetting the Romans and their church."

"What is an Uther Pendragon?"

"Pendragon means head of the dragon. The dragon is the ancient symbol of the power of the greenwood. The pendragon serves as king over all the other tribal kings during times of conflict. The King of the kings, so to speak."

The musicians, having returned, struck up a tune and the bells on the knees of the dancers matched the beat of the drums as the colorful and noisy dance began. Margaret and Aria watched two sets of dancers before returning to join the other grandparents under the apple tree.

Roger and Maud graciously hosted their picnic but Aria was fast losing her appetite as she thought about the impending ride on a submarine. Did she hear that right? She hoped desperately that she had heard it wrong and she would be spending the night tonight over at Appleby Castle and waking up tomorrow in this new Eden. She hoped that if she asked Roger and Maud enough questions about their castle they would want to take her home with them to show it off. They patiently answered her questions about the English weather and what apples graced the sauce for the roast and how old Appleby Castle was. As it turned out, there had been only three owners of the castle, Roger and Maud being the third. All three owners had served as Sheriff of Westmoreland and Lord of Appleby. The castle had an omphalos stone which served as a marker for the center of a kingdom. This one being Eden where Appleby Castle sits squarely in the center of the Eden Valley and is encircled by the convergence of two rivers, the Eden and the Eamont.

"This would be a fun place to spend the night", Aria suggested trying to steer the conversation. "My home is called Eden, you know."

Roger, ever the sheriff, saw right through her ruse as if she were transparent. "We know that you are apprehensive about riding on the submarine. That problem is being worked on right now. We would love to have you as a guest in our home but it is vital that you stay as close to your schedule as possible. For your safety, of course."

For her safety? What the heck did that mean? From here on out she would run a little faster when following a guide. Embarrassed that he had so easily discovered her ploy to stay, she was quick to change subjects. "Catherine said this place has another name too. Something like Appleby but not."

"Avalon" Roger stated. "The Plain of Apples is its meaning. It is the Otherworld. The Underground Country."

"We aren't underground."

"The veil is thin here in Appleby. Reality is more than you perceive. The apple trees live in both realms at once. It is the oldest cultivated tree in Europe and a member of the rose family. There is an age when the deliberate felling of an apple tree is punishable by death."

Aria chuckled to herself. "I'm back to thinking about my grade school education when they taught us the little story about George Washington chopping down the cherry tree and then admitting it like he had committed some sort of cardinal sin."

Margaret responded to her remark. "That's because a cherry tree is of the rose family too. Cousin to the apple. The Washington ancestors of your President have their home on our Strickland land just south of Sizergh Castle. And yes, it does seem a bit of a sin to cut them down, the apple trees. They are not from this world."

"What world are they from?"

"Hyperborea", Roger answered, "where summer never ends." His look alone let Aria know that his authority on this matter was forbidden to be questioned.

"Where is Hyperborea?"

"At the back of the North Wind", he answered in all seriousness.

"It is an eternal spring far to the north bordered by the earth encircling river, Oceanus."

"Is this a romantic way of saying that it is on another planet?"

"It's an ocean voyage. That's how the Hyperboreans get here."

"What does a Hyperborean look like?"

"They look much like the five of us sitting here at this table. They have Rh negative blood."

Aria gasped! "That's my blood type! My strange blood, yes?"

"It is rare and alien to this reality and happens in no other species on earth. The vast majority of the population of the world is Rh positive. It becomes necessary to produce a vaccine for saving the life of an Rh positive fetus from being destroyed as an alien invader in the womb of an Rh negative mother."

"Are you talking UFO alien? Am I from off planet?"

Roger looked irritated with her. "You need to listen closer and not rely on old fictions so readily. I told you that the Hyperboreans come by ship. By water."

"So did these Hyperboreans come here to Appleby, or Avalon or Eden or whatever it was called then?"

"Yes, and to Iceland, France, and Scandinavia. In fact wherever you are likely to find high concentrations of Rh negative blood. The people of the British Isles are at one time called the Hyperboreans."

"Did they leave the omphalos stone where your castle sits?"

"I wasn't here when the castle was built so I don't know about the stone. Your ancestor on your father's side, Ranulf le Meschines III, builds Appleby Castle."

"Again, I am amazed by the interactions of my parent's linage so long ago. My dad's ancestor builds the castle and two owners later it belongs to my mom's ancestors?"

Elizabeth nodded in agreement and spoke to Aria. "It is mysterious, isn't it? I too descend from Ranulf le Meschines, whose mysterious wife, the Countess Lucy, has inherited the island in the center of Eden, from her second husband. Ranulf is her third."

"What is mysterious about the countess?"

"For one thing, she isn't a countess at all and yet everyone calls her one. Her name is Lucy Turoldsdottir but no one really knows who Turold is. It is often speculated that he is the elf named on the Bayeux Tapestry."

"Is that the tapestry with the unicorn in the fence?"

"No. The Bayeux Tapestry depicts the Norman Invasion of England in 1066. It is very long and detailed and for some reason only three people on the tapestry are named on the tapestry and Turold, the elf, is one of them."

"Was Lucy's second husband an elf?"

"He is Roger de Romara and I don't believe he is an elf", Elizabeth remarked with nonchalance. "Roger acquires the land in the center of Eden from the first Earl of Huntingdon, Tostig Godwinsson. But the Council wants you to hear that story from the bears since the earldom passes to them."

"Bears, Elizabeth? Bears? Did you mean to say that?"

"Oh dear!", Elizabeth said quite flustered to have said too much.

Aria felt instant empathy for Elizabeth who had the demeanor of a kitten and wanted only to put her at ease again. "No worries, Elizabeth. What's a few bears among the elves and the mermaids, right? Tell me now who the Norman's are. I know nothing about the Norman Invasion of England."

"I'll tell you, Child" Margaret said, "since my husband, your grandfather, is descended from them. The Norman Invasion is headed by William the Conqueror who is the son of Rollo the Viking. The Normans are the Norse. The Vikings. Appleby is a Norse word that means apple farm. The Norse influence is all around us. Even Ranulf le Meschines is affected by their culture when he gets involved with the ring. Ranulf is a wealthy land owner in Westmoreland but also in the adjoining county of Cumberland. It is in St. Bees in Cumberland that he donates some of his land so that his brother, William, also your grandfather, can build the priory to house the ring."

"I have two grandfathers who are brothers?"

"Yes. Your lineage passes through both brothers."

"Why did a ring need a priory to house it?"

"Because there is a time when St. Bees is known for the ring and pilgrimages are made there. In your time, St. Bees will only be famous for being the birthplace of Edmund Grindall, the Archbishop of Canterbury."

"Hey!", shouted Aria, "I know that guy! John Wilson from Inverary is related to him…er, I'm related to him. An uncle I think. But why a pilgrimage to visit a ring?"

"There is an overlay story that an Irish princess named Beaga or "Bees", flees to the English coast to escape an unwanted arranged marriage. According to her, she is given a bracelet by what she calls "a heavenly being" and a cult develops around the bracelet. The narrative insists that the cult develops around St. Beaga, but when the princess moves away from the village, now named after her, the cult persists with the veneration of the bracelet, or ring. In Norse the word for ring is beaga."

"What do you mean by cult?"

"The ring is a touchstone, a power object. It's a ring of power and truth. People swear oaths on the ring. If one is to break an oath that has been sworn on the ring, retribution will be swift, just, and happen of its own accord."

"Wow! That would be a priceless object. Is it still in that priory?"

"Wetheral Priory that William le Meschines builds to house the ring still stands in modern times but the ring is no longer there. When it is there, Wetheral is the richest priory in England."

"Who was the second owner of Appleby Castle?"

Maud spoke answering, "The second owner of our castle is Robert de Vieupont. He is sheriff of Westmoreland like Roger and Ranulf but he is a particularly harsh one. When Ranulf is appointed Earl of Chester, he bequeaths Appleby Castle to King Henry II. Henry then gives it to his son, John. John appoints Robert de Vieupont as one of his hundreds of sheriffs and gives him Appleby Castle."

"That story reminds me of King John and the Sheriff of Nottingham", Aria expounded. "is this the same John or is he even real?"

"Maud", Roger said to his wife, "recite that little poem you know about Ranulf."

"I cannot perfect my Lord's prayer", Maud recited,

As the priest sings it.

But I can

Rhymes of Robin Hood

And Randolf, Earl of Chester!"

"I take it that is your way of telling me that not only is John real but so is Robin Hood since he is lumped in there with my real grandfather. Don't tell me he's my grandfather too!"

"Okay I won't", Maud said, "because he isn't. We all know him as Robert de Ver. He and Lytol John and their band often come to hunt in Inglewood Forest where Margaret's husband, Robert Lowther, is the keeper."

"You will meet de Ver tomorrow", Roger said to her and rose from his seat. "I hope your anticipation of that will make your passage to France less worrisome. I'm sorry to say that it is time for you to go."

"Are you sure I need to travel all the way to France to meet an English folk hero?"

Aria couldn't help but make one last stab at avoiding a ride on a submarine.

"Robert de Ver's ancestors are French, as are Maud's. Why such fear of a submarine?"

"I really like fresh air", she squeaked apologetically. Still, it was true.

"Maud is making the crossing with you." Aria perked up considerably at his words.

He continued, "Her father, Thomas de Beauchamp, is your next guide."

Butterflys were flying kamikaze missions in her stomach as Aria worried over her impending ride deep beneath the sea. She attempted to make small talk to hide her irrational fear. "Perhaps someday I will return to Warcop as a tourist to watch the Morris dancers here at St. Columba's again."

Margaret tried to cheer her, sensing her distress. "You might also want to visit the Appleby Fair as well. It also survives into the modern age."

"An apple fair?" Aria said this still distracted by fear and commented half-heartedly, "That sounds like fun."

"Not an apple fair, Child. Appleby Fair is the oldest fair in England and was originally a fertility rite of the horse goddess, Epona, whose other name is Eden. The fair is dominated by the gypsies who come to sell their fine horses."

Aria and Maud climbed into the black and white carriage with the black and white team and left Warcop and the rush bearing behind. Aria, now overtaken by an odd exhaustion, asked Maud one last time if it was imperative that she leave for France.

"Na biodh eagla ort, Child. It will be some time before we reach the transport station. Maybe you should rest."

"Temple Sowerby is only minutes away", Aria whined.

"But the submarine station is at Settle in Yorkshire. There is sufficient time for rest."

The gentle clip clop of the horses hooves as they fairly meandered along put Aria at ease. At least they weren't racing to the submarine. In this time squished world in which she was traveling the stars were already popping out with their nightly display. The heat was gone and Aria reached for the cloak from where she had left it and wrapped up in its delicious warmth. Clip clop. Clip clop. Within moments she was sound asleep.

Reverend John Wilson
Massachusetts Bay Colony

MINISTER – FIRST CHURCH OF BOSTON

Ancestor of Joseph of the New England Company

Majorie de Bruys
Countess of Carrick

Mother of Robert The Bruce

Ancestor of May of the Moon Men

Robert the Bruce

King of Scotland

Ancestor of May of the Moon Men

Elizabeth le Despenser

Great Granddaughter of King Edward I

*Ancestor of Nancy Ann of the Virginia Company and
Joseph of the New England Company*

Maud Beauchamp Clifford

daughter - Thomas de Beauchamp

Ancestor of Joseph of the New England Company

CHAPTER THREE

"It's like being a Knight of the Garter, it's an honor, but it doesn't hold up anything."

Bishop Fulton J. Sheen

Robert Earl of Huntingdon
Lies under this little stone
No archer was like him so good
His wildness named him Robin Hood.

November 8, 1247
Headstone of Robert de Ver
Northern England

"Knowledge is power"

Sir Francis Bacon

MORNING LIGHT PENETRATED the carriage and woke Aria from her deep slumber. "How on earth did we get to France in a carriage?", she asked Maud in a sleep stupor.

"It isn't France. We are still in Northern England. This is Settle in the Ilkey Moors.

The Council altered the schedule to accommodate your fears regarding the submarine. Such things are more easily faced in the light of day after a restful night's sleep.

Maud's tone held not a hint of judgement concerning Aria's cowardice but still it cut her to the quick. "I'm so sorry to have disrupted the plans. I've always been claustrophobic and I don't know how to overcome it. I feel terrible about this."

"Now we are behind schedule", Maud said without any accusatory tone.

Aria slumped in her seat with shame. They rode the rest of the way to a building called Giggleswick in silence. The building looked too new to have existed during Maud's time in history so Aria inquired as to the dichotomy of this.

"This building does not exist here in my era. However, the portal is always here and so is the transport station for the submarine. Don't ask more about it and don't look the man in black at the door in the eyes." After this odd remark, Maud jumped out of the carriage leaving a stunned Aria staring at the imposing figure standing guard at the door and wondering how she could look a man wearing sunglasses in the eyes. Sunglasses? She jumped out of the coach and ran to catch up.

Scurrying through the door and past the man in black, Aria was shushed again by her guide and told not to talk. Maud led her silently to a small room where a fresh set of clothes and toiletries had been set out for her. "Be quick", she whispered, "and meet me at the elevator, first hall to the right."

Aria re-dressed and re-braided her hair in a frantic hurry, desperate to make up for the wasted time that she had caused so that whoever was watching, the Council, would not be so ashamed of her. The new outfit consisted of some sort of pants or leggings with a wool tunic over them, slit to the waist on the sides and tied with a small belt. Boots replaced the embroidered slippers she had been wearing. Her hair needed washing more than re-braiding but a bath, or better yet, a shower, may never be made available to her so she was grateful for the perfumes and powders that were always left for her use. She barely availed herself of these sweet treasures in her haste to get out the door and meet up with Maud. She did indeed leave so fast that she left the Silver Branch in the changing room and was forced to backtrack in order to retrieve it.

When she did reach the elevator Maud was already inside waiting with her finger on the button. Aria rushed in beside her and the door closed and they plummeted to the center of the earth. Or at least it felt that way. The G forces were too strong and prevented Aria from conversing with Maud. She wanted to ask about the sunglasses and this elevator and even the working toilet that was in the changing room but when the door slid open again she forgot all about her questions because there was the submarine, bobbing on the water in its bright yellow glory. It was an exact replica of the one the Beatles sang about in Yellow Submarine. Written large across the side in blue lettering was the word Wavesweeper. Aria smiled in appreciation and noticed the small smirk that Maud was attempting to conceal.

The women hurried up a set a stairs to a plank walkway out to the open hatch and climbed into the submarine. If the appearance of the outside of the submarine had put Aria's fears to rest, then certainly the Council had outdone themselves with the inside. For here also was an exact replica of a comforting sight, the library in Iverary Castle, complete with wood paneled walls, books, and soft lighting. This interior was just big enough for two over stuffed chintz covered chairs flanking a loaded mahogany tea cart. The honey pot next to the warm rolls was shaped like the yellow submarine in which they stood. Walt Disney couldn't have done a better job at staging the happiest place on earth. So instead of being terrified to be on a submarine, Aria felt only delight and gratitude. Na biodh eagla ort.

Maud sealed the hatch and they sat down to tea. The submarine plunged beneath the water in a flotilla of bubbles while Maud filled the tea cups and Aria spread golden honey on her fragrant roll.

"Is Giggleswick the same sort of establishment as Temple Sowerby?"

"I'm not at liberty to say much about that but I am permitted to answer one question only."

"Hmm" Aria pondered for a moment before speaking. "Why are there gold stars on a bright blue ceiling in the sanctuary?"

"They represent the world in which you live."

"Outer space?"

"No. Stars stuck to the ceiling."

Aria had no idea what that cryptic reply might mean but her question had been answered so she moved on. "I think I need to hear again about Tarzan and Robin Hood being real." Was she really going to meet a story book character today?

"All that has a name exists, Child. Robert and Lord Clayton have a life just like you. The stories carry a message based on their lives. There are many stories in the world. In your modern time there is a story that Neil Armstrong walks on the moon and this too carries a message. These individuals seem larger than life because the message is larger than life."

"Do the English worship the moon like the Scots?"

"Our heritage contains an understanding of the moon and its importance in our lives. Notice that I don't say the word worship. England's original name is Albion. Albion is the Milk White Moon Goddess."

"Is Tarzan immortal?"

"Just long lived. He is no more immortal than Odin, the progenitor of the Grebson line of John's family."

"The Norse god?" Aria couldn't hide the skepticism in her voice.

"Do you believe him to be only a story too, Child? That proof you can look up for yourself in the Encyclopedia Britannica where it clearly states that Odin is an actual person. There is a cult of Odin which the Grebsons, his heirs, follow. A cult at odds with the high Roman church who sought to extinguish it. The Grebsons are burned at the stake for four hundred years accused of witchcraft. And so the people of the Deira like to live very private lives. I speak of John and his family. Deira is another name assigned to the Grebsons. It means waters. Deira is a town near Appleby. Margaret Strickland, from yesterday's picnic is the heiress of Deira but she she doesn't give that village to Roger!", Maud laughed.

"Maybe its more valuable", Aria said and laughed too.

"It may well be. The little island in the Derwentwater River that runs by it is inhabited by St. Herbert. He is a people's saint. Roman Christianity is very slow to take root in Northern England just as it is in Scotland and Wales. Another people's saint, St. Cuthburt, is St. Herbert's best friend. St. Cuthburt is the Prior at Melrose Abbey where Robert the Bruce's heart is buried. Herbert and Cuthburt die at the same moment on the same day, one at Deira, one at Melrose. And yet they live on in this story."

"Why did the heart of Robert the Bruce get buried in Melrose Abbey?"

"Melrose Abbey is the mother church of the Templars and the Cistercians but that is a story for later today. There is one last roll so you should finish it before we dock."

"Dock? Where? On an island? We just left Northern England minutes ago!"

"We are arriving now at the transport station in France. It is imperative that you not fall behind schedule so the Council has no alternative but to condense this crossing. Since the use of the submarine will be availed to you on another occasion, it is also imperative to quell your fears so as not to lose additional time later. However there will be physical effects and for that I apologize. You should adjust and be feeling rested again by tomorrow."

Aria, with renewed humiliation over her stupid fear and the trouble it caused, left the last roll uneaten and followed Maud up and out of the hatch. A gentleman waited for her on the walkway in the near darkness. Maud introduced him as her father, Thomas de Beauchamp, before getting back into the submarine. What a difference a few minutes makes, now all Aria wanted was to get back into the coziness of the submarine with Maud instead of standing here in the gloom with a strange man.

Thomas took Aria's elbow and led her down the stairs and across the dim platform where a small train sat at the bottom of spiral train tracks leading up into complete darkness. The train was only two cars long. One was the engine without an engineer and the other a tiny car with two single seats facing each other. It was a wonder that the small trainlet could even pull itself up the winding tracks, but with great strain and effort, it did. The noise of the strain however prevented conversation so Aria tried not to make eye contact with this new grandfather. He was quite handsome and wore a tunic much like the one she was wearing. An insignia had been embroidered on his, it was the ball and cross. The logo of the sacred tribes.

The trip to the surface probably took longer than the time spent crossing from England to France and Aria was relieved when the train finally leveled out and deposited them into yet another cave. However sunlight was streaming into this one.

"Where are we?", Aria asked Thomas as she followed him toward the sunlight.

"This is called Abbeville. It's a prehistoric site that is millions of years old. Outside this cave is Gamaches. We are expected at Castle Gamaches which is owned by your twenty-fourth-ago grandfather, Thomas de St. Valery. Thomas is not a contemporary of my wife, Katherine, and I. You will meet her too this morning. He is closer in time to the other relative you will meet, Llywellyn of Wales. Also, Elizabeth Dispenser's mother, Eleanor, is there. Are you up for riding?"

"Absolutely!" Aria agreed as quickly as she could, trying to sound enthusiastic. She was not going to make another fear based error that would slow her progress to wherever it was that she was going. She needed to get there and get home and if she had to do it fast then she was willing to climb into a spaceship if need be.

She didn't feel quite so enthusiastic once they had walked out into the warm sunshine of western France and Aria saw just why it was that she was wearing pants. Two horses were tethered under the shade of a large tree. Aria loved horses but how many decades must have passed since she last rode one?

"You do ride, don't you?", Thomas asked.

"Yes", she answered simply and put on the most sincere smile she could manage.

Thomas did not spur his horse and race to another castle of another grandfather like Aria thought he might do. Their horses walked side by side enabling Aria to ask her questions. "Will Robin Hood be coming to meet me?"

Thomas smiled. The first one she had seen. "You will go to meet Robert."

"Is it far from here?"

"Very. But I'm sure you're already aware that it doesn't matter."

"Is it in Sherwood Forest where I'll meet him?"

Now Thomas laughed a little. "Sherwood Forest is in England. This is France. After our stop at Castle Gamaches, we will continue riding to Poitiers. If you have trouble pronouncing it in French you may call it Pictavia.

"Are you French?"

"English. Born at Warwick Castle. It's Maud's mother, Katherine de Mortimer, who has the French connections. She is descended from the Lusignans of Poitiers."

"Yet you serve as my guide and not her?"

"I have my own connections to France. I am the Marshall of England, head of security for King Edward III and I serve as his commander in a place near here called Crecy de Ponthieu in the opening battle of the Hundred Years War."

"Did it really last for a hundred years?"

"One hundred sixteen to be exact."

"What could you fight over for that long ?"

"Gascony."

"Who is Gascony?"

"Not who but what. Gascony is an autonomous region of Southern France."

"What was England doing? A land grab from France?"

"Eleanor of Aquitaine is its heiress. She bequeaths it to King Henry II of England when she marries him. It passes through generations of English kings before King Philip of France decides that the matrilineal inheritance of the Plantagenets is no longer applicable and declares that Gascony once again belongs to France."

"And what is a plantagenet?"

"The Royal line of Henry II and Eleanor. The title comes from the broom plant. Henry's grandfather, Henry I, is an avid hunter and he plants acres of it to broaden his hunt. The nickname sticks."

"Gascony must be one heck of a state for the fight over it to last so long."

"The remarkable thing about it is that it isn't a state at all. And it's not a county or a provence or any other thing belonging to the French. Basqueland, it is called in your time, but you will never see it designated like that on anyone's maps but their own. It is where the Basque people live and even that name is our designation and not theirs. They call themselves Euskara speakers, meaning those who speak the language of the sun, Ak, in Hyperborea."

"Where summer never ends? Did these Basque people want to be French or English?"

"I would imagine neither but they fight alongside the French."

"Did you win?"

"No."

"Why do you wear St. Columba's cross embroidered on your tunic?"

"We call it the Creator's Cross. It's the emblem of the Knights of the Garter."

Aria gasped in surprise. "You're one of those knights? Highest honor in the world thing? Limited to twenty five? And you are one of them? How did you get nominated?"

"I am the co-founder with Edward III." He trotted out ahead of her as Castle Gamaches came into view and when they had both reached the doors, stable hands were waiting to care for the horses. Aria dismounted and wondered if it looked like she was walking like a gnome because that is how it felt. Regardless, she rushed gnome-like into the castle after her famous grandfather.

Katherine de Mortimer met them inside and introduced herself. Thomas appeared relieved of his conversational responsibilities since his wife was in the room. He sat down in the sunlit space. Katherine introduced Aria to Eleanor de Clare who was the mother of Elizabeth from the picnic and to Thomas de St. Valery who was the owner of Castle

Gamaches. The final grandparent introduced to Aria was Llywellyn the Great, King of Wales."

Aria was speechless. A King? A Great King? She, ordinary Aria, was descended from a royal personage standing right here in front of her? What was she supposed to do? Bow? Curtsy? Kiss his ring? Was he wearing one? Katherine saved her and led her to a chair near the fireplace. It might be warm outside in the sun but the temperature was considerably cooler indoors. Aria worked on controlling her trembling and tried not to look at her royal grandfather.

She was glad when Katherine took the time to explain a little about all these new grandparents. "My husband, Thomas, is a descendent of Thomas de St. Valery although he will never admit to being French. As you know, we are the parents of Maud Beauchamp of Appleby Castle. Eleanor is the mother of Elizabeth Dispenser and the wife of Hugh le Dispenser. She is also the granddaughter of King Edward I, Hammer of the Scots. Eleanor is an ancestor of Nancy Ann of the Virginia Company. I am descended from Llywellyn and his wife Joan and we are the ancestors of Joseph of the New England Company as is Thomas de St. Valery. Our common denominator in the room is King John of England. King Edward I is his grandson. Llywellyn's wife Joan is his illegitimate daughter and Thomas de St. Valery saw his half-sister murdered by him.

"King John from Robin Hood, right?"

"There is ever only the one. No monarch wishes to give their child his name."

"Is the Sheriff of Nottingham real too?"

"We all know him as Roger of Hell. Roger de Lacy. Maud marries his descendent, Roger de Clifford. You are descended from him, Child."

"What about you, Thomas? Are you a descendent of John?"

"Almost", he snickered, "my marriage to Katherine needed papal dispensation due to our being too closely related."

Katherine reacted with a bit of sarcasm in her tone. "Sure, that needed papal dispensation but nobody seemed to mind that I was being married off at five years old."

"Five years old?', Aria said alarmed. "How old were you, Thomas?"

"Twenty-three", he answered shamelessly.

Katherine was noting the look of disgust on Aria's face. "It is a different time and we are a different culture, we ruling elite. Arranged marriages are considered normal. The protocol is that betrothal at eight years of age is accepted, with marriage at twelve and consummation at fourteen. Probably even that seems distasteful to you."

"I apologize for appearing judgmental. However, wasn't even the standard protocol violated if you were married off at five?"

"Elfael is at stake. It is my inheritance and my marriage portion. There is a tug of war over who will gain the legitimate lordship of Elfael. and our marriage grants that title to Thomas."

"Is Elfael some place in fairyland?"

"It's a province in Wales. Cadwallon ap Madog, son of Prince Madog who discovers America, is the one who feels he should have the lordship of Elfael. His brother, Eineon, is already the prince of Elvenia. In the end though, Cadwallon barely protests. The marcher lords are really more of a threat. It is the marcher, Pain fitzJohn who builds Painscastle there in Elfael."

Thomas de St. Valery added his thoughts to the conversation. "It's not Painscastle anymore! It proudly wears my half-sister's name now, Matilda's Castle."

"Why is that?"

"Because she earned it!" He appeared filled with pride for his half-sister. "Without her husband's aid she fended off thousands of Welsh Gwenwynwyn in an attack that lasted for three weeks."

"Her husband let that happen?"

"Happily", Thomas answered. "My half-sister marries none other than the Ogre of Abergavenny, William Braose, who is perfectly content with sticking Matilda in Painscastle and then conveniently disappearing."

"How did a little woman fend off thousands of Welshmen?"

Everyone in the room laughed at her question but none more so than Thomas de St. Valery. "Moll isn't little", he said.

"Who is Moll? I thought we were talking about your half-sister, Matilda?"

"Moll Wallbee is my half-sister. That is her folk name. Her real name is Matilda de St. Valery. And Moll isn't little because Moll is a giant."

"Like six feet tall or something?"

"No. Taller. An actual giant. She builds Hay on Wye Castle in a single night by carrying the stones in her apron."

"Oh, I see now. A folk hero is based on your sister called Moll Wallbee. Just like the character of Hester Prynne is based on Anne Hutchinson but Hester Prynne isn't real. So Moll isn't real."

"She's as real as they come", Thomas corrected. "Katherine just told you that King John murders her. Clause thirty-nine is added to the Magna Carta due to how John kills her. No noble person ever wants to suffer such a death at the hands of a monarch again."

"What did he do to her?"

"Bricks her up in the castle with her son, William, and starves them to death."

This information sickened Aria. "That has to be the worst possible death!"

"I know of worse", Eleanor chimed in. "My husband's death and that of his lover, King Edward II, come to mind. Do you know what it means to be hung, drawn and quartered, Child?"

"Fortunately I do not."

"Well, one is hung by the neck until almost dead but not quite. Cut down from the gallows they are then placed on a table where all four limbs are tied to four horses who take off in four different directions. This is the death meted out to my husband, Hugh le Dispenser. Don't ask me how Edward dies."

"Who could be so barbaric as to do such a thing?", Aria asked in revulsion.

"My father", said Katherine de Mortimer.

"Aren't the two of you on opposite sides of my family? Is one side killing the other now?"

"Yes", Katherine said to her. "Your Celtic braid of a genealogy weaves tight in our time. Eleanor's Uncle Edward II, lover of her husband, Hugh le Dispenser, is deposed and then killed by both sides of your family.

Edward's son, Edward III, co-founds the Knights of the Garter with my Thomas. Edward III is placed on the throne as a child after his mother, Isabella, the She Wolf of France, and her lover, Roger de Mortimer, who is my father, dépose and murder Edward II. Edward II is weak and loses the Battle of Bannockburn against Robert the Bruce. He is unpopular. Once deposed, Father and Isabella are the de facto rulers of England until Edward III puts an end to it. And an end to my father when he hangs him."

Turning to Thomas de Beauchamp Aria asked, "How could you serve the king who killed your father-in-law?"

"My father-in-law killed his father. Edward III is his own man. He establishes the order of the Garter, doesn't he?"

"Why are you called the Knights of the Garter? Is it like the ring at St. Bees and oaths are sworn on it?"

"The garter, the blue garter specifically, is the most magical article of clothing worn by a priestess of the Elder Faith. However, wearing one sets you up for heresy charges. It is Joan of Kent, the Countess of Salisbury, whose garter is accidentally revealed placing her in a potentially lethal situation. Joan is the wife of the Black Prince, the son of Edward III."

"Why is he called the Black Prince?"

"His mother is black. Phillipa of Hainalt is the wife of Edward III. Father and Isabella seek warships when they go to depose Isabella's husband, Edward II, and they procure them from Phillipa's father, the Count of Hainalt. In exchange for this favor, Phillipa is promised as wife to Isabella's son, Edward III."

"What ended up happening to Joan who wore the garter?"

"Edward III is there when it happens and he snatches up the offending garter and puts it on himself and proclaims, "Shame to him who sees wrong in it." That is still their motto even into the modern age. The mission is to protect women. The Knights are dedicated to Mary Magdelene."

"So it is the Elder Faith that puts the Creator's Cross on your tunic, Thomas. And you, Katherine, inherit Elfael from your father who is running England?"

"I inherit Elfael from my mother", Katherine explains. "My mother is not Isabella, wife of Edward II, who is my father's mistress. Father is legally married to Joan de Geneville, one of the richest heiresses of the Welsh marches. Her inheritance, Ludlow Castle in England where I am born, is built for us by our de Geneville ancestors, the de Lucys. Roger de Lucy is Roger of Hell, Sheriff of Nottingham."

"I thought Thomas said that you were born in Pictavia."

"My mother's mother is Jean de Lusignan of Poitiers. Llywellyn's wife, Joan, grows up in the Lusignan family home and not in her father's court, although King John acknowledges her as Princess of Wales. Her stepfather is Hugh X de Lusignan, our ancestor."

Aria wondered if Joan was as wicked as her father, John. She tried to steal quick glances at her grandfather the king who hadn't uttered a single word yet in this conversation. It couldn't have been much fun to have King John as a father-in-law.

He caught her glances and commented, "You are wondering if the apple falls far from the tree."

"No Sir, Your Majesty, Sir."

"Yes you are and don't call me majestic. Just call me Llywellyn. We have our troubles, Joan and I. It's well known that I discover her in my own bed with William Braose."

"Moll Wallbee's husband?"

"No. Same family, same name, different man. But you, Child, are descended from both of them."

"Is adultery a crime in your age? Did John punish him?"

"He punishes Joan. He puts her under house arrest for two years and takes away her title during that time. He doesn't get the opportunity to punish Braose because I do it for him. I drag the horse's ass out of my bed and into the marsh behind the castle and hang him. Enough said."

Llywellyn didn't seem to be interested in any more recounting of his wife's sordid past so Aria looked around the room for someone else to talk to. Her gaze landed on Eleanor. "Your daughter, Elizabeth, seems like such a sweet person."

"She is only six when Hugh is murdered, poor dear. She becomes a nun. Not surprising really. I am only fourteen when Hugh and I are married. He has just been knighted at the Feast of the Swans."

"What is that?"

"A mass knighting staged by Edward I. Grandfather knights Uncle Edward and then Uncle Edward knights two hundred sixty six more men. Katherine's father, Roger, is one of them. Imagine that! He knights the very man who deposes him as king."

"What do the swans signify?"

"The new knights all swear an oath on the two swans that are at the feast."

"Like Beaga's ring? What was the oath?"

"Grandfather wants revenge for the death of John Comyn by Robert the Bruce."

"But the Bruce and John Comyn were the joint guardians after your grandfather murders William Wallace. There are politics at work here that I don't comprehend. Was it going to take two hundred and sixty six men to kill Robert the Bruce?"

"He also wants the Armstrongs dead. And any other Scotsmen who oppose him."

Aria stopped asking questions. Killing ran rampant in both sides of her family. It should have felt honorable to discover so much royalty in her bloodline but her real descent was from grandfathers who killed grandmothers and grandmothers who killed grandfathers and grandfathers who killed other grandfathers, ad nauseam. They were killers who wore crowns perhaps, but still, they were killers. Was that a genetic gift from John?

Thomas de Beauchamp stood and looked at Aria. "It's time to ride, Child" He turned and hurried out the door with a bewildered and startled Aria on his heels.

Aria and Thomas rode for miles through French countryside. It was a warm day under a cloudless sky and Aria remembered all over again how much she enjoyed riding a horse. Thomas rode just far enough ahead of Aria that no conversation was possible and she was glad for the silence and the soft breeze and the occasional butterfly that passed by. She was lost in her thoughts about beautiful Scotland, beautiful Northern England, and now beautiful France. She pushed her impressions about her ancestors that inhabited this land as far from her thoughts as possible. The only intrusion into her reverie about the beauty of nature in Europe were the words of Roger de Clifford at yesterday's picnic, "Tomorrow you will meet Robin Hood". Now it was tomorrow and he waited at the end of this long ride. It had been thrilling to meet a royal grandfather but now she was going to meet someone that she had always thought was imaginary. It was akin to being told that she was going to meet Peter Pan. Oh goodness! Was he real too?

Thomas turned his horse toward a dark thick expanse of trees with Aria and her horse following. He reined in his horse and stopped before entering the thick woods.

"Is Pictavia in there?", Aria asked.

"No. This is Y, Somme, Picardie, France."

"Why did you say that like it's some sort of address? Is it a village or something?"

"Not a village. This is the Mametz Woods."

"So why did you use that address?"

"Because you are discovering your genealogy and genealogists will know this place."

"A genealogist would know my genealogy?"

"All genealogies refer to this place. They call it the place of death." He urged his horse in under the canopy of trees and they entered the Mametz Woods.

A thick carpet of grass covered the ground under the old trees muffling any sounds the horse hooves might have made as they walked through. All sound disappeared the deeper they went. No birds, no chattering squirrels, no breeze through the leaves. Nothing. Being a child of the modern world, Aria had always wondered what it would be like to hear silence. This was it. And it wasn't pleasant. But perhaps it was something beyond the silence. Whatever it was bothered her because it was palpable and eerie. Hoping they could pick up the pace and leave this place, Thomas reined his horse to a stop.

"What now? Why are we stopping?"

"This is Y."

"There is nothing here but trees."

"It's beneath you. It's called the Y Ravine. When the woods disappear you can see it from above. The ravine is shaped like a Y."

"I don't understand, Thomas. It's definitely spooky in here but what does that have to do with genealogy or this being a place of death."

"I think that those who record genealogies only use this as a symbol", Thomas surmised. "Naturally, not all who are listed as having died here did so."

"Since this place even seems devoid of wildlife, I'd hazard a guess that nothing ever died here."

"Then you would be wrong, Child. The single deadliest battle of all time happens right here in the Mametz Wood. It is called the Battle of the Albert, named for a nearby village. It is the opening battle in the Battle of the Somme in what is called World War I. Fifty seven thousand people die here in a single day. Even the Mametz Wood is destroyed. Every tree, save one, dies. A hornbeam that is renamed the Danger Tree." The look on Thomas's face said that he had seen more death and killing than he ever needed.

"Did you die in the Hundred Years War, Thomas?"

"I die of the plague. Before that happens though, I'm imprisoned in the Tower of London. I have the dubious honor of having my tower named after me, Beauchamp's Tower. Some honor, huh?"

Aria wanted to ask how one progressed from being the Marshall of England to imprisonment in the Tower of London but considering what she was discovering about court intrigues, there probably was no point. Besides, she didn't want to remain even one moment longer in this oppressive atmosphere by making conversation. "Will I be spending the night in Pictavia tonight?" Aria asked this in the hopes that it would serve as the clue to be moving on.

"I wasn't told. I am entrusted to deliver you to the tower."

"Beauchamp's Tower?", she gasped.

"The Tower of London is in England, Child. We are still in France. I am taking you to the Tower of Maubergeonne. It's not a prison. It is built by William IX, the Duke of Aquitaine for his mistress, Maubergeonne.

You are dining with her and her guests tonight. We should leave now as the day grows short."

Happy to be leaving this doomed environment, she was happier still when the dark canopy of leaves began to thin and sunshine once again filled her vision. The oppressive gloom was now left behind in the woods that were destined for destruction. Yet a great weariness clung to her anyway and she wasn't sure if it was because of the information she was digesting or the push put on the submarine to play catch up.

After a time a city appeared on the horizon that Aria assumed must be Poitiers. The sun was already low in the sky when the horses reached the door of the tower where Aria was to dine. The staff awaiting their arrival were women, two of them. They were exotic beauties with caramel colored skin and warm brown eyes. Once Aria had dismounted, one of the women pulled an apple from the pocket of her skirt and showed it to Aria's horse who happily followed her around the corner and out of sight. Thomas turned silently and rode away.

The other beauty held open the door to the Tower of Maubergeonne. Aria walked through and the heat hit her like Palm Springs in August. This was heat that Aria knew well. This was desert heat. And sure enough, it was! The tower stones had somehow dissolved into the billowing walls of a canvas tent. A tent in the desert. She could see miles of desert and dunes outside the billowing tent door. The shock, combined with the sweltering confinement of the wool tunic and leggings made Aria feel like fainting.

The attendant pulled back a curtain wall to reveal a large copper tub. "A cool bath is drawn for you, m'lady, with the oils of lavender and lemons for your comfort."

Aria would not have allowed the attendant to leave without an explanation concerning this high strangeness except that it was becoming an emergency to get out of her wool tunic before she suffered heat stroke.

"Madame will be waiting for you to join her once you are feeling refreshed again. You are not to feel rushed", the beauty said as she scurried out.

Aria was already attempting to peel the heavy un-breathing tunic over her head in a desperate attempt to lower her body temperature.

"Wait please!", she called out from deep inside her wool prison. "How will I find your Madame?" Finally free of the dress, she started pulling off the leggings that were sticking to her sweat soaked body like a second skin. A half second later she was in the cool fragrant water.

The attendant stuck her head back through the canvas opening. "You will smell gingerbread." And then she was gone.

I'm losing my mind, Aria thought as she slipped under the water that was the perfect temperature to provide relief from the stifling heat. Relief not only from the oppressive heat but also the welcome relief that comes from contact with blessed water. That which washes things away. A baptism. A renewal. A cleansing. A bath at long last. She sank to the bottom of the ample tub and wished with all her heart that she could go home. She washed her hair and scrubbed her feet and looked out at the pink and blue sunset appearing and disappearing through the wind rustled tent walls. It wasn't home. Her Eden had no sand dunes. But it was the desert and she knew the scent of it, and the wind of it, and the heat of it, and it made her so homesick she thought she might die. She stared out from her perch in the tub until darkness began creeping into the tent. She wanted to quit but there was no quitting. She wanted to change her mind but it was too late. So she got out of the tub and slipped into the long white linen dress that had been left for her once her equestrian outfit had mysteriously disappeared. She would never get used to that nor to being called Child by people who were younger than her. If shoes had been left for her she couldn't find them in the deepening dark. She re-braided her wet and tangled hair because she couldn't find a brush either. She began groping her way barefoot along the curtained walls that all felt the same and led nowhere. Again convinced that she was losing her mind, she sat down on the Persian rug beneath her bare feet and gave up. Even Robert's little spider was not going to convince her to move from this spot. It was then that she smelled the gingerbread.

The smell led her to a light that was escaping from beneath a wooden door and the wooden door led back into the reality that was France. The tent was gone. The stone walls of the tower had returned. The woman removing hot gingerbread cookies, however, was nobody's grandma as far as Aria was concerned. The woman was ravishing. A diva. A goddess. She wore the same long white linen dress that Aria was wearing but the similarity stopped there. The mistress of the tower was far from ordinary. Aria stared at her slack jawed and didn't know what to say.

"I am Dangereuse", the goddess said, "your twenty-ninth-ago grandmother through Newt and Nancy Ann and Joseph too. Would you like one?", she said holding out a basket of split-tailed mermaid cookies.

"I thought I was to meet Maw Bear somebody."

The woman laughed and explained, "I have more than one name. Maubergeonne is one. In the language of Ak, however, it is Dangereuse or Dangerosa."

Aria swallowed her bite of cookie and asked, "the sun in Hyperborea?"

"Excellent! Can you help fill the baskets? It's a local tradition here in Poitiers." The two exotic women appeared and the four of them began filling several baskets to overflowing with the delicious gingerbread.

"What local tradition calls for gingerbread mermaids?"

"The mermaid is Queen Melusine, a famous citizen here in Poitiers. She is also a grandmother of yours."

"My grandmother was the queen of France and a mermaid?"

"Melusine is the Queen of the Elves during the time of Charlemagne."

"Elves are mermaids?"

"It is a curse. She is only a mermaid one day out of each week. Saturday, I believe."

Dangereuse relayed this information as if trying to remember the mermaid's work schedule.

"Did Charlemagne know her?"

"I would imagine. She and her husband, Raymond de Ver, build Chateau de Lusignan here in Poitiers near her forest pool."

"That name…de Ver, that's Robin Hood's name, isn't it?"

"Yes. Melusine is his grandmother as well."

Aria's eyes kept drifting over to a shield that hung prominently on the wall behind where Dangereus stood filling baskets. A portrait of her in all her voluptuousness was captured there in vivid detail. The motto, written in English naturally, made Aria blush. It said, "Above Me in Battle, Likewise in Bed".

Dangereuse caught the blush and the glance and explained, "That shield belongs to your grandfather, the Troubadour, William IX, Duke of Aquitaine. He steals me and puts me in this tower that he builds and then names for me. Our step children, of sorts, marry each other. That is why you are related to us both. He also steals these women here in this room in one of the Crusades and gives them to me. It sounds worse than it is. I too am a troubadour, a trobairitz. A female troubadour. But William is THE Troubadour. He invents the love song. He is the first to sing in the vernacular of the common man. Women throw themselves at his feet. Can you even imagine?"

"Regardless of all that, the three of you are prisoners here, aren't you?"

"We prefer to think of ourselves as family. These sister of mine teach me magic, the very magic you experienced when you arrived. William never knows what he is walking into when he enters my tower and it drives him wild with desire. Perhaps he is my prisoner."

"That was pretty amazing magic. How can it feel so real?"

"The magic they know is beyond your comprehension. They teach me the Language of the Birds and how to count the stars in the night sky to form verses of hidden chant."

"Are you speaking poetically?"

"I am speaking of the Music of the Spheres. It is caused by the movement of the stars."

"The Music of the Spheres is just a metaphor, isn't it?"

"Then you have never heard it, Child."

"Where did your sisters learn this magic?"

"From the Magi."

"And you taught it to the Troubadour?"

"No. It is more fun to leave it in plain sight and let him find it. He does know the Language of the Birds however. All troubadours know the Language of the Birds. But he doesn't get the other magic. He has magic of his own. He has the love song."

"I wish people would leave magic in plain sight in my day."

"You have all been looking at magic for hundreds of years and are only just beginning to recognize it."

"What magic is in plain sight?"

"The Mona Lisa."

"Da Vinci's painting? It's magnificent, for sure, but magic? I don't get it."

"The science that enamors modern man is discovering the painting's impossible reality. Like other paintings of old, the portrait is created in thin, overlapping layers of paint and glaze. Modern scientific instruments can view each separate layer. It is determined that there are thirty such layers used to create the Mona Lisa."

"What is magic about that?"

"All thirty layers together are only forty microns thick. Forty microns, Child, is one half the thickness of a human hair. Such a feat is still impossible to achieve in your modern times. Even with scientific machines."

"It makes you wonder who they were, huh, Da Vinci and the Mona Lisa?"

"The model is your grandmother, Isabel of Aragon. She is the first-ago grandmother of Isabella, the She Wolf of France, mother of Edward III. Remember that it is the She Wolf who chooses such a cruel death for her husband King Edward II after she and her lover, Roger de Mortimer, depose him."

"I don't know what that death was and please don't tell me." Aria hadn't fully digested the information from this morning about the overthrow of Edward II who had lost the Battle of Bannockburn against Robert the Bruce. Obviously he had also lost the love and respect of his wife since she ran off with Katherine de Mortimer's father. But come on, he was in love too with the father of kitten-demeanored Elizabeth Dispenser that Aria had met at the picnic in Warcop. Now she had new information to process knowing that the Mona Lisa was her grandmother. And the painting of her grandmother was magic and hanging in plain sight. And this gingerbread mermaid baking grandmother talking to her right now had magic of her own. Perhaps all the troubadours were magic too. They knew the Language of the Birds. "How many troubadours are there? Are you all singers?"

"We are primarily of the noble class. But we are a renegade nobility. We sing and we play music but we sing about unearthly love. We are followers of a religion called Catharism. Before we are wiped out, our numbers swell to nearly four hundred fifty."

Aria reached for another mermaid cookie but Dangereuse took it out of her hand.

"We don't expect you to dine on gingerbread alone. You have other ancestors waiting for us in the dining room so let's join them now." She led Aria down a long hallway looking as beautiful as a runway model but all Aria could think about was the possibility that Robin Hood was in the dining room and her hair looked a fright.

When they entered the dining hall, four men stood up from the table. Not a single one of them noticed Aria. All eyes were riveted on the hostess. Aria was relieved since she was standing there barefoot and her hair was still wet. At least, thank goodness, she smelled deliciously of lavender and lemons. And since they weren't looking at her, she could look at them. Which one was Robin Hood? Probably the one with the green jacket draped over his chair. Didn't Robin Hood always wear green?

The women joined the four men at the table and Dangereuse began the introductions. "Fulk V, twenty-ninth-ago, is King of Jerusalem. Robert de Sable, twenty-fourth-ago, is the eleventh Grandmaster of the Knights Templar. William Marshal, twenty-second-ago, is the Marshall of England and the greatest knight who ever lived. Robert de Ver is a cousin to you and the third earl of Oxford as well as Lord of the Greenwood."

Aria was right, Mr. Green Jacket was Robin Hood. Robert de Ver. Her cousin. But what of the others? King of Jerusalem? The greatest knight who ever lived? The grandmaster of the Temple Sowerby and Giggleswick people? She wished she wasn't already so tired. She wished she had shoes on. Dangereuse elaborated on the histories of the men sitting around the table.

"Fulk V is the grandfather of Henry II of England. Henry is the one who marries Eleanor of Aquitaine and inherits Gascony from her marriage portion. They are the parents of King John and his brother, Richard the Lion Heart. Eleanor is the granddaughter of William and myself, being the child of our respective children. Fulk also has the dubious honor of being associated with the only two women to ever rule Jerusalem, his wife, Queen Melisende, and their granddaughter, Sybilla."

"You married the mermaid?", Aria blurted out.

"I'm not THAT old, Child!", the king said as he sat up rather stiff. "Queen Melusine is the Elf. My wife, Melisende, is the Queen of Jerusalem."

"I'm sorry, your Majesty."

"Now there's no need for formality", he responded, "just call me Fulk."

"Let's continue", Dangereuse suggested. "Robert, the Grandmaster, is famous for becoming the Grandmaster before he even bothers becoming a Templar Knight. The order needs someone dangerous in charge due to a die off of the non-dangerous ones. Robert is recruited to NOT get killed off. And then he is also known for giving the island of Cyprus to that half wit, Guy de Lusignan, who marries Sybilla." Turning to de Sable she said, "I'm sorry Robert, but my dislike of the Lusignans aside, I cannot fathom why you would do such a thing."

The grandmaster said nothing in his defense.

Now turning to William Marshal, her demeanor softened and a purr entered her voice. "The Marshall, as he is known all over Europe, is called the Flower of Chivalry. He is the Earl of Pembroke, the Sheriff of Westmoreland and the embodiment of paratge."

"You don't live in Appleby Castle, do you? I have a later grandfather who is also the Sheriff of Westmoreland that lives there."

"I am awarded Cartmel Estate in Westmoreland, very near to Appleby."

Dangereuse finished her history lesson with Robin Hood. "Your cousin, Robert de Ver, that you know as Robin Hood, is descended, as you are, from the Elf King, Aubrey de Ver, immortalized as Oberon in the Shakespeare work A Midsummer Night's Dream. Robert is the Hereditary Master Chamberlain of England and also an outlaw. He is surety for the Magna Carta and Pretender to the Earldom of Huntingdon."

Dangereuse's sisters of the Levant entered the room heavily laden with delicious smelling food on plates to set before them. Conversation ceased as the meal began.

Finally buoyed by the infusion of food energy Aria felt ready again to ask her questions. She looked at her storybook cousin and commented, "I've heard the title of the Earldom of Huntingdon mentioned on more than one occasion already. Or did I hear that wrong?"

"You heard it in reference to Lucy Turoldsdottir, wife of Ranulf le Meschines. Her second husband acquired Appleby from the first Earl of Huntingdon. The second Earl of Huntingdon is the Fairy Bear and that is why the name stuck in your head."

"Why were you pretending to have the Earldom?"

Robert smiled and corrected her. "It simply means I have a right to it. Siward Fairbairn is the first Armstrong to have the earldom after he takes it from Tostig Godwinsson. I'll let him tell you how that happens. Anyway, the earldom is passed from one Armstrong to another until the last Armstrong earl dies without on heir. So the Empress Matilda, mother to Henry II, offers it to our mutual grandfather, Aubrey de Ver. He turns it down and takes the earldom of Oxford instead. That is when the earldom of Huntingdon goes vacant. Since the offer of the earldom is made to my grandfather, by rights it should pass to me. And don't think I don't want it. I do. John seizes all my lands from me. A long time passes before the earldom is offered to anyone again."

"De Ver is a French name I assume. Yet I thought in the stories you are called Robin of Loxley. Is that here in France?"

"I am born in England. Loxley is close to Stratford upon Avon."

"That's where William Shakespeare lived", Aria exclaimed, happy to be able to show off her knowledge about something.

"William Shakespeare is a group of men writing under the name William Shakespeare. My relative, Edward de Ver is one of them."

Aria stared at him for a moment in disbelief. "A group of men? How many men? Who were they?"

"About half a dozen. They all work for Queen Elizabeth I and call themselves the Entity. Ben Johnson is one and Christopher Marlow.

Even Edmund Spenser, who pens the Fairy Queen about Elizabeth, is a member. And of course, her son, Sir Francis Bacon."

"I thought Elizabeth never married. I didn't know she had a son and I certainly didn't know it was Sir Francis Bacon."

"She does not marry. Yet still, she is hopelessly in love with a grandfather of yours, Robert Dudley. They are the parents of Francis Bacon but she does not recognize him as legitimate. John could do the same with his daughter, Joan, but he chooses to recognize her anyway and proclaims her the Princess of Wales. Francis wants to be recognized and even petitions the court of Spain to assist but to no avail. His father, Robert, is a womanizer and eventually marries a woman living in the court of Elizabeth. The granddaughter of that marriage is your grandmother, Constance Hopkins, who is an invited passenger on the Mayflower. She is a young woman then and travels to America with her father and step-mother."

"Why did Edmund Spenser fictionalize Elizabeth into the Fairy Queen? Did she request it as his employer?"

"Elizabeth is the Fairy Queen. He writes it about her, not for her. It is Edward de Ver who crowns her as Fairy Queen in the early dawn at Windsor Castle on the same day of her coronation as Queen of England."

"Why did your relative do the crowning?"

"Due to his descent from the Elf King, our ancestor, Aubrey de Ver. The de Vers are elven and it is Edward's responsibility to perform the Right of the Kingship of the Caledonians, the People of the Forest, the elven folk."

"Are you an elf, Robin…er, Robert?"

"Are you one, Oh-she-of-the-strange-blood?", he said and winked. "Why even little Joan of Arc, whose title la Pucelle, proclaims her a practitioner of the Fairy Faith. I have another relative who rides with Joan on her mission that she swears is given to her by the Fairy Ladies. It is the reason they burn her at the stake."

"I thought the reason was political because she headed some battle or something like that."

"That is the mission. It takes place during the Hundred Years War. She sides with France."

"What does it mean that you are Lord of the Greenwood?"

"It's very flattering that our beautiful hostess thinks that's me, but it isn't. The Lord of the Greenwood is Robin Redbreast."

"A bird?"

"Not just a bird, the King of Birds."

"Did you steal from the rich and give to the poor, Robert?"

"I sure do steal from the rich. The rich clergy! The money supports the heretics once they become poor because they are labeled heretics by the rich clergy. I have a forest sanctuary for them and a band of men who help me protect them."

"Did you live there with Maid Marion?"

"My wife's name is Isobel de Bolebec. Maid Marion is a reference to Merry the Gypsy. And Merry the Gypsy is the reason that my band is called the Merry Men. Friar Tuck performs the ceremonies which are illegal because the veneration of Merry the Gypsy is banned. Yet the people know that her Merry Men are in Sherwood Forest, or Ingleside Forest, or any of the Greenwoods and can be utilized."

"I thought a gypsy was someone from Egypt."

"The gypsies are the minions of the moon. They have their own culture. They are a people who live without a fixed address and therefore they live beyond the reach of authority. They have their own savior, Alako, who ascends to the moon which is the place to which all gypsies believe they will go when they die. In their wedding ceremony they use an apple for the giving of the heart saying, "I am your nourishment, you are mine, we are the feast." Nice, huh?"

"Very nice", Aria said and then after a brief awkward silence she realized that she had reached the bottom of her vast reservoir of things she knew about Robin Hood. So she initiated a conversation with the King of Jerusalem instead. "Do you agree with Dangereuse that your granddaughter's husband was a half wit or whatever she called him?"

"Wholeheartedly!", he bellowed. "Guy de Lusignan is a worthless twit but evidently our granddaughter is clueless of this obvious fact.

Sybilla annuls her marriage to him so she'll be awarded the monarchy of Jerusalem and afterwards the little scamp turns right around and remarries the horses's ass. Bingo, he's co-ruler. Both a couple of twits, if you ask me."

"Did she meet him in Jerusalem?"

"No. Henry II is Sybilla's cousin and Guy is his regent. And a lousy one at that but she marries him anyway. Guy is Princess Joan's half-brother. John's girl. She grows up with their mother and Guy's father, Hugh X de Lusignan."

"I met her husband Llywellyn. He's not real fond of Joan."

"That, Child, is an assumption. You may assume that because he caught her with another man, he does not love her. In truth, he loves her to the end of his days."

Aria wondered how many times a day she made assumptions and didn't even know she was doing it. She had so many character flaws to work on when she got home. If she got home. Feeling chastised by the King of Jerusalem Aria turned her attention to the Grandmaster of the Templars. "Why did you give Cyprus to Guy?"

"I will never live that down. Twit or not, Guy has no lands of his own. Considering his unpopularity, I know he never will. I'm not hired to make good business choices. Although I do buy Cyprus for only twenty five thousand pieces of silver. I think that is a pretty good deal. Why I'm even being held accountable for this is a moot point. They hire a warrior, they get a warrior."

"Who sold it to you?"

"Richard the Lion Heart. John's brother. He is a Templar but only an honorary one. Full fledged members give up everything to belong. Richard is too wealthy but he sells us Cyprus at a good price."

"Why does Richard the Lion Heart own Cyprus?"

"He claims it when his wife-to-be and his sister are shipwrecked there. The island has a romantic history like that. Antony gives it to Cleopatra and her sister. And before it is Cyprus, it is Ia-Dan. The Isle of Dan. The Tuatha de Danaan live there. The Shining Ones. And before them the Phrygians are there, the blue folk, the Picts."

"As in Pictavia?"

"Yes. Like Pictavia. Eastern Scotland is occupied by the Picts, the Caledonians. Melusine is their princess and in line to be queen because she is the oldest of the triplets. When the girls are exiled, Melusine comes here to Poitiers and marries Raymond de Ver and together they build Chateau de Lusignan."

"Guy de Lusignan is descended from Melusine?"

"The Lusignans are born at Chateau de Lusignan and so take its name but they are not of Melusine's de Ver line. The Lusignans are the Crusader Kings of Jerusalem."

"How many crusades were there?"

"There are seven if you don't count the Albigensian Crusade."

"Why is that one different?"

"The seven are fought in Jerusalem. The Albigensian is fought in Gascony against the Cathars for the most part."

"Isn't that your religion, Dangereuse?"

"Yes. All the troubadours are champions of the Cathars."

"Where does the name, Cathar, come from?"

"St. Catherine", she answered. "She spins the stars to create the sound energy of existence. The moon is her spinning wheel."

"So you guys worship the moon?"

"Of course we don't worship the moon, Child", Dangereuse chided. "Catharism is a religion of love."

"Why a crusade against love? And why call it Albigensian? The elf thing?"

"The culture of the elves is a threat to a government that espouses a different culture. The Roman church is the government. The Roman church orders the Crusades."

"Were the crusades in Jerusalem also about an attempt to squelch a culture that was different?"

Fulk answered her question this time. "The crusades in Jerusalem are all about getting the treasure back."

"What treasure?"

"Solomon's treasure! The Rex Deus families hatch the idea for the crusades in the first place so that they can cause a long enough distraction to dig for the treasure under Solomon's ruined temple. The Lusignans are descended from the Rex Deus so that is why they serve as the crusader kings."

"The Lusignans dig for treasure? What is a Rex Deus?"

"The Templars dig for the treasure. The kings just make it possible for them to set up shop next door to the temple and dig for nine years. The Rex Deus are the Zadokite priests of the temple when it is first built."

"You guys found the treasure?", Aria asked and gaped at de Sable.

"I'm not the first Grandmaster, Child, I'm the eleventh. So, of course, I didn't find the treasure. It is well hidden by the time I come around. Do you think they are going to trust me with it? I give Cyprus away!"

"Then the crusades were successful if the treasure was found", Aria assumed.

"The crusades are not successful militarily except the first one. If one can judge success by the massacre of the entire Jewish and Muslim population of Jerusalem."

"All in the one crusade?"

"All in one day, July 19,1099."

Aria thought back to the Battle of the Albert in the Y Ravine. Such carnages as these should be unthinkable, let alone possible and accomplished. What a world. She sighed and dropped her head in disgust. She lifted it again when she heard Fulk speaking.

"I'm sorry to say that we all have blood on our hands. Even our sainted knight, William, who is the very embodiment of paratge, cannot say otherwise."

"What does that word mean?", she asked William Marshal.

"He won't tell you", Dangereuse said to her, "it disturbs his sense of paratge to do so. Therefore I will explain. In the modern age you might call paratge Karma or Cosmos. It is a conviction that one should do the right thing whether it's called upon or not. Then, having done the right thing, one can live in a personal state of harmony and contentment knowing one took responsibility for one's own actions."

Looking uncomfortable, William added, "I am not the only one yoked with that distinction."

"That is true, my pet" Dangereuse assured him. "Interestingly enough", she said to Aria, "the only other person 'yoked' with such a compliment, for there are only two, is the opposition leader against the crusaders, an Egyptian sheik named Saladin."

"Before you go sticking a damn halo on my head", William interjected, "keep in mind that the bishop of Ireland places a curse on me and my entire family."

Dangereuse patted the hand of the Marshall of England and said, "Consider the source, Darling. You are still our saint."

"Fulk is right." William spoke. "I too have blood on my hands. Where is the paratge in that?" William didn't look all that harmonious or content in his admission.

"How did you become known as the greatest knight who ever lived? Or was she just flattering you?"

"He isn't going to respond to that question either", Dangereuse stated, "and I'm not flattering him. It's a real title. In your modern age you watch boxing matches where two men fight until one is declared a winner. The competitions in our age are great and deadly staged battles. These are not jousting tournaments, you understand. If you do not best the other knights in these battles, they best you. Our talented William bests over five hundred knights. Including the Lion Heart. He is the only knight to ever do so. He unhorses him but spares his life by taking the life of the horse instead. This act wins him the position of Marshall for Henry II and later for Richard and for John and even for John's young heir, Henry III."

"You are the Marshall for John?", Aria said with a bit too much disgust. How did he live with his paratge in that situation?

"William is instrumental in getting John to sign the Magna Carta", Dangereuse defended. "He and John are family since William's daughter, Isabella, marries John's son, Richard, Duke of Poitiers."

"Was is common for royals to marry the children of the household staff? Oh dear, How rude of me. I'm very sorry, William."

Dangereuse spoke again before William could respond. "William is one of the wealthiest, most powerful and influential men in Europe. His position goes far beyond that of household staff."

William decided it was time to speak for himself. "Wealth and power are handed to me. The Lion Heart gives me Isabel de Clare to marry. Her father is Richard Strongbow de Clare and he is given Isabel's mother, Red Ava, in marriage after helping her father reclaim his throne in Leinster, Ireland. Unfortunately this act is the cause for the Norman Invasion of Ireland. Strongbow is made the king of Leinster and becomes very very rich. Isabel and I inherit those riches. Henry II gives me Cartmel near Appleby and I am even awarded the earldom of Pembroke."

Dangereuse's captive sisters walked into the room carrying pitchers wrapped in thick toweling and handed cups to all at the table. When the toweling was removed Aria caught the scent of coffee.

"You have to be kidding! It smells like I'm in a Starbucks back home. I certainly wasn't expecting coffee!"

"We honor your modern day beverage company because they honor Queen Melusine", Dangereuse said and smiled.

"Are you really serving Starbucks coffee? What is the connection with the elf queen and Starbucks coffee?"

"She emblazons their paper drinking vessels. The split-tailed mermaid queen is their logo. I know that you long to hear de Sable tell what he knows of the treasure, but let's enjoy this warm beverage that you moderns are so fond of and indulge in a mermaid cookie or two, shall we?"

The cookies were indeed a sweet indulgence, a perfect partner to the hot coffee that only reminded Aria more than ever of the life she had left behind. She was so very grateful however for the pick me up that the coffee provided since she was again experiencing the effects of the quick crossing this morning on the submarine and attempting to stifle her yawns. She was very much looking forward to a good night's sleep here in her grandmother's tower. But right now she needed to hear about Solomon's treasure. "Who dug up the treasure, Robert?"

The Grandmaster swallowed his cookie and drained the last of his coffee before answering. "Hughes de Payn and eight others. The original Templars. They are primarily from Gascony."

"My father-in-law, Baldwin II, is king of Jerusalem at the time", Fulk added. "Baldwin already knows Hughes so he just agrees to the plan they dream up for tourist security services. The nine knights will provide security for the European tourists flooding into the holy land. They are getting clunked over the head and their money stolen upon arrival if not before. The Templars put an end to that."

"I thought they spend nine years digging under the temple. Where did they find the time to run security as well?"

"Banking", de Sable answered. "They invent banking, plain and simple. Put your money in the bank in Europe and take it out again from the bank in Jerusalem. So all the Templars need to spend their time on is digging."

"For nine years? That's a long time. What did they find?" Aria realized she was a bit breathless waiting for the reply.

"I don't know", de Sable answered. "I never saw it."

"But you are the Grandmaster! Surely you were told."

"I have an idea But really I'm the military arm of the Templars."

"Why do you need a military arm?"

"We are bankers. What is more likely to get stolen than money? And we find the treasure. Can you imagine how many people want that? Even William joins our military arm."

"You are a Templar Knight, William?"

"Only honorary, I'm afraid. Like the Lion Heart, I can't just give away all that land and wealth and the responsibility that goes with it. I am only a Templar on my deathbed. I swear an oath to those in the military arm that I will die as one of them."

"So you guys are the military arm. What's the other arm called?"

"Theocratic", de Sable replied. "The whole enterprise is funded by St. Bernard and the Cistercians and the Benedictines."

"Then the treasure must be religious artifacts, right?"

"The treasure consists of many things. We know from what has already been stolen that they are of a magical nature."

"Someone beat you to the treasure?"

"The Romans loot the temple in the year 66 and then the Goths sack Rome in 410 and steal what they stole. The Goths stash it in Languedoc in Gascony, their new homeland."

"What was it?" What did they get?"

"Two books of spells."

"Do you mean magic spells?"

"All of what is unearthed under the temple can be considered magic. But then I believe ancient manuscripts, both Syrian and Hebrew, are discovered as well which predate anything the High Church has to validate its dogma and the manuscripts are in conflict with that dogma. It's why the church lets Bernard build his magical cathedrals. He blackmails them into it. Every one of them is dedicated to Mary Magdalene. I speak of the Norte Dame, "Our Lady", cathedrals. There is even a statue of Mary in one of them calling her Our Lady Under the Earth."

"Magical cathedrals?"

"Buildings prior to the cathedrals are short and squat. Bernard's masterpieces have flying buttresses and domes. The knights find sacred geometry under the temple and apply it to the cathedrals. Even the stained glass has otherworldly properties. Its affect on light, even in your modern age can't be explained."

"Where are the cathedrals?"

"Only in France. The home of Mary Magdalene after her time with Jesus. She lives out her life in France and the French people are tremendously proud of this association."

"So the treasure is spells, manuscripts and sacred geometry?"

"Much more than that. For one, instructions for understanding the Language of the Birds."

"You and the troubadours know that magic, don't you Dangereuse? Can you talk to sparrows?"

"Better than that, Child, the sparrows can talk to me and I can understand. In the Elder Faith, the bird is king and queen. Their language, their green language, is considered angelic and even Enochian by some. With it they can communicate with the initiated."

"Solomon must have known it too since he had the instructions."

"Of course", she said. "As do Odin and Aesop and others. The Picts know it and the troubadours too. Naturally, Enoch speaks it and is even called the Bird Man."

Turning back to de Sable, Aria continued with her questions. "Okay, bird language, geometry and what else? What other treasures did they find?"

"The Ring and the Stone. Solomon is a Ring Lord and is considered the greatest magician of his time. It is with the ring that he is able to control demons. But Solomon is only one of the Ring Lords. Many come after him. Odin is one and so is Ragnar Lodbrock's father-in-law, Sigurd, in the Norse tales. Daire Dornmar of Ireland is a Ring Lord and so is Aedan macGabran, the Pendragon."

"That is who St. Columba crowned. Just how many rings are there?"

"I'm not sure. There are the lesser rings and greater rings. Solomon's is the latter."

"Who wears the lesser rings?"

"I'm not sure about that", de Sable admitted.

"The Lion Heart has a ring", William said. "I don't know if it is one of the lesser ones but a special ceremony is needed to place it on his finger. It is called the ring of St. Valery, the personification of Aquitaine, whose devotees are the Plantagenets."

"If a number of people wore the greater of the rings, how did it end up buried under the temple?"

"How indeed? I do not comprehend magic and as I already said, I do not see the treasure."

"What is the stone?"

"As with the ring, I can only speculate. Stories of the Stone are legend. The Hebrews speak of the stone called Shekinah that can transform matter to spirit. The Hyperboreans bring the Philosopher's Stone. The Chintamani Stone is taken to Shamballa. The Tuatha de Danaan bring the Lia Fal, the Stone of Destiny, to Ireland and call that land Inis Fal, the Island of the Stone. Even the Ka'aba, still encircled in Mecca in modern times, is brought to earth by Aliah, the Moon Goddess."

"Is there an owner of the stone, like there is an owner of the ring?"

"I've never heard of one."

"When you speak of the greater ring are you speaking in the same vein as the pendragon who binds all the other tribal kings to his authority in conflicts?"

"The owners of the greater rings guard portals."

"Solomon's Temple is a portal?"

"I imagine it is but Solomon's Temple also houses the portal maker, the Ark of the Covenant."

"I thought the Ark of the Covenant held the Ten Commandments."

"That is never its function. It is a storage facility for orbitally rearranged monatomic elements. What the Bible calls manna."

"The stuff Moses feeds to the Isrealites?"

"That's correct. He makes the manna by melting down the Golden Calf. He turns it into the white powder of the Alchemists. He turns it into exotic matter."

"What is exotic about it?"

"Heated to a certain degree it disappears. Once cooled again, it reappears."

"Where does it go?"

"To a different dimension."

"Oh I get it! It's a portal for metals. You can't stick people in a furnace and melt them down to send them through a portal. So what is the point in sending metals to a different dimension?"

"King Nebuchadnezzer sends some folks through. He robs the treasure too so having found the instructions, he builds a furnace to make the manna. The prophet Daniel has appointed three master Masons to administer Babylon for the king. They are Shadrach, Meschach and Abednego. But these three Masons refuse to serve Nebuchadnezzer which greatly angers him so he throws them into the furnace. Not only do they not burn up as you suspect, but a fourth gentleman walks back out of the furnace with them."

"That could be a parable. The Bible is full of them."

"Perhaps. Yet a scientist in the modern age, Nicola Tesla, proves that high frequency electrical fields, hot enough to melt metals, have no effects on the human body."

"Did you Templars find the Ark of the Covenant under the Temple?"

"I don't know, Child. I told you that I never saw it."

"But I'll bet you know where they put it", Aria speculated hoping she would be taking home some very valuable knowledge.

"Originally it is taken to Languedoc and added to what the Goths have retrieved. But they keep moving it. I think at one time it is in the Chapter House Treasure Vaults in Paris but it does not remain there. We take it to Scotland and give it to Robert the Bruce to hide. He gives it to his cousin and military commander, Angus Og macDonald, and has him hide it."

"Where does he hide it?"

"Not sure. Probably Mt. Heredon because it's so near to the mother lodge of the Scottish Knighthood. The other name for Mt. Heredon is the Fairy Hill of the Caledonians. The Fairy Hill is a pure quartz portal to the Otherworld. It is one of a trio of mystical mountains, the other two being Mt. Sinai and Mt. Moriah."

"I've heard of Mt. Sinai. Where is Mt. Moriah?"

"It is the Temple Mount, where Solomon builds his temple. It is named for Enoch, the Bird Man. Moriah is the new name given to him after he is translated by God and becomes an angel. Templarism is Enochian. In fact, the Book of Enoch is rediscovered after fifteen hundred years by a descendant of Robert the Bruce."

Aria yawned but certainly not because she was bored. The submarine effects were beginning to weigh her down and she was so relieved that she would be curled up asleep in this tower very shortly. She yawned again.

"I'm your guide to the transport station", Robert de Ver said as he stood up from the table. "Soon you may collapse so we should go now."

Disappointment hit her like a thunderbolt as much as her marching exhaustion. But she wasn't about to voice her dismay after what the Council went through to accommodate her submarine fears. She would just have to sleep in the carriage, like the night before, and at least get a little rest before she transferred to whatever she was catching to ride at the transport station.

Resigned to her fate, Aria also stood and Robert put his green coat over her shoulders. They quickly exited the room and walked down several flights of stairs making Aria wonder why she had no memory of ever climbing up. Too tired now to contemplate the strange magic at work in this tower, she blindly followed her cousin out the door. No carriage was waiting and the cold penetrated her bare feet making her shiver and wrap the blessed coat even tighter. Robert took her elbow and led her rather briskly into a very dark forest on foot. She might have actually fallen asleep while he supported her arm and navigated through the near complete darkness. She heard what sounded like birdcall but it seemed as if it was coming from Robert. She became alert again and opened her nearly closed eyelids when a light appeared in the distance. A green glow could be seen approaching but Aria was too sleepy to even feel concerned. Robert knew the forest, what could go wrong?"

The dim green illumination was being emitted by a large animal with an enormous rack of antlers. Aria was fully awake again by the time it stood majestically before them. With no effort at all, Robert scooped Aria up and placed her on the animal's back. "We'll ride the hart to the daleth", he said as he climbed on behind her.

Fully absorbed in the idea that she was really riding atop a supernatural deer of some sort with her cousin, Robin Hood, Aria just knew that she would not be falling back to sleep now, but moments later she was.

Robert was forced to shake her out of her deep slumber which she fought against wanting only to remain in her very necessary sleep state. "Wake up, Child. We have to go into the pool."

"Into what? A pool? A swimming pool?", Aria asked groggily but waking up very fast over this new information. There was no way she was getting into some cold dark swimming pool in the middle of a cold dark forest in the middle of a cold dark night. "What happened to the daleth, the transport station?"

"The pool is the daleth. A daleth is a portal through a sacred pool. This pool is named Lucina after our grandmother, Melusine. She and

Raymond build Chateau de Lusignan here. I know that you are tired but we must use the daleth to reach the transport station."

Aria fought back tears as she dismounted from the animal who had carried her through the forest. She realized now why she was dressed in lightweight linen and wore no shoes. She would be expected to hold her breath and have to swim through countless cave openings before finding the exit and air again just like in the myriad adventure movies she had watched over a lifetime. Only Aria always closed her eyes during that part of the movie. She couldn't hold her breath very long and could never understand how the characters managed to do it. So, knowing that she was about to die, Aria closed her eyes and let Robert lead her to her death.

But Aria didn't die and she didn't even get wet. Braced for the cold and the wet, she was baffled when she didn't feel it. Certainly they were in the water by now. But when she opened her eyes she found herself once again in a tunnel underground with another little train sitting silent on its tracks. Like the one she rode with Thomas de Beauchamp up from the submarine, this train also only had two cars, the engine now puffing in preparation for departure, and behind it a small sleeping car softly lit and inviting.

"There is a comfy bed piled high with soft blankets in there for you", Robert said as he motioned toward the train. "You should feel good as new by morning. Don't fret over watching for the station. The train knows when to stop. I will be needing my coat back though. You can't use it where you are going anyway."

She didn't know what that might mean and she was too tired to care. As soon as she had stepped foot inside the sleeping car, the little train began to move. Turning back to see Robert still standing by the tracks she asked, "Where am I going?"

"Gascony. Bugarach Station."

Aria tumbled onto the soft welcoming bed and disappeared under the warm covers without even bothering to remove the branch from her waist. Click clack, click clack, click clack, sang the train. Sleep had never felt better or arrived quicker as she and the train sped south to Gascony.

Thomas de Beauchamp
Marshall of England

Co Founder · Knights of the Greater w/ King Edward III

Ancestor of Joseph of the New England Company

Eleanor de Clare
Lady of Glamorgan

wife of Hugh le Despenser

*Ancestor of Nancy Ann of the Virginia Company
and Joseph of the New England Company*

Hugh le Despenser

*Ancestor of Nancy Ann of the Virginia Company
and Joseph of the New England Company*

Llywellyn the Great

King of Wales

Ancestor of Joseph of the New England Company

Joan Princess of Wales, daughter of King John, wife of Llywellyn the Great

Ancestor of Joseph of the New England Company

*Ancestor of Nancy Ann of the Virginia Company,
Newt of the Massachusetts Bay Colony
and Joseph of the New England Company*

King Edward I Longshanks

*Ancestor of Nancy Ann of the Virginia Company,
Newt of the Massachusetts Bay Colony
and Joseph of the New England Company*

King Edward II

*Ancestor of Nancy Ann of the Virginia Company,
Newt of the Massachusetts Bay Colony
and Joseph of the New England Company*

King Edward III

Founder-Knights of the Garter

*Ancestor of Nancy Ann of the Virginia Company,
Newt of the Massachusetts Bay Colony
and Joseph of the New England Company*

Lover of William IX
the Troubadour

Dangereuse
l'Isle Bouchard

Ancestor of Nancy Ann of the Virginia Company,
Newt of the Massachusetts Bay Colony
and Joseph of the New England Company

Fulk V of Anjou
King of Jerusalem

Ancestor of Nancy Ann of the Virginia Company,
Newt of the Massachusetts Bay Colony
and Joseph of the New England Company

William Marshall
Marshall of England

Greatest Knight who ever lived

Ancestor of Joseph of the New England Company

Robert de Ver
3RD Earl of Oxford

Robin Hood
Lord of the Greenwood

Ancestor of Joseph of the New England Company

Ancestor of Joseph of the New England Company

Eleanor of Aquitaine
Heiress of Aquitaine

wife of Henry II, mother of King John and Richard the Lionheart

*Ancestor of Nancy Ann of the Virginia Company,
Newt of the Massachusetts Bay Colony
and Joseph of the New England Company*

Henry II King of England

husband of Eleanor of Aquitaine

Plantagenet

*Ancestor of Nancy Ann of the Virginia Company,
Newt of the Massachusetts Bay Colony
and Joseph of the New England Company*

CHAPTER FOUR

"It's just a choice. No effort. No worry. No job. No savings and money. Just a choice between fear and love."

Bill Hicks

"Love is my religion."

Bob Marley

An Inuit hunter asked the local missionary priest, "If I did not know about God and sin, would I go to hell?" "No", said the priest, "not if you did not know." "Then why", the Inuit asked earnestly, "did you tell me?"

Annie Dillard

ARIA WOKE UP in the semi-dark, the train still click clacking down the track. She was no longer tired but she had no desire to get out of the warm bed. As the stories she had heard over the last couple of days swirled around in her thoughts she realized that it was draining her emotionally. The stories of death and massacre were unsettling as were all the elven connections. It's fun to pretend that elves are real but it was impossible to wrap her brain around the idea that it may be truth. Robin Hood was a character in a book and women, giants or not, did not build castles in a single night by carrying stones in their aprons.

Yet it was possible that the Robin Hood character could have been based on Robert de Ver, an ordinary man. An ordinary man who can call for a ride from a green illuminated stag through the forest at night to the magic pool portal of their shared ancestor, the split-tailed mermaid elf queen. Sheesh!

Aria knew now that she had made a serious error in judgement when she agreed to this adventure. She may as well be Dorothy in the Wizard of Oz and just like Dorothy, all Aria wanted was to go home. Tears welled up in her eyes and she rolled over hoping that sleep would overtake her again and release her from this growing nightmare. But it was the Silver Branch she rolled over on top of instead. Panic hit like a heart attack. She had destroyed the one thing, like Dorothy's red slippers, that insured she could go home again, the little apple branch with its living bells. Leaping out of bed like a prick eared hunting hound, she untied the branch and held it up in the dim light to inspect the damage. It looked completely unscathed from its time under the covers and crushed beneath Aria. In fact, it still had that same appearance of having just been plucked from the tree with the tiny blossoms just getting ready to bloom.

The linen tunic Aria had slept in did not fare as well, so she pulled it off over her head and looked around for the next outfit that she knew would be laid out for her. She found it folded neatly next to her toiletries, a simple black dress. A pair of black shoes was all there was to finish off the ensemble. Perfect. It fit her mood to a tee. She dressed and tied the branch back onto her waist which softly played a melancholy tune in minor notes.

Where was she going, she wondered? What was this place, Gascony, that inspired a need to possess it with such passion that it would be fought over for one hundred sixteen years? Perhaps it would be here that she would discover the Beginning of Things and then be allowed to return to her Eden. As she sat on the bed and re-braided her hair she wondered what she had actually learned from her ancestors. King

John killed Moll, the folk hero. Llywellyn the Great killed the lover of his wife, Joan, the daughter of John. Edward I killed William Wallace and the Armstrongs. Roger de Mortimer killed the lover of Edward II, husband of his lover, Isabella, the She Wolf of France. Isabella killed Edward II in some fashion so obscene that it couldn't be mentioned. Edward III, son of Edward II and Isabella, killed Roger de Mortimer. Why even the sainted William Marshal must have killed or maimed at least five hundred knights in his career of the Greatest Knight Who Ever Lived. Killing. That was what she had learned from her ancestors, killing. Maybe at the Beginning of Things, it would be made apparent why it was necessary. Yes, Aria thought, she was sorry that she had come here. No one ever got killed in her Eden.

The little train car began to fill with stronger light as the vehicle moved into a huge cavern and slowed to a stop. The sign overhead read Bugarach Station. A woman dressed identically to Aria was waiting on the platform. Good, she thought, a woman will be a better guide considering her emotional state. Judging from their stark attire, she thought perhaps they were headed for a convent or something which seemed a blessing in her current despair.

The woman introduced herself as Esclarmonde de Foix, sister to Aria's ancestor, Rohese de Foix, wife of Thomas le Dispenser, the ancestor of the ill fated Hugh le Dispenser, lover of Edward II.

"So you are an aunt, and not a grandmother. Are you my guide to my grandparents here in France?"

"I am not your guide. I am your destination here is Gascony."

"Am I staying with you here at your convent tonight?"

"My convent? Oh, you are confused by our clothes. I do dress this way for religious reasons but I don't live in a convent. Oftentimes I live right here. In fact, I have a small meal prepared for us if you will follow me", Esclarmonde said as she turned to walk across the cavernous room somewhere beneath the earth.

"What is this place?"

"It is called the Holy Mountain of Bugarach. The uncle of Jesus, Mary's brother, lives here when he is twenty years old."

"Aren't we a long way from Nazareth?"

Esclarmonde stopped and thought for a moment. "Not really. I think it's only a few hundred miles north of here."

"Galilee is a few hundred miles north of here?" Aria was attempting to pull up maps in her head in her confusion.

"I'm sorry, I am speaking of Nazareth, France."

"I assumed that Mary's brother would also be from Nazareth in Galilee."

"There is no Nazareth in Galilee. You can look it up in the Talmud, I believe. It names all sixty three towns in Galilee and I'm pretty sure Nazareth isn't one of them".

Here we go again, Aria thought to herself, no moon landing and now no hometown of the blessed savior. "Why is this holy mountain hollow?"

"It's an anomaly. This is an inverted volcano meaning that the rocks on the top are older than the rocks on the bottom."

"How can a volcano erupt into the center of the earth?"

"That is probably the question Jules Verne, the modern writer, ponders when he comes to live here."

"Jules Verne will live in Gascony?"

"Jules Verne lives in this volcano."

"Does he write Journey to the Center of the Earth here? Do you think you can get to the center from here?"

"His friend, Berenger Sanuiere, gives him the maps to the entrances."

"How is it that his friend possesses such a thing?"

"Sanuiere is the priest at Rennes le Chateau here in Gascony. It is the place to which the Goths and the Templars bring the treasure of King Solomon. Perhaps the maps are part of that. I'm making an assumption since I never see the treasure." Now on the far side of the cavern, she ducked behind a large boulder jutting out from the wall and Aria followed her into a smaller chamber.

The simple meal of small loaves and nuts, apples, milk and honey was carefully set out on a table-like stone in the center of the chamber. Light filtered in softly from somewhere above and they both sat down on a rock bench and began eating their breakfast.

"You actually live here?", Aria asked wondering where the bed and the blankets might be that she would be needing if she were to spend the night.

"I use the caves to elude the heresy hunters. Yet, I too, know of entrances to places that others do not."

"Are you persecuted by the Puritans?"

"Not the Puritans. The Catholics. You assumed I might be a Catholic nun living in a convent. In truth, I am a Perfecti of Catharism."

"That is the religion of Dangereuse and the Troubadour."

"The Crusade wipes out the culture of the troubadours along with paratge and even the veneration of St. Catherine. In time, it kills over five hundred thousand people in Languedoc alone. Half the population of France is exterminated. For these reasons we call the high Roman Church, the Church of the Wolves."

"Half of France were Cathars and didn't want to be Christians?"

"We Cathars are Christians, Child. That is our name for ourselves. But half of France does not adhere to Catharism. The heresy hunters care little for whom they murder. The Pope's abbot, Amalric, is famous for his proclamation, "Kill them all, God will know his own", in an attempt to force the public to accept a church it doesn't want. The Roman church has its own army, the Dominican Black Friars and the Franciscan Greyfriars. Torture is given papal sanction."

"What kind of Christians are you?" Aria had never heard that Christians killed other Christians in the Crusades.

"We are called heterodox which simply means unorthodox. We are often referred to as Gnostics or Manicheans. Our neighbors call us the "Good Christians" in comparison to the High Church clergy."

"Where are your churches?"

"You are sitting in one. Caves and forests serve as our sanctuaries. We have only one rite, the consolamentum, which is a laying on of hands."

"Who do you lay hands on?"

"The Credentes, the believers. I am a person who performs this rite as I am the Perfecti, the priest."

"What are the beliefs that have you guys labeled as heretics?"

"They are legion, according to the Catholics. But evidently our greatest offense is in our belief that it is wrong to judge one as being above or better than another, therefore we do not call Jesus divine. Yet the very foundation of our faith is given to us by Jesus in our book called AMOR."

"AMOR? Why, that's another name for love. The religion of Love, like Dangereuse said."

"Yes it is. And in the Elven tongue a reverse spelling of a word is also a reverse meaning."

"Roma? Oh my gosh, Jesus reversed Roma?"

"No, Child, Roma reverses AMOR."

"What are the tenants of the religion of Love, of AMOR?"

"We believe that suicide is not a sin and neither is contraception. In fact, we believe that non-procreative sex is better. We believe that euthanasia is a kindness and reincarnation is a fact. But perhaps it is what we don't believe that is more upsetting to the church of Rome. We do not believe in the Eucharist or the Last Judgement. However our heaviest offense is not taking oaths or paying tithes to the Church of the Wolves. Each of these tenants are punishable by torture and death so I spend thirty years of my life outrunning and outsmarting the army of the church. It is why they call me the Fox of Foix. My name, Esclarmonde, means the Light of the World in the Occitan language. I serve as hope and inspiration for the members of our faith who nearly to a man will pay with their lives for these beliefs."

"Do all Cathars wear black?"

"No, only the Perfecti. It is to show our discontent with earthly life."

"What other life is there?"

"The one in AMOR, where the good spiritual world of light exists. This place is an evil material world of darkness. It is also one of our beliefs that a struggle goes on between the good creator God and the evil adversary, Luzbel."

"So if I'm here with you then this Crusade against the Cathars must be happening now. I'm dressed like you." Aria said this at the precise moment that she realized what the implications were of her all black clothes. Her fear for her own safety was sudden and acute. "I'm not a Perfecti. Shouldn't I be dressed in street clothes or something? You know, non-religious clothing?"

"We will appear in public, you and I, when we rise to the surface today. The heresy hunters strike fear in the Credentes. All who are strangers could be a heresy hunter. My mission is to instill encouragement, hope, and blessings on the faithful so that they have the courage to face another day. One that may well turn out to be their last. Their reaction to seeing Perfecti among them should be a cause for joy and not terror that death has found them. That is why you are dressed like me."

"Why do you have to go to these people in broad daylight?", Aria asked still deeply concerned for her own survival. "Couldn't you meet them in the woods at night or quietly in someone's house?"

"If I am not seen in public, it will be rumored that I am dead. I understand your fear. Unlike you, I choose this path. Your grandmother, Rohese, and I are noblewomen. It is my choice to become a Paladin Ranger and spend my life opposing my enemies simply by continuing to exist."

"What exactly is a noblewoman?"

"The ancestors that you are meeting are primarily of this class, the ruling class. The upper class. Or whatever they come to be called in your era. The de Foix family are the Kings of Aquitaine and the Lords of Gascony. This is the Elven bloodline. As it is with the Troubadours and the Plantagenets, the Morris clan, the macDonalds, the Bruces, the de Mortimers, the Beauchamps, the de Vers and the Grebsons of Greystokes and others that you have still to meet. In any family tree there will be countless thousands of branches. This branch is an especially interesting one, don't you think?"

"I guess by my time, where I live anyway, this class doesn't rule anymore." Aria felt rather ordinary again.

"I wouldn't be so sure of that. Every single American President, with the exception of a Mr. Van Buren, are able to claim ancestry through the Plantagenet King John, son of Henry II and Eleanor of Aquitaine."

When the meal reached its conclusion, Esclarmonde gathered the bowls and cups and hid them in a satchel behind a rock. Aria was glued to her place on the stone bench.

"Noli Temere, Child. We have to go. Our swan is waiting."

"What did you say?"

"I said, be not afraid, in French. To not fear death is a crowning achievement in our lives."

Aria put on her bravest face and followed her aunt to her fate. They recrossed the cavern space to where the train had stopped and Aria was shocked to see that the tracks were gone. Best not to miss any of these connections, she realized with alarm. Esclarmonde opened a door in the cavern wall and Aria was sure that it would disappear too as soon as they passed through. Just inside the door was the swan boat, or one identical to it, bobbing on the surface of the turquoise canal water.

"Where on the surface are we going?"

"To the Village Troglodytique de Madeleine in the prehistoric center of the world."

"Madeleine? Who is she?"

"It is French for Magdalen, which translates as tower. The village is the home of the Magdalenians."

"Is that where we will spend the night tonight?" Aria knew with certainty that her crowning achievement to not fear death was no where close at hand. How on earth was she going to be able to sleep knowing she might be murdered?

"Tonight you will take your rest on the Wave Sweeper as you travel on to Joyous Garde. You will be met by others here in Brittany who will accompany you. It is not safe for you to remain with me for long."

Esclarmonde's words had Aria's heart singing with joy. What a difference a day makes. The very words, Wave Sweeper, caused a flood of jubilation to pass through Aria where one day ago special arrangements had to be put into place just to deal with her fear of it. Now her fondest hope was to avoid being killed before making a safe return to the once dreaded submarine. But her joy evaporated when she thought of her aunt spending thirty years avoiding a violent torturous death.

"Will I go back to England after visiting Joyous Garde?"

"Joyous Garde is in Northern England. In Caledonia. Tomorrow you will return to Scotland as well."

Aria perked up tremendously at this news. "To Inverary Castle?" She hoped that her departure point for home was the same one where she had entered.

"No. Inverary is on the Scots side of Scotland. You will be visiting the Palace of Scone on the Pictish side."

"I thought I would be seeing more of Gascony."

"You will see very little of Gascony while spending time with me. But you will return one last time."

Back and forth, back and forth. How long was this journey to the Beginning of Things going to last? She knew for a fact now that it wouldn't be tomorrow since she was slated to return to France. This only added to Aria's growing depression but she said nothing of her paltry fears to her brave, courageous aunt.

"The name Mary Magdalene keeps coming up." Aria forced herself to use her time with Esclarmonde in the little boat to ask more questions. "The Magdalenians can't be named for her, can they? She wasn't prehistoric."

"I do not know why the researchers named them the Magdalenians. Perhaps it is for Mary Magdalene who makes her home in Gascony. The French are extremely proud of that association. Mary has other names as well. Stella Maris, Star of the Sea, is one. We Cathars know her as St. Catherine. Names change. Even when Mary lives here Languedoc is called Septimania, the Jewish Kingdom."

"You would think that more people living outside of France would know about her living here."

"Her veneration is purposely killed off over the years. Just as the Cathars and the troubadours and even our book of Love are wiped from existence. Mary Magdalene is immortalized as a harlot, a whore. And who cares where a whore lives out her life or raises her offspring?"

"The Church of the Wolves did that?"

"They did worse. It is our belief that they substituted a false Christ for the real one. The modern Jesuit Order of the church performs acts and deeds that are so antithetical to the teachings of Jesus that the very fact they call themselves the Society of Jesus is wrong."

"And you are called the Cathars after St. Catherine who is Mary?"

"In the original center of her cult, Mt. Sinai, the priests are called Kathari, meaning the Pure Ones."

"Mt. Sinai is one of the three mystical mountains, isn't it? If Mt. Moriah is named for Enoch, who is Sinai?"

"The Akkadian Moon god, Sin. Sinners worshiped Sin instead of Jehovah."

"Akkadian?"

"Ak or Oc is the name of the black sun in the Lands Beneath. The name Languedoc means Language of Oc or occitan. Aquitaine is pronounced the same. This language is how the Basque of Gascony refer to themselves, as the Euskara speakers."

"What the heck is a black sun?"

"In your modern age you would think of it as a sun deity. Electromagnetic in nature, it gives life and form to all that is, both in Hyperborea and on earth. It becomes known as chi or orgone or dark energy. Regardless, we know it as the spark of the Creator."

"I'm confused, Esclarmonde. You say that you don't believe Jesus was divine and yet you call yourselves Christians. What about your St. Catherine? Was she also not divine?"

"She is one of those through the ages who performs the "Dance of Time", for she spins the endlessly circling Silver Wheel that controls the stars."

"It sounds like you are waxing poetic and it sounds very nice but I'm assuming you speak of the moon."

"Yes. The Wheel of the Stone. The Wheel of Light. The Cosmic Spinning Wheel."

"I think it's a ball and not a wheel. A wheel is flat."

"A ball is round. A wheel is round. How can you tell which one it is?"

"Well because Neil Armstr….oh", Aria said and stopped mid

sentence. "Well because you can look at it through a telescope and see that it is a ball."

"If you saw a painted moon on a theater set would you assume it to be a ball? Could it just as possibly be flat and propped up from the back with boards?"

"You are trying to tell me that the moon is a stage prop. How can a stage prop control the stars that are a billion miles away and probably don't need controlling anyway."

"Stars do not need to be controlled. People do. Time is what offers that control. Time is measured by the stars."

"Which like I said are a billion miles away from here and unaffected by a stage prop."

"Actually", Esclarmonde added in her patient and gentle manner, "they are affixed to the ceiling."

"I'm not going there", Aria exclaimed and crossed her arms. "You are talking about a flat earth and a flat moon and a firmament over our head. You live a very long time ago, Esclarmonde. I realize that primitive cultures had a different cosmology than we have in my era but our science disputes such beliefs. You'll see."

"Is this the same science that is able to hurtle men through the Van Allen Radiation Belts in 1969 but cannot reinvent the technology in 2018? Perhaps science is the Church of the Wolves in the modern age. The primitive culture from which mankind received their geocentric cosmology belongs to the Sumerians, a people who come from a place they call Dilmun and speak an unknown language. They teach other things as well, writing, forging metals, building arches, weaving cloth, baking bread, measuring things, making instruments to measure things. They bring to us astronomy, the calendar, genealogy, schools, medical science, written proverbs, history, congress, taxation, laws, social reform, money, the 360 degree circle, the zenith, the horizon, the celestial axis, the Procession of the Equinox, a zodiac based on their gods and last, but not least, the wheel."

"Okay. So maybe not so primitive. But I still think a heliocentric earth makes a lot more sense."

"That is because it is easier to fool someone than to convince them they have been fooled. You can easily suspend your belief that water seeks it own level in order to make it bend around a ball."

"Now see, that's what I'm talking about. You obviously don't know about gravity."

"But I do. It is invented by Jesuit interests. Who is your most exalted scientist?"

"Albert Einstein, I would imagine. Who incidentally proved gravity."

"What does Mr. Einstein say when asked what it feels like to be the smartest man in the world?"

"I don't know."

"That's exactly what he says. "I don't know, you'd have to ask Nicola Tesla that question." And do you know what Nicola Tesla says about gravity?"

"No."

"Gravity is a theory that cannot be proven because it doesn't exist", is his observation. The hammer is denser than air, Child, and so falls to the ground. But the soap bubble does not. Gravity affects water and hammers but not soap bubbles?"

Aria could not come up with an answer for that so she fell back on her old stand by changing the subject. "Didn't the Catholic church appear foolish changing their cosmology that is certainly geocentric in the bible?"

"An explanation can be presented for any eventuality. The church uses their scholar, St. George Mivart, to declare that God purposefully leads the church into error over the geocentric cosmology in order to teach that astronomy lay outside their jurisdiction."

All of this was becoming too much for Aria. She wanted to go home so badly she could scream. But Esclarmonde would never understand such behavior. So she soldiered on and pretended that discovering the earth was indeed NOT spinning into the infinite void, had no effect on her. "Are all the Cathars elves? Is that why the crusade against you is called Albigensian?"

"The Cathars protect very ancient knowledge of the bloodline of the elves, a unique genetic strain of humanity descended from an other-than-human race. There are two branches that exist here. The Knight Ranger class who are far more interested in the magic and build the Notre Dame cathedrals. And the Ffayrie Branch of the Illuminoids whom we believe descend through St. Catherine. Their symbol is the moon's creature, the unicorn."

The swan slowed to a stop below a sign which read Lasceau Station. "This is the village?", Aria asked as her heart jumped into her throat.

"Not yet. This stop is a gift to you from the Council. As I said, the oldest traces of civilization found in the world are here in the Pyrenees. There are over two hundred prehistoric sites, some dating back hundreds of thousands of years. This is the place where the small Magdalenians mix with the tall Cro-Magnons. The Council thought you might benefit from seeing their art."

"Lasceau Station? Are you telling me the Lasceau Cave art is here? I've always wanted to see these paintings." In her excitement, Aria forgot that she may be getting killed later today.

They both left the swan and entered the cave. A light that shouldn't have been there and probably wasn't, illuminated the images painted on the walls. Regardless of their incredible antiquity, the word primitive never once entered Aria's mind. She read once that an acclaimed artist viewed these paintings and remarked, "We have invented nothing." Having now learned about the contributions of the Sumerians, along with getting to view this art, she thought that might be correct.

Esclarmonde allowed Aria to take in the magnificent works of art without a sense of being rushed for which she was deeply grateful. If she managed to survive time with her aunt and found a way home again, she would definitely want to remember that she got to see the cave art of thirty thousand years ago. Leaving through a different opening, the women found a small train waiting to assist with their rise to the surface. Similar to the one Aria rode in with Thomas de Beauchamp in Gamaches, this too sat on a spiral track leading up and out of sight. However it turned out to be far slower and much quieter, again filling Aria with gratitude.

Determined to enjoy her last minutes of life she let out a long sigh and relaxed.

"So this is the place where the Cro-Magnon man evolved, huh?"

"Do you mean evolved from a knuckle dragger?", Esclarmonde laughed softly. "No evolution happens here or anywhere. The likelihood of life forming from inanimate matter is one to a number with forty thousand zeros after it. The Cro-Magnons, the early modern humans, come here from some place else. They are not a species. They have dark hair, blue eyes and an olive complexion. They make baskets and cord thread and you just viewed their art. They have a very deep connection to the moon and use a lunar calendar. You, Child, have their blood."

"What?"

"That's right, the population of Gascony, the Basque people, have the highest concentration of O blood type in the world and they also have the highest concentration of Rh negative blood in the world."

"I'm O positive, Rh negative!" Again Aria was left pondering her strange blood.

"The Rh negative is an aquatic, copper based blood. It is considered a mutation."

Certainly this should be the Beginning of Things. This land of blue eyed moon people artists. Sadly, Aria knew this wasn't the case. Sunlight began flooding the spiraling tracks and its light was both welcoming and alarming. They must be near the surface. The train continued laboring upwards inside a tower dotted with windows which revealed a river and a valley below. When the train stopped, they were several stories high where residences had been carved into the sheer cliff wall. It reminded Aria of the Mesa Verde cliff dwellings she had visited in the American southwest. Except that in Mesa Verde there were no heresy hunters waiting behind heavy oak doors like the one she and Esclarmonde were about to pass through, heavy laden with swords, hatchets, battle axes, spiky iron balls swinging from chains or whatever else they might have devised.

'This place looks pretty old. Certainly no people are living here now", Aria said and could not disguise the trembling in her voice.

"People have and will live here continuously for nineteen thousand years. The people I have come here to bless are working inside this room. You are welcome to remain quietly standing near the door if you wish and will not be faulted if you feel compelled to leave. My visit here is very short, as they all must be, and then we will take the train back down to the swan."

The room they entered could have been the inside of another castle, although one stripped of its elegance. The dozen or so people in the room were absorbed in their work, which Aria recognized as paper making. So involved were they in their efforts that they did not seem to notice the entry of two women dressed in black into their midst. These people, also stripped of any elegance, wore faces of strain and worry.

Esclarmonde moved across the room to stand next to a woman whose hands were busy working a screen in a tub of watery pulp. The Perfecti reached over and took the deckle screen from the woman's hands and tapped out a sheet of wet paper on a long table where other wet sheets lay drying. The woman looked at Esclarmonde and a look of shocked recognition crossed her face. Her involuntary gasp alerted the others in the room of the unexpected visitation.

Aria not only couldn't find the courage to leave the safety of the door, she couldn't even find the courage to take her hand off the handle. A man now standing near her stared in disbelief at the famous Perfecti in his presence. "Esclarmonde", he spoke in a barely audible voice crackling with surprise and wonder. Leaning closer to Aria, he whispered, "How did you get here?"

"We came up on the train", she whispered back.

"What is a train?" But fortunately for Aria he did not wait for a reply as he too hurried to be close to his Perfecti, now completely surrounded by her adoring believers. The men wiped at the their eyes and the women cried openly in silence as one by one they received their consolamentum blessing from the Light of the World. The tears fell silently from Aria's eyes as well as she watched the effect her aunt had on all these brave souls who would probably lose their lives rather than compromise long held beliefs. What a coward I am, Aria thought, as she continued with her death grip on the door handle. As soon as each person in the room had received their blessing, Esclarmonde, true to her word, turned to leave. Tears ran anew at the idea of her departure. When some insisted on whispering their gratitude to Aria for her appearance as well, it only made her doubly ashamed of herself. She was both relieved and humiliated when she shut the door on them and boarded the train.

Her depression only deepened as she rode the train back down the spiral tracks.

Safety and relief would never again be a part of the lives of the people they just left. Aria did not feel at liberty to indulge in hers. If she made it back to her safe and ordinary Eden, it would be forever tainted by the memory of this place. When the train stopped Lasceau Cave was no longer there because it had more than likely never been there in the first place. If she got lost on this journey, Aria would never be able to find her way home and now she was just as frightened for herself as for the papermakers. A veil of fresh tears kept her from noticing that the swan now bobbed on dark green water instead of illuminated turquoise.

The two women sat in silence as the boat drifted slowly toward a dot of sunlight.

Aria's emotions were still on overload so the dark of the water and the dark of the cave were balm to her senses. One profound revelation per week could probably take her down, but an endless stream was becoming more than she could stand. She was told that you were never given more than you could bear but that theory was collapsing like all the others she had held so dear for so long. She watched dejected as the sunlight opening grew steadily larger. When the boat glided majestically onto the emerald colored lake shining in the warm sun like a bowl of jewels, Aria's heart soared at the sight. Feeling the sun for the first time this day lifted her up like it always did. Birds flew overhead and shouted their delight at just being alive.

"I love this place. Where are we?"

"It is called the Lake of the Trouts or the Lake of the Sins."

"Akkadian moon god?"

"No, an actual sin. Brennus, a Celtic chieftain, along with a couple hundred thousand of his soldiers steal the treasure of the Temple of Delphi. The lot of them settle here at the Lake of the Trouts. But the treasure is cursed and the thieves start to die in droves from an inexplicable illness. Their druids, who abhor material possessions anyway, advise them to offer the treasure to the chthonic deities by throwing it into the lake. Which they gladly do. The water turns inky black and the thieves are cured. The water returns to the emerald color you see beneath us."

"What is a chthonic deity?"

"Chthonic means subterranean, indicating the Lands Beneath."

"Was the Temple of Delphi treasure like Solomon's?"

"Magic? No. Just diamonds and gold and jewels and such."

"What is a druid?"

"The Men of the Trees. Magi from the Black Sun. They are practitioners of the Elder Faith, known as gatekeepers or Aria."

Aria was shocked to hear the sound of her name. No one here called her anything but Child. "Well I'm feeling healed just floating on this water", Aria remarked and meant it. Her sense of doom and gloom was lessened in this bright day and the beauty of this place.

"Gascony is quite famous for its healing waters. The river you saw running alongside the village Troglodytique has a strange spring which empties into it. It is called the Source de la Madeleine. What makes it strange is that it only flows during times of great drought. But, of course, the most famous is the healing spring at Lourdes."

"I know that one. I saw that movie. It's about St. Bernadette."

"Yes. Bernadette Soubirous, a simple Basque girl is led to it."

"Yes, by the Virgin Mary", Aria added drawing from her store of Hollywood cinema knowledge.

"Bernadette only ever referred to the apparition as That Thing."

"Why did they build Lourdes there then?"

"The apparition repeatedly sends Bernadette to the local church authorities to request the building. Naturally they are put off by the use of the moniker, That Thing, so they repeatedly refuse. But she is unrelenting so they tell her that the apparition must identify itself before they will consider the build. So Bernadette asks for a name."

"What is it?"

"The Immaculate Conception. That's what she is told to tell them. And since the divinity of Mary is being hotly debated in the church at the time, and whether or not she is holy enough to be considered the mother of Jesus, it is suggested that she be declared immaculately conceived. Now how on earth can a simple Basque peasant girl know of such a thing? So they build the cathedral where millions of pilgrims come to the healing waters of the well. In fact, only Paris, in all of France, has more hotels to facilitate tourists.."

As Esclarmonde elaborated on the healing waters of Gascony, the swan boat traversed the emerald water and entered a cave on the opposite side of the lake. "The mountain we are within now is called St. Barthalemy", she explained to Aria as they floated into the dark. "Many of our consolamentums are performed here and that is why I am here today. And that is why this is where we will be parting ways."

The sign for St. Barthalemy Station appeared and the swan slowed to a stop.

Esclarmonde got out but remained standing on the platform.

"I shall remember you, Esclarmonde. I pray that you stay safe."

"It is meant to be, Child. St. Catherine is with me."

"I shall remember her too then."

"She will be easy to remember. Her name changes to Juno Febreata, whose life is celebrated on Valentine's Day. Her symbol is the heart. Take heart, Child."

The swan slowly pulled away from the platform. "Where am I getting off?"

"Techorentuec Chapel Station in Brittany." The canal curved and the Perfecti disappeared from view.

Aria thought about how she was not taking heart at all. Her head hung down and her mood was as melancholy as the dark water around her. Her core belief systems, like the Twin Towers on 911, had pancaked down upon their own footprint leaving her standing bewildered in the dust. She resolved, as the swan carried her to the next ancestral meeting, to not let this whole experience defeat her. Instead, she would channel her Aunt Esclarmonde and be a woman of great courage and determination.

Right now though, Aria needed solitude to digest her thoughts. She hoped the ride to Brittany would be a long one as she was used to time alone and craved it now more than ever. But alas, the station sign appeared and there was not one but three guides waiting for her on the platform, two men and a beautiful little woman. One of the men stepped forward to assist Aria as she got out of the boat and introduced himself as Judacael. The other man, he said, was Ebalus, and the petite woman, oddly enough, was named Papa.

No conversation ensued as they all moved to the elevator in the cavern wall. The silence continued during the long drop to the submarine station. Aria stole many quick glances at the delicate woman and couldn't help but wonder who she might be.

When the elevator doors opened Aria sighed when she caught sight of the bright yellow Wave Sweeper lit from within like a welcoming cabin in the winter woods. She wondered how all four of them were going to sleep in two chintz overstuffed chairs but in her emotional exhaustion she hardly cared. Even this minor worry was put to rest when they climbed through the hatch for somehow the interior, still appearing like the library at Inverary, now was roomy enough for a table set for four. And the man, Ebalus, walked around the table and opened a narrow door in the aft of the sub revealing sleeping quarters for Aria.

The woman, noticing the look of relief on Aria's face upon seeing her room, said to her, "You may retire for the evening if you wish. Or you might like to take a shower and rejoin us for a supper of seafood chowder. It is your choice and one that we accept."

All of what the woman just said surprised Aria. Her deepest desire was to retire for the evening but then the woman said that she could take a shower. A shower? She could take a shower and retire for the evening? Heaven. But then again, why were they allowed to forfeit their opportunity to share their histories with her? Right now, none of that mattered. She was going to take a shower. You don't know what you've got till it's gone, she thought, and walked past whoever these people were to get to it.

She tossed the Silver Branch on the narrow bed and took off the oppressive black dress. A gown of sea foam green had been left for her with opalescent pink pearls sewn with care onto the bodice. She felt guilty in her love of its material finery as she thought of Esclarmonde making a statement about the world with her dark depressive clothing. But no amount of guilt would have her putting the black dress on again. She stepped into the hot shower and felt as revived as if she had bathed in the healing waters at Lourdes. Perhaps all water is curative.

By the end of the long blessed shower, curiosity had overtaken Aria's desire for solitude and she wasn't about to miss finding out who the three people were sitting at the table in the other room. And besides, seafood chowder sounded way too good to turn down.

Judacael ladled steaming soup into Aria's bowl once she had joined them and Ebalus handed her a basket of warm bread. She was so hungry that she was half way through the bowl before she asked her first question. "How is it that someone so delicate and feminine as you, came to be named Papa? In my age that is a name for fathers and grandfathers."

"It is a different spelling. P O P P A. It means doll. I am remembered as the Doll Queen."

Aria stopped eating and stared at her. "You are the queen of France?"

"I am not a queen at all. It is just what I am called. I am the Dutchess of Bayeux before Rollo marries me."

"Is that the same Bayeux as the tapestry fame?"

"Yes. Our son is the commander of the Norman Invasion of England. That is why he is remembered as William the Conqueror."

"What's a Norman? I forget."

"A Norse man. A Scandinavian."

"It's a damn Viking, sister" Judacael hissed. "Call them what they are."

"You are siblings? Is one of you my grandparent?"

"All three of us are your grandparents", Poppa answered. "Judacael is the Count of Rennes and succeeds our father, Berenger."

"Because your damn husband kills him!", Judacael snapped.

"He wasn't my husband at the time, brother. Perhaps in your next life you can return as a woman and experience what it is to be a trophy of conquest."

"Are you a brother too, Ebalus?", Aria asked in hopes of dissipating some of the sibling rivalry in the room.

Poppa spoke for him. "Ebalus's son, William III Towhead, is married to our daughter, Adele of Normandy. Ebalus is the Count of Poitiers. Ebalus and I are on your father's side. Judacael is on both. We are approximately your 30th ago grandparents."

"I am descended from the Meschines of Appleby", Judacael pointed out.

"Adele's daughter, with Lambert de Lens, not the Towhead, is Judith de Lens and Judith is married to Waltheof, the son of the Fairy Bear."

"And who is Rollo?"

Poppa quickly glanced at her brother as if daring him to remain silent. "Rollo is a Viking. He is also an outlaw and a cattle thief who is banished from Norway to the Hebrides of Scotland. In Norway it is prophesied that the bear will marry the princess. That is me."

"Your husband is a bear too?"

Poppa giggled slightly. "He certainly is the size of one. His name, Rollo, means the walker, because he is too big to ride a horse. He calls me Poppie, she said and giggled again.

"You're disgusting, sister!"

Ebalus entered into the conversation in an attempt to squelch the tension between the siblings. "I'm not the greatest fan of Rollo either, I have to admit. I tried in my own pathetic way to oppose him but I failed so it could just be sour grapes. However, our mutual granddaughter,

Adelaide, does marry Hugh Capet, King of France, and brings glory to us both."

"Did I hear Poppa say that you are the Lord of Pictavia?"

"I'm the Count of Poitiers. I should be the Prince of Aquitaine. My father is the King of Aquitaine. But I am called Manzer, meaning the bastard, so the highest honor I can claim is Count of Poitiers. Regardless, I still marry Elfgifu, the granddaughter of King Alfred the Great."

"What does the name Elfgifu mean?"

"Elf gift. And Alfred's name means elf advice. A good choice for his name, being as how he is the greatest of all of England's lawgivers. Elfwyn or elf friend, is Elfgifu's cousin and both she and Elfgifu's mother, Athelflaed, rule England after Alfred."

"Then the barbarian ends up ruling England?"

"Who are you calling the barbarian, Child?", Poppa asked her.

"Why, Rollo, of course. He murdered your dad."

"So in modern times a barbarian is a murderer?"

Feeling suddenly self conscious by her limited knowledge of history, Aria, for some inexplicable reason blundered on anyway. "Well…um…. not just that…um…a barbarian is a ruffian of sorts. Rough around the edges so to speak. Potentially dangerous. Very dangerous. Living out in the wild." Aria knew that her image of a barbarian was derived from a movie poster of an Arnold Schwarzenegger movie that she never even bothered to watch.

"Interesting interpretation", Poppa commented. "In reality the barbarians are the Goths. The Scandinavian tribes who marry the Germanic tribes are the barbarians. They are not unlike the Picts who inhabit the great forests and the greenwoods. Both are the Albigens, the elves. They do not live so much out in the wild, as you say, as they do apart from formal civilization. It is a choice not to live a settled way of life with stored necessities and shared labor, but still it is a deep, rich, and authentic culture whose many traditions are adhered to into your modern age."

"What barbarian traditions do we adhere to?"

"Well, a twelve based mathematical system, for one. And Santa Claus and the Easter Bunny too."

Aria laughed at the absurdity of it. "So then that St. Nicholas guy from Russia or wherever, that Santa Claus is based on, is really a barbarian?"

"Nicholas of Myra is from Turkey. He has no business being labeled a saint. When the Council of Nicea is called by the high church to determine the tenants of the fledging Christian faith, the proponent and founder, Arius, of the very popular Christian sect named Arianism after him, stands up. But his postulation of beliefs is never heard because Nicholas of Myra also stands up and punches his lights out. It is declared, while Arius lay unconscious, that Arianism is heretical."

"Punishable by torture and or death?", Aria asked.

"I told you, Nicholas is no saint."

"Pretty easy to wipe out established belief systems, huh?"

"Not as easy as all that. The Picts, the Irish and the Basque refuse to convert for another thousand years. Celebrations of Santa Claus and the Easter Bunny still exist in your era."

"Are the Picts, the Irish, and the Basque the strange blood people?"

"Yes, and the Icelandic as well. Rollo's daughter, Kaolin, is married to Bjolan of Iceland who is a king in Scotland. And it is Bjolan's sister, Aud the Deep Minded, who is married to Olaf the White. But that is a story for tomorrow, so we will leave it for then."

"Oh my gosh. I'm not going to Iceland tomorrow to meet Olaf the White, am I?" Aria's voice had a bit of that old whine in it and she knew she was getting tired and impatient for a conclusion to her journey. What if it went on forever? What if she had to visit every ice covered god-forsaken country in the world before she reached the Beginning of Things?

"Olaf the White is not Icelandic. Olaf is Basque and the son of Mari, their chthonic deity, with her lover, a white bear."

Aria could not even respond.

"You need rest, Child", Judacael told her. "It is a long passage to Bamberg Castle so you have sufficient time."

"Bamberg Castle? Oh no! I'm on the wrong boat. I was supposed to be going to Joyous Garde." She wanted to cry but she was still too fresh from her meeting with the always courageous Esclarmonde to indulge in such selfish luxuries.

"Joyous Garde is the name for Bamberg Castle when it is occupied by Lancelot du Lac. Bamberg is the home of the Armstrongs, the descendants of Olaf. Noli Temere. You have not missed your boat."

"My brother is right. You need your rest. Those used to fresh air, sun rays and starlight can be adversely affected by too much time spent beneath the surface. Your mood will rise with your ascent. Take heart."

Aria's mood did not rise as she changed into a sleeping gown and tumbled into the welcoming bed. Tomorrow is another day. Isn't that what Scarlett O'Hara was so famous for saying? She had no idea what tomorrow would bring but she did know that she would be reunited with fresh air, sun rays and starlight. And that was enough to be grateful for in her confused, exhausted, emotional state. She welcomed a good night's sleep but for once it didn't come. She stared out at the inky black water and could think of nothing else but home and how desperate she was to get back there. She was glad that Esclarmonde could not see her here in the dark with her salty tears streaking her face. She would probably have cried all night but the Silver Branch on the nightstand could be heard tinkling the faintest of tunes. She thought it might be Somewhere Over the Rainbow but then she fell asleep so fast that she couldn't be sure.

Esclarmond de Foix
Cathar Perfecti

The Light of the World

Ancestor of Nancy Ann of the Virginia Company

Rollo the Viking

father of William the Conqueror

husband of Poppa

Ancestor of Nancy Ann of the Virginia Company

Hugh Capet
King of France

Ancestor of Nancy Ann of the Virginia Company

Alfred the Great

King of England

Ancestor of Mariah of the Masons and Nancy Ann of the Virginia Company

CHAPTER FIVE

"It takes courage to be happy."

Irma Armstrong Carnahan

Ride a cock horse to Banbury Cross
To see a fine lady on a white horse
With rings on her fingers and bells on her toes
She shall make music wherever she goes

Northern English Nursery Rhyme

THE SUN DID not come up to announce morning's arrival because Aria was sleeping on the submarine. Yet when she opened her eyes, she knew for a fact that a new day had begun. It probably didn't matter if she slept for two hours or ten, once she was rested a new day would begin because time was custom ordered for her here. She was being rushed from place to place but her time resting at night seemed to be under her control so she considered taking advantage of the fact by rolling over and going back to sleep. Maybe if she slept some more she would wake up with enthusiasm instead of dread. She was experiencing the opportunity of a thousand lifetimes and all she cared about was home. Where was Esclarmonde's home? How did her aunt face each dangerous day without dread? It was so disappointing to Aria to discover that she had not even acted like the heroine in her very own story. Perhaps a hero is simply someone who daily swallows down their fears and perseveres regardless. She could be at least that much of a hero. She was done disappointing herself and if she ever saw Esclarmonde again she would be able to hold her head high, so Aria got up and got dressed.

Poppa, Judacael, and Ebalus were no longer in the main cabin of the submarine which was no longer larger enough to accommodate a dining table for four. The chintz chairs and tea cart had returned and a new woman sat waiting patiently for Aria's appearance. She stood and introduced herself as Aud the Deep Minded.

"I heard your name mentioned last night but I'm embarrassed to say that I don't remember the connection", Aria said shaking her hand.

"I am the sister of the Icelandic King of Scotland, Bjolan. My sister-in-law, Kaolin, is Rollo's daughter."

"I remember now. I thought I would be traveling to Iceland to be meeting someone named Olaf."

"Olaf the White is my husband. You are meeting me instead. Olaf is not Icelandic. Even Scandinavian countries think of him as an Irish Sea King and the king of Dublin. The Basque people think of him as Juan Zuria, the White Lord, first Lord of Biscay. He is the child of Mari and a white bear, Bjorn the Old."

"I have trouble with this, Aud. Sex with bears is beyond my comprehension. I find it to be repulsive. Sorry."

"It is not part of the culture that you know. In Scandinavian, Germanic, and Basque cultures there exists a long tradition in a belief of a descent from bears. These beliefs remain encapsulated within these cultures in your modern era and are not spoken of freely. You will probably assimilate this information more readily from the bears you will meet here today before returning to France tonight."

"France?", Aria said aghast "I just came from there! And Bears? I'm terrified of bears!"

"Your journey is presented to you in a linear timeframe like the one in your reality. "You will meet the bear descendants of Olaf at Bamberg Castle before you meet Mari this evening."

"And who is Mari?"

"Olaf's mother who is the Basque chthonic deity. The name Mari is the Basque, or Euskara, word for love. You will return to France with her tonight."

"I'm going to ride on the submarine with an underground deity?"

"Of course not. Mari does not use the submarine." Aud gave her a little Mona Lisa smile and climbed up to and out of the hatch. Aria reluctantly followed.

An elevator carried the women to the surface and deposited them into yet another cave. Disappointed to still be under damp, dark earth Aria asked, "Where is the castle from here?"

"Over our heads. These caverns lie directly beneath Bamberg Castle, or what you are told is Joyous Garde. When it existed as Joyous Garde, these caverns are used by Lancelot to free the maiden from the vessel."

"King Arthur's pal? That Lancelot?"

"Lancelot is Arthur's knight. The story of the maiden is an alchemical reference to an even earlier name, Castle Corbenic. Corbenic being the Chaldean word for Holy Vessel."

"What is a Chaldean?"

"Chaldea is a place in Mesopotamia. Among its citizenry are magicians and alchemists to such an extent that the word Chaldean in time refers to them. You know what a magician is but you may not know what an alchemist is."

"They turn lead to gold", Aria clarified.

"They do indeed transform matter. It'a a difficult subject to explain and even more difficult when applied to the maiden in the vessel. Faust writes about it. I can quote a bit if you would like."

Aria knew for a fact that she would have difficulty quoting Dr. Suess, let alone an author she had never read so she encouraged Aud the Deep Minded to proceed.

"There is a red lion", Aud began, "a bold youngster, married to the lily in the lukewarm bath, and then with an open fire, chased from one bridal chamber to another. Next, with motley colors, the young queen appeared in the glass vessel."

Now Aria knew why she had never bothered to read Faust because she hadn't understood a single word of his quote. Confused, she asked, "That's the girl that Lancelot rescues?"

"It is in actuality Sir Gawain, Lancelot's most trustworthy friend, who witnesses the dove bringing the vessel out of which emerges the beautiful maiden."

Aud led Aria along close smooth rock corridors until they reached a door in the cavern wall. Once opened, sunlight and the scent of the briny sea assaulted Aria's senses. She stepped outside to a view of the Eastern Shore of Northern England and reclaimed her joy. She drew in great breaths of nature's anti depressant, fresh air. She looked up at the castle behind her. "Is Lancelot in there now?"

"Lancelot is before today's timeline. The Fairy Bear occupies it today. The Armstrongs possess it even in the modern era."

"How did it manage to change from French to Scottish ownership?"

"I don't understand your question, Child."

"Well, Lancelot du Lac, right?, the French guy, had it and then the Armstrongs end up with it."

"Lancelot is an Englishman and du Lac means 'of the waters', and signifies the Desposyni family. The Armstrongs are descended from the Fairy Bear who becomes the original owner of the Armstrong name right here in Northern England."

"There were no Armstrongs before the bear?"

"He is the first."

Aria was worried. Her own grandma, Irma, was an Armstrong. Was she too descended from bears? Best not to ask. "What is the Martini family?"

"You ask of the the Desposyni. The Desposyni are descended from the Holy Family."

"As in Mary and Joseph type holy?"

"Lancelot is descended from the brother of Jesus, James the Just."

"What? Am I related to Lancelot then?"

"You are of his descent on your mother's side."

Hearing this took Aria's breath away. She wasn't even going to ask if it were really true that she could be descended from the brother of Jesus, making Jesus her uncle. And she wasn't even going to ask if she was slated to meet this uncle. She had met two aunts, Catherine Greystoke and Esclarmonde. It wasn't beyond the realm of possibilities but it seemed sacrilege to even think about it. Jesus would naturally be way too busy helping all those billions and billions of people who called on him endlessly for help with their troubles. She said a quick prayer to him herself asking would he please tend to his important work and not take precious time for her. She was fine. And in that moment she realized she was. She stared out over the water with its diamond sparkle and the breeze that brushed her face was warmed by the sun and she felt the tiny beginnings of bliss. Which turned to embarrassment when she realized that Aud was standing silent, watching her.

Her shame was unfounded because no one was watching her. While she stared out to sea and ruminated over her connection to the Christ, Aud had vanished. Aria searched the perimeter of the castle with her eyes in hopes of catching a glimpse of her waiting by the door. At last, she spied her heading for the nearby tree line at the proverbial rapid clip. Thinking that Aud was trying to give her the slip because she also was afraid of bears and didn't want to go inside, Aria hiked up the skirt of her gown and took off after her. By the time she reached the forest entrance she was breathing hard and had broken into a sweat. Aud was sitting peacefully on a tree stump waiting for her. "I'm not going in there to meet that bear without you", Aria panted."

"You aren't going into Bamberg Castle now at all. First we shall travel to Scotland." Later we will return to Bamberg where you will dine."

Trying not to look as relieved as she felt, she casually looked around and asked, "Where is the transport station?"

"We'll walk."

"To Scotland? I don't think we'll get back in time for dinner!" Now Aria was even more relieved that the meeting with the bear would be further postponed. Maybe horses and submarines could travel at unnatural speeds but she couldn't. In fact she was a slow walker. Aria smiled.

"You are on the borderland of the time squished world. You will dine with the bears, don't fret. You are unraveling from within and require time in nature to repair yourself. We journey through the land of the Picts. You cannot know them if you do not connect with their sanctuary."

And so they walked and they walked in silence. This was not the Mametz Wood with its war atrocity energy. This was more akin to the cottonwood grove of her Eden where she and all the faithful dogs through her years had traversed its ancient solitude. This was peace, plant scent, and birdsong and before long she lost herself in the majesty of it and could no longer tell if she was walking through Scotland or scuffing the clean white sand of the little dry wash bed just beyond her own front door. For the first time in days, the world disappeared. Just as it always did on her daily walks in the early dawn, and then later in the growing twilight. This was what home felt like.

They walked for a very long time. The path was too easy and the forest too gentle to probably be real but it didn't matter at all. The further she walked, the deeper her silence, the better she felt. At last the forest thinned and the path widened to a meadow under another clear blue sky.

Aud broke the morning's silence when Aria spied a man approaching from across the meadow. "That building yonder is the Palace of Scone. It is the seat of the Picts. The man walking to meet you is Kenneth macAlpin. He is further back in your ancestry than the others inside awaiting your visit. His father is Dal Riata and his mother is Pict. Since he can lay claim to both thrones he unifies the two. He commits treachery against his mother's people to do it. You are descended from him by May of the Moon Men, Nancy Ann of the Virginia Company and Newt of the Massachusetts Bay Colony. He is also the ancestor of Wilson of the Silver Branch."

"I feel bad now, Aud, that I didn't spend our walk through the woods asking about your history. I had no idea you would be leaving me so soon."

"I will return shortly with a carriage to take us back to Bamberg. The walk through the woods was not meant for questions."

Aria and her Emery's Scottish king grandfather walked up and shook her hand. She no longer felt like a first grader meeting the principal when in the presence of her royal lineage. They were, after all, human beings like herself. She walked beside him as they crossed the meadow toward the Palace of Scone.

"Is your name Alpin a form of alpine, like the trees?"

"Alpin is another spelling of elfin."

Okay, Aria thought to herself, maybe not so human after all. He looked human. Did all elves look like humans? Whatever he was, and king or not, she wasn't afraid of him. Whoever these people were they didn't seem to intend any harm to her. They created yellow submarines and enchanted forests just to make her feel better. But she didn't ask him any other questions so they walked in silence.

Three more ancestors waited inside. A woman named Bethoc introduced the other two as St. Margaret and Margaret's husband, Malcolm Canmore. Bethoc explained that Kenneth was the ancestor of both she and her grandson, Malcolm. Kenneth was Aria's thirty-fifth-ago grandparent whereas Bethoc was her twenty-ninth-ago and Margaret and Malcolm, her twenty-seventh-ago. Malcolm was also a king in Scotland and Canmore meant big head.

A serving girl arrived with a basket of scones. Aria tried to conceal her smile as she thought that once again the Council was humoring her. Like serving Starbucks coffee in Poitiers. Hungry from her walk, she ate two before speaking. "Aud told me that this is the seat of the Picts but that you, Kenneth, united the Picts and the Dal Riata. Isn't this the seat of the Dal Riata too?"

"I declare Scone the capital but I rule from Dunkeld. The center of the Dal Riata kingdom is in a little village called Gretna Green."

"That's not too far from Appleby, right?"

Bethoc spoke, "Yes, It's on the western side of Scotland which is the Dal Riata, or Scots, side. Scotland is divided by the Drumalban mountain range with the Scots on the west and the Picts on the east. Kenneth is titled Rex Pictorum, King of the Picts, because the Picts are an older clan than the Dal Riata."

"I was told that the Picts and the Basque speak the same language. Did the Picts migrate from France?"

"They migrate to France and Ireland from Thrace, where they are known as the Phrygians from Agartha. In Ireland, they are known as the Cruithne, or the people of the designs, because they tattoo their bodies with blue ink. When they are thrown out of Ireland, they migrate to Scotland."

"Why the blue tattoos?"

"In honor of their descent from the blue people."

"The Phrygians?"

"Yes. You might best know them by their hat, their Phrygian cap. It's an odd red cap that curves up over their head. In your time, pixies are depicted wearing them."

"Oh my gosh! A blue pixie wearing a curved red cap? You just described Papa Smurf! The little blue Smurfs are cartoon characters on television. Papa Smurf became my dad's nickname because he was short and had a wonderful white beard." Aria smiled at the memory of her father fondling his beard.

Bethoc smiled too. "What is your father's name?"

"Brownie. Well, that's his nickname. His grandma named him that when he was born because he was so teeny and dark."

"That is the name for an elemental. The brownie is the unseen helper at hearth and home. But what is his given name?"

"He always hated it", she laughed, "it's Fay."

"Fay is the name for the fairies. Words, especially names, are important. This appears to you as a coincidence, but is it? Even the word pixie is merely a bastardization of the words, Pict, and Sidhe (shee). The Sidhe are the Tuatha de Danaan who are the ruling elite over the fairy class."

"So the Tuatha de Danaan are the elves?"

"The elves are inter-dimensional like the Tuatha de Danaan. The Picts are of this class. This class rules over the fairies who are the elemental earth spirits, like the brownies and the gnomes."

"Where did you say the Phrygians came from?"

"Agartha. The Underground Country. The Lands Beneath."

"Is there some way to get there?"

"By boat. And in your age, also by air. You can read the accounts left by those who make the journey but they are few. It's really 'invitation only' being a fifth dimensional world where third dimensional beings don't necessarily fit in."

"Where is the fourth dimension?"

"In the dream world."

"What about the Dal Riata, Kenneth? From whom did they descend?"

"We claim our descent from the Beastie", he answered in all seriousness.

"A bear?" she guessed.

"No. A water horse, Epidion. Some would call it a kelpi. It sports the mane and tail of a horse but has the bill and flippers of a duck. Pictures of it are left by the stone carvers."

"And you think this is your ancestor?" Aria didn't even want an answer. It was preposterous to even consider.

"Perhaps you can dine with Epidion as well, after you've met the bears!" Kenneth's words were meant to sting and they did.

Aria shriveled at his remark. Once again she had embarrassed herself by her insistence on overlaying modern beliefs onto this mythological world with such blind certainty. Her eyes brimmed with tears.

Bethoc, like all good grandmas, came to her rescue. "Cultures are obliterated by history's victors leaving no record for future generations. The concept of a descent from kelpies and bears is no longer given credence in the modern age. The Great Knight, William Marshal, causes the cultural collapse of my mother's clan in Ireland, the People of the Deer. But even larger groups, like the Picts, add to their own cultural demise by the habit of not writing any of it down for posterity. The

Picts leave no written accounts of their lives. No chronicles, no stories, nothing. And the Scots are as guilty as the Picts. Once they finally learn the error of their ways and begin to record their history and beliefs, the Vikings come along and throw it all into the sea. So they write it again and Edward I of England comes along and steals it. So you see, a lot of effort goes into your not knowing these things."

"That's my ancestor, I guess, Edward I. He's a thief as well as a torturer?"

"He takes what he wants. He takes Margaret's rood."

Turning to Margaret, Aria asked, "You are a contemporary of Edward I?"

"Edward is our descendant. That is why he takes the rood because he feels that it belongs to him", Margaret explained.

"Do you see why they label her a saint?" Malcolm sighed and shook his head. "She sticks up for everybody. Why, she won't even eat her dinner unless she knows that the orphans and the poor have been fed. But you are correct, Child. Edward is a thief. He even steals the Stone of Scone."

"I don't know what either of those are, a rood or the Stone of Scone."

"The rood, or the Black Rood as it is called, is a crucifix with a piece of the true cross in it."

"That's a torture device, you know, the cross. Your rood must be Roman Catholic."

"I am canonized a saint by Pope Innocent IV and I will be considered a saint by the Anglican Church as well. And yet it is I who pours the blood of St. Catherine into the well at Roslyn enabling her great healing to continue."

Dumbstruck for the hundredth time, Aria did not know what to say. Her grandmother was a bonafide saint, not a popular saint of the people. She stared at her in awe expecting her to glow. And why was that? Did being bonafide by the Church of the Wolves give one glow rights? And what about the blood in the well reference? Did the church know she was venerating the not-to-be-venerated St. Catherine? Things weren't exactly black and white here. "What about the stone? What is that?"

"The Coronation Stone from the Temple of Solomon" Bethoc replied.

"That must be it!", Aria exclaimed, "the stone in the treasure that Robert de Sable couldn't recall! But what is it?"

"Kenneth, you brought it here, why don't you tell her." Bethoc said to her ancestor.

"Alba. It means stone. This whole country is called Alba after I bring it here."

"You stole it from the Temple of Solomon?"

"I inherit it from our ancestor, Fergus, who brings it from Ireland to Argyll. Fergus is the first Dal Riata king."

"The Irish stole it from the temple?"

"It is hidden in Ireland from Nebuchadnezzer when he sacks the temple. There is an Isrealite tribe living in Ireland descended from the Tuatha de Danaan who call themselves simply the Tuatha de. They continue to use it as the Coronation Stone in the same location as the Stone of Destiny, at Tara, seat of the High Kings. It roars out when the proper monarch stands over it. Doesn't work anymore, of course. Edward I builds the Coronation Chair to fit over it. Still, it does not roar for a single one of those English monarchs. But then it doesn't roar for Robert the Bruce, or MacBeth, or the forty others who are crowned over it here in Scotland either. England and Scotland share it, believe it or not."

"Did it ever work?"

"Of course. The last monarch it roared for is Conn of the Hundred Battles in Ireland."

"Were you talking about the MacBeth that the Shakespeares write about?"

"He's my brother-in-law", Bethoc said. "My sister and I are the princesses of Scotland. My sister is married to MacBeth. Malcolm here kills him."

Aria's head whipped around to look at Malcolm Big Head. "You killed MacBeth?"

And before the words were fully voiced she realized that she had let the cat out of the bag that she had never read MacBeth.

"He kills my father."

"That's true" Bethoc said. "My dear sweet son, Duncan, has far too mild and gentle a disposition to be ruling a country as turbulent as Scotland in the first place. MacBeth kills him to take the title."

"My Uncle Siward helps me get it back", Malcolm told her. "It's where your Armstrong name comes from. Before the Battle of MacBeth he is Siward Fairbairn, or Fairy Bear, my mother's brother. Uncle Siward comes up from Northumberland with his troops for the battle. He loses one of his sons, my cousin, Osberne Bulax, in the fight but he saves me. My horse falls on me and crushes me so I can't walk. Uncle Siward fights his way out to me, picks me up with one arm, brandishing his big sword in his free hand, and carries me back to safety. I start calling him Siward of the Strong Arm after that. He is living at Bamberg, his wife Elflaed's place, but I give him Mangerton Castle on the border in Liddesdale. Now the Armstrongs are in Scotland."

"No Scottish blood?"

"It doesn't take long. Uncle Siward's granddaughter, Maud Armstrong, is married to our son, David. She is down at Bamberg waiting to meet you."

Aria was afraid to ask if Maud might be a bear. She didn't want to think about the bears.

"Even David is not fully Scottish", Margaret pointed out, "since my mother is a Hungarian princess and I am born there at Castle Reka. Father is Edward the Exile, the uncrowned king of England. I am raised in the English royal court being the granddaughter of six of the kings of England, from Edmund Ironside back to Alfred the Great. This is where the influence of the High Church comes in. The royal court is already Christianized by them. But when Father is killed in the Norman Invasion of England, I flee here to Scotland with my brother, and heir to the throne, Edgar Atheling, along with Siward's grandson, Siward Barn the White. Malcolm is our protector." Margaret smiled warmly at her husband.

Malcolm saw the look on Margaret's face and blushed. "Don't go trying to make me some sort of saint, Margaret. I still can't figure out why you agreed to marry me. Some things make no sense at all."

Bethoc observed this interchange between her grandson and his wife. "No one could love you more, Malcolm. She dies of grief from the loss of you in only four days."

Malcolm was visibly upset by her words.

"Margaret", Aria jumped in saying, "tell me about your St. Catherine connection. Where did you get her blood to pour into the well?"

"These things are not uncommon and are procured for a price. I get the vile at the monastery on Mt. Sinai."

"Where did they get it?"

"It is also not uncommon to find zealots who, using a sponge, soak up the blood of saints when they die and hide them in wells to be stored until sold. St. Pudenziana is one such individual. She and her assistant, Pastorus, Shepard of the Stars, are well known for this."

"A saint soaks up the blood of a saint?"

"Not only a saint but the niece of the first Bishop of Rome."

"Do you mean the first pope? Peter had a niece who was a saint?"

"Peter is never a Bishop of Rome, or pope, as you call it."

"Of course he is. He's the first one."

"Linus is the first Bishop of Rome. He is the grandson of the first Pendragon."

"Italy has pendragons too?"

"There are only pendragons in the British Isles. The first pendragon, Cymbelline, is in Wales. The Shakespeares write about him."

"Why would the High Church choose a Welshman for their first pope? Doesn't that seem an odd choice?"

"Not really. England is the first country to embrace Christianity", Margaret explained.

"Embraced it? I thought the Romans forced it on you."

"There are two Christian sects in England, one Roman, one Nazarine. The bishop of the Nazarines is James the Just."

"The brother of Jesus! Now that's a good choice. Who picked him?"

"The Apostles of Jesus."

"You would think that the Romans would pick amongst one of the other Apostles instead of going all the way to Wales to find someone."

"No one goes anywhere. Linus lives in Rome. His grandfather, Cymbelline, opposes the Romans and winds up captured by them in Northern England and hauled off to Rome. Linus and his sister, Claudia, are basically raised as Romans. She is married to Rufus Pudens, half-brother to Paul. They are followers of Paul and his Pauline doctrine. The High Church is based on it. And St. Pudenziana is the daughter of Rufus and Claudia."

"Where is your rood in my time, Margaret? Can I go see it?" Aria needed a simple response to something. There never was a moon landing, there never was a Nazareth, Peter was never the pope. It would be quicker to ask what's real than what isn't.

"Edward gets it stolen from him and it is displayed in the Shrine of St. Cuthbert.

Henry VIII steals it from there and it vanishes. In modern times it is said to be in Roslyn Chapel which is built over the well. The chapel, built by freemasons, is also constructed directly over a megalithic underground chamber, an otherworld portal. All nine of the original Templar Knights are buried there. The floor plan is the same as Solomon's Temple. I doubt if you go there though, that you would see the rood."

"David's wife will probably have to finish this narrative", Kenneth said as he stood to leave, "since it's time for you to leave for Bamberg now. I'll walk out to Boot Hill with you."

"Boot Hill? Are we off to Dodge City?", she laughed and stood up too.

"We are just going outside" Kenneth responded not understanding the reference. "It is the place of coronation. One must stand on the dirt that has been carried from one's home inside one's boots while being crowned on the hill. Boot Hill."

Aria will never have a memory of Boot Hill or what it even looked like because she saw nothing and was aware of nothing once she spied the carriage awaiting her. It was minuscule. So tiny, in fact, that she was surprised to see Aud stuffed inside. Yet even that was not the focus of her attention. It was the team of six horses harnessed to the carriage that shocked her. They too were minuscule, really no bigger than spaniels. But strangest of all, they were green. The wee horses were green!

Kenneth held the door while Aria wriggled in beside Aud and the little team took off like a shot, green manes flowing and re-entered the forest south of the palace. This was not the idealized peaceful forest of this morning's walk. This forest felt primeval. It was dense and dark so that only the diminutive horses and carriage could have navigated such tight confines. The shade was deep and pervasive. The sounds of birds and animals was hushed and sporadic. The earth smelled ancient and alive. Cold air embraced the travelers.

"Why the Mythic Woods atmosphere?" Aria asked flippantly but really was so grateful for the tight quarters inside the carriage where she felt safe butted up against Aud so that she was warm against the advancing cold. She would love to have her tartan cloak now.

"This is a truer representation of the home of the Caledonians, the Picts. It is the place where the earth dream meets the otherworld. Here you are more likely to see the White Hart, the Forest King, or catch a glimpse of a Pict abode."

"The houses of the Picts? What do they look like?" Aria intently scanned the landscape for a sighting.

"Beehive shaped. Thick walls covered with turf to make them water tight. Doors about three feet high."

"What about windows?"

"No need of them. They do all their work at night because they lose their strength during the day so that is when they sleep."

"A three foot high door implies a three foot high person. Kenneth is normal height so I'm confused."

"The Picts are known for marrying outside their clan, unlike the Basque, who practice just the opposite. Here in Kenneth's Alba a change takes place over time."

"Is the Beastie real, Aud?"

"You have never heard of the Loch Ness Monster?"

"Nessie is the Beastie?"

"The Beastie is associated with Loch Fyne, Loch Argyll, and Loch

Awe, all on the Dal Riata side of the Drumalban range. The poet, William Butler Yeats, says that these creatures are placed by subtle enchanters to watch over the gates of wisdom."

"Of course he would say that. He's a poet and that sounds poetic."

"Or maybe he was given this information when he met the Queen of the Fairies."

Aria did not know that Yeats had ever met the Queen of the Fairies so she didn't want to respond. The cold accelerated and she was rubbing her hands together in her lap to produce some heat. She couldn't even imagine not having this carriage in which to ride and was so grateful for the modicum of heat and safety it provided. "It looks dangerous out there."

"It can be dangerous. Hadrian and the Romans have to build a wall between England and Scotland to protect themselves from the inhabitants of these forests. Enchanted people who disappear into the woods like magic are difficult to conquer. They think that a wall will contain them inside Scotland. It doesn't work. They end up using a series of castles along the border. Castle Greystokes is commandeered for this."

"I can certainly see why the Romans were too frightened to come here to fight the forest people." Aria shivered to think of having to get out of the carriage for a stroll let alone a battle.

"The Romans have no fear of the Picts. At least not initially. And they do come to do battle. Four thousand of them at once. Not regular soldiers either, but what you might term super soldiers. They are the IX Hispanic Legion. The Unlucky Ninth."

"What happened?"

"They march through the village of Dunblane on their way to do battle and continue marching straight into nothingness. All four thousand of them disappear and are never seen again."

Aria looked out the window and didn't doubt for a moment that could happen in this place. "You know a lot about the Picts for an Icelandic girl."

"Iceland is colonized by the Scots and the Norse so our cultures are similar. And in essence, the Picts are my husband's people because he is the son of the Basque deity and there are many similarities between the Basque and the Picts. They both speak the language of Ak, Euskara. They both know the Language of the Birds. They are both aware of the Golden Mean and the Golden Number. Both are steadfastly matrilineal. The major difference between them is that the Picts are exogomatic, marrying outside their clan, and the Basque all but quarantine themselves."

"Why is your Basque husband considered to be a Viking?"

"His father is Norse. Bjorn the Old is descended from Ragnar Lodbrock."

"Is he a bear too?"

"Ragnar? Have you never heard of him, Child? His exploits are legendary. He is a Viking."

"I'm ashamed to admit that I really don't know much about history."

"It is the least studied subject of all. The majority of people never learn any more than what is taught to them in their early education years. History is easy to manipulate when the controlled are unfamiliar with it. In your era you are studying His Story, history."

"I'm afraid to meet your mother-in-law!", Aria finally blurted out. "She lives underground and has sex with animals!"

"You make her sound like a ground squirrel. Chthonic does not mean that you live in the dirt. We are trying to teach you that there is another reality beneath this one, but it isn't a hole in the ground. If you could imagine the earth as a disk instead of a ball, and you flipped it over, you would find another world there. As above so below."

"I won't know how to act around someone from another world." There was that annoying whine again.

"Well then you are in for a treat. Her name is Mari, Basque for love. What could go wrong? You worry too much, do you know that?"

Aria agreed with her while silently worrying about her upcoming meeting with the bears.

The little carriage and its occupants exited the forest just as the sun was beginning to set, casting a rosy glow over Bamberg Castle. Aria was deposited at the door where another woman awaited her arrival. She was another living doll, like Poppa.

"My grandmother?", Aria asked the lovely woman.

"Twenty-ninth-ago through Joseph of the New England Company."

"Are you Maud Armstrong?"

"No. She is waiting for you inside. My name is Godgifu. My husband, Leofric, serves on a triumvirate of earls with the Fairy Bear."

"Triumvirate?"

"Three earls working together. The third is Godwine, Earl of Wessex."

Aria walked through the door expecting to faint. But to her great relief, what she saw were two massively large men sitting on a long bench and another woman, who must be Maud, walking over to greet her. So relieved was she that the so called bears were not covered in hair and sported long sharp teeth and four inch claws that she nearly fainted anyway. The younger of the two men had pale blue eyes and a thick blond beard. By the time Maud had taken her hand to shake it, Aria discovered the swiveling, white, fur-covered bear ears on the sides of the second man's head. And her knees went weak. Maud supported her by the elbow and led her to a chair near the window overlooking the water.

"Quick, Papa, get her some mead!", Maud said to the bearded man.

The little cup all but disappeared in the big man's hands as he handed it to Aria, "It's honey wine, Child. A favorite of ours, naturally. Sorry if my father frightened you. I'm Siward Fairbairn, by the way, ancestor of May of the Moon Men and Newt of the Massachusetts Bay Colony. This is my granddaughter, Maud Armstrong, and the gentleman with the disturbing ears is my father, Bjorn. And of course, you have already met Godiva."

"Godiva?", Aria asked looking over at the little beauty while simultaneously chugging her mead like it was iced tea on a hot day. "Didn't you say it was Godgifu?"

"Godiva is a variation of the name Godgifu", Maud pointed out. "She is more often addressed as Lady Godiva."

Aria, shocked, continued staring at her gorgeous grandmother until she realized that she was undressing her in her mind, then embarrassed, looked away.

Siward poured his father and himself tankards of mead and let Maud tell Aria who they were. Maud refilled Aria's empty cup and began the introductions as the last rays of sunlight danced over the water outside the window. "Your descent from me is through both my first and second husbands. My second husband, David I, is the son of Malcolm and St. Margaret. They call David a saint too but it's just a nickname and isn't official like his mother's. What kind of a saint commandeers the Earldom of Huntingdon away from its rightful inheritor, his step son, Simon?"

"Am I in line for this earldom?", Aria asked, now a little bit tipsy.

Maud poured a little more mead into Aria's cup and ignored her. Even though the sweet liquor had relaxed her jagged nerves, Aria couldn't help but steal glances every few minutes at the darkening horizon in search of Mari's ship. She fought to stay focused on these people in the room. "In my age, Godiva", Aria slurred a little, "you are an expensive candy bar. Did you really ride through town in the buff?"

"Yes, I do"

"And your husband didn't care?"

"My husband is the cause. He is the Earl of Mercia and he puts his own citizens under oppressive taxation. I don't like it so I nag him to stop. And I nag and I nag and I nag. I nag until he can't stand it anymore so he offers the challenge that I ride through town "in the buff", as you say, and he'll lower the taxes. Imagine his surprise when I call his bluff. He does, however, tell everyone to shutter their windows so they can't see his naked wife."

"And Tom peeked!" Aria squealed.

"Yes. Tom peeks. Tom is our tailor."

"Did your husband lower the taxes?"

"I'm pleased to say that he does."

"Did you embarrass your kids?"

"We only have one son together, your twenty-eighth-ago grandfather, Aelfgar. It is not our way to inquire as to the emotional states of our children so I do not know whether I embarrassed him or not. Interestingly, even Aelfgar is tangled in with the Earldom of Huntingdon that is Maud's inheritance. His daughter Edith is married to Harold II Godwinsson, King of England during the Norman Invasion, and Harold is the son of Godwine, third earl in the triumvirate. Harold's brother, Tostig, is the first Earl of Huntingdon."

"Siward lops off the head of the horse's ass", Bjorn pipes in gleefully. "Let me tell you how it happens. I love this story."

Siward pretty much growled at his bear-eared father, "Enough! She's already afraid of us. I can tell her with far less drama and embellishments."

"Oh, I'm not afraid of you guys anymore. And I do want to hear the story."

"Do you see that, Son? She wants me to tell her your fairy bear stories."

"Stories? There are more than one?"

"Well there's the one about him killing the dragon. Single handed, I might add."

"Oh for Heaven's sake", Siward said and shook his head in dismay.

"Did you really do that?", she asked Siward.

"Look at the size of me!", he exclaimed. "My father makes it all sound so dramatic. My crew of fifty men and I sail from Denmark to the Orkneys in Scotland. That is where we encounter the dragon. If I need help I certainly have it. I don't need any. It's kinda fun, actually. I want to go find another dragon to slay so I land here in Northern England."

Aria had finally learned not to ask if things like dragons were real. "Did you find one here?"

"He finds Odin instead!", Bjorn added with obvious pride.

Siward went on before his father could continue. "That is who I think it is. He counsels me to give up the dragon slaying thing and offer my services to Edward the Confessor who is the king. He gives me a banner, Ravenlandeye, to display on our ship and points me toward London. So Edward takes one look at the size of me and offers me the moon to stay and help him retain his kingship. That is where I meet Tostig."

"He was in Edward's court?"

"No. He is on a bridge. The one leading in and out of the castle. I am returning from a meeting with Edward and the horse's ass, as my father so aptly calls him, throws dirt on me."

"What?"

"It's a form of insult", he explained, "like thumbing your nose at someone."

"So you kill him for it?"

"Of course not! I don't acknowledge him at all. Just keep on walking. But later when I have to return to see the king, there he is again, waiting for me. And throws dirt on me again. That's when I lop his damn head off. Carry the bloody thing to show Edward what I've done and am immediately given the Earldom of Huntingdon since the king is that pleased with the beheading. He even throws in the Earldom of Northumberland where we are now."

"Edward owes you a debt, Son, and you know it", Bjorn interjected in all seriousness. "Tostig's uncle, Swein, murders me and Edward knows he has to make good on it. Siward deserves those earldoms too. He gets the earldoms of Cumberland, Westmoreland, and Bamberg too. He's one of the most powerful men in all of Britain. Famous in his own time, he is!"

"Stop it!", Siward demands of his father. "I get the earldom of Bamberg just by marrying Elflaed, the earl's daughter. And it passed back to her uncle, Gospatrick, once I was done with it anyway."

Bjorn snorted and laughed. "Only until William the Conqueror takes it away from him and gives it to Waltheof."

"Who is Waltheof?"

"My father", Maud said. "And the brother of Osberne Bulax, who dies in the Battle of MacBeth."

"What did William the Conqueror have to do with your father?"

"My mother, Judith de Lens, is the Conqueror's niece."

"Well that was nice of him to give his nephew-in-law the title."

"He doesn't seem quite so congenial later when he cuts my father's head off", Maud said in disgust.

"Maud!", Siward barked at his granddaughter. "Your father's

punishment was expected. Even by your father. He willingly joined the group plotting William's overthrow."

"Father already discovers the error of his ways and even confesses to Uncle William. He could show leniency but chooses not to." She looked angry and crossed her arms. "At least the rest of the world knows what a saint Father is."

"Another saint?"

"With proof", Maud continued. "Father's decapitated body is thrown into a ditch to rot. Later when the remains are removed for reburial, he is found to be incorrupt and his head reattached."

"Do you see, Maud?", Siward says to her. "You have your vindication. And you inherit the Earldom of Huntingdon as well."

"If you are related to William the Conqueror, Maud, are you also descended from Rollo and Poppa?"

"My grandfather, Lambert, is their son. He is also the great uncle of Queen Melisende of Jerusalem."

"That's Fulk's wife! Wow! One big happy family, huh?"

"Tell her where they bury you, Son", Bjorn said ignoring her remark. "Better yet I'll tell her. Right inside the very church that Siward builds in York, St. Olaf's. Right inside! He is the only non-royal person in this country ever to have such an honor. They even hang the banner in there with him."

"That's wrong", Siward said. "It is of the Eldrich world and should be returned there."

Aria figured the Eldrich world was where bear people originated, or Norse gods, or inter-dimensional folk or whatever and decided not to ask. She did, however, need to inquire as to how people could be descended from bears. "How can you be both a man and a bear, Bjorn? Isn't there an incompatibility in the DNA?"

"We are descended from the Great Old Ones, also called the Outer Ones, those outside and beyond the tree of life. The ones with eleven strands of DNA. You can read this for yourself. It is all contained in the pages of the Vita Waldevi, the Life of Waltheof."

Aria was now spending as much time scouring the dark surface of the water looking for her next ride as she was paying attention to the people in the room. When Maud announced that a meal was about to be served she relaxed visibly knowing that she still had time before the inevitable fetching. Servants handed individual bowls of stew to them all right where they sat. This pleased Aria as she did not want to move from her place by the window while she kept watch.

The food was delicious and invigorating and for a time she lost herself in the meal.

Finally her curiosity about her ancestors returned. "How did you manage to marry the King of Scotland, Maud?"

"It is an arranged marriage by Henry I. My first husband, Simon, is a Crusader and is killed. Henry knows I am a widow. He is married to David's sister, Matilda. David and I go to live in their court after we are married. We are even Normanized. David gets set up in Carlisle, near Appleby. His brother, Alexander, who rules Scotland before David, grants him the right to rule Cumbria."

"Where is Cumbria?"

"Westmoreland. It's another name for Westmoreland. David is the Prince of the Cumbrians."

"Why do you say he's a saint?"

"Margaret is the only Scottish royal who ever officially attains sainthood. It's just a nickname for David. He really is a good guy. He founds a lot of religious institutions like Holyrood and Melrose. They put the Black Rood in one and the heart of Robert the Bruce in the other. David is gentle and just and chaste and humble but he still introduces feudalism into Scotland."

"What is feudalism?"

"It's a kin based system of land ownership."

"Is that bad?"

"It is when the 'kin' are French knights immigrating to Scotland during the Norman Invasion. Now all the property is passed to their kin."

"Who are they?"

"The Bruces, the Comyns and the Stewarts. The Stewarts get that name because they serve as David's stewards. The first steward, Walter fitzAlan, comes in and defeats the native Scots under the protection of another of your ancestors, Somerled (Sorley), and I seriously doubt that Somerled's people think of David as a saint."

The room began to fill with a rosy light that distracted Aria from the conversation. She looked out the window to see that the light was emanating from the rising moon. The rising red moon. Not a pink moon in atmospheric haze either, but a huge bright blood-red moon. Aria's spoon clattered in her empty bowl and she rushed up to the window in complete disbelief at what she was seeing.

"Mari is here", Bjorn announced.

She whipped her head around to look toward the door but it was closed and only she and the grandparents were in the room. Turning back to the view outside she assumed that she must have missed seeing the ship. But no vessel was visible in the bright red moonlight. Suddenly a flashing meteor shot across the sky. When it traversed in front of the enormous moon Aria gasped. Backlit by the bright red orb Aria could see that it was not a meteor at all but a sickle shaped cart trailing contrails of flame and being pulled by four horses. It was Christmas Eve on steroids and more than Aria could wrap her mind around. Her knees buckled again and she was going down. Siward had her before her crumple was complete. Who would have thought that such a large man could move so fast? Like a bear. He caught her before she hit the floor and still holding her, carried her quickly out the door and into the cool Northern English night. She felt like a child in his strong enormous arms as he moved rapidly away from the castle and onto the rose lit shore. Mari glowed in the moonlight as she sat in her landed cart, reining in her overly excited team of matched red stallions, pawing at the shallow surf, anxious to rise again into the air. Siward placed Aria gently on the bench next to Mari who remained silent. A blue-black raven sat perched on the edge of the open cart beyond Mari and watched Aria intently. A baby goat lay sleeping on a sheepskin blanket on the floor at her feet. Siward picked up the the little animal and placed it softly on Aria's lap and wrapped the blanket around them both. She couldn't even find the nerve to steal a glance at the chthonic goddess sitting next to her but she was instantly overwhelmed by her scent. It was both very foreign and at the same time familiar and beautiful beyond words. She closed her eyes and inhaled deeply, again and again and again, never wanting to stop.

The baby goat stirred on her lap breaking the scent stupor she was in so she opened her eyes. They were already high in the sky and Aria could just make out Siward far below them on the rosy shoreline, watching their departure. Her bear sized grandfather now looked like an ant.

The quickest of glances told Aria that Mari was a redhead. The oddly cool flames surrounding the cart cast enough light to let Aria know that she was a beautiful redhead perfectly at home behind the reins of her team. There was a sign written in English tacked to the inside of the cart. It was a list of the things that Mari does not tolerate and read as follows:

1. Lying
2. Robbery
3. Pride and Boasting
4. Breach of Word
5. Being Disrespectful
6. Denying help
7. Getting into Mari's homes without permission

Fearing that she might be disrespectful if she didn't say something about the ride, Aria squeaked out a note of gratitude, "Thank you for coming to fetch me."

"It isn't out of my way."

"I wasn't expecting to be flying since I've heard that you live underground."

Mari chuckled at her comment. "It is correct that I spend very little time in this reality but I am associated with Ilargi and I enjoy flying when she is full."

"Who is Ilargi?", Aria asked thinking it might be the goat or the raven.

"The moon. To the Basque, Ilargi is the moon and the moon is red. It is why I am called Mari Gorri or Red Mari, because of our close association."

"Are you really a deity?", Aria asked timidly.

"There is no need for aging in the Lands Beneath. Humans mistake longevity for immortality and immortality for divinity."

"Are you human?"

"No. I come because of my connection to Ilargi and Ilargi spins the stars."

"You came from the stars?"

"I come with the stars. They are not always here. We call the light of the Golden Sun, Ost, the god of the firmament. Ost belongs to the day and the natural world. But Ilargi emerges from hidden things, from the hidden side of existence. She belongs to the night and the dark. To the supernatural."

"Are we going to your home in the Lands Beneath?"

"No. I am delivering you to Prats de Mallo le Preste."

"Where?"

"It is a village in Gascony. In the Pyrenees."

"Why are we going there?"

"Because tomorrow is Bear Day!" She snapped the reins to make the horses fly faster.

The little goat started to shiver. Or was that Aria? She pulled the blanket tighter around herself and the baby to protect against the chilly wind and just like the baby, within moments, fell fast asleep.

Kenneth macAlpin

King of the Scots and the Picts

Ancestor of Nancy Ann of the Virginia Company,
Newt of the Massachusetts Bay Colony,
May of the Moon Men
and Wilson of the Silver Branch

*Ancestor of Nancy Ann of the Virginia Company
and Newt of the Massachusetts Bay Colony*

Maud Armstrong

wife of King David I of Scotland

Earldom of Huntingdon

*Ancestor of Newt of the Massachusetts Bay Colony
and May of the Moon Men*

St. David I
King of Scotland

Husband of Maud Matilda Aemstrong

*Ancestor of Newt of the Massachusetts Bay Colony
and May of the Moon Men*

Siward Fairbairn Armstrong

2nd Earl of Huntingdon

*Ancestor of Newt of the Massachusetts Bay Colony
and May of the Moon Men*

CHAPTER SIX

Before the beginning had begun, before mountains became mountains, the Basque were Basque.

Basque belief

"If you have a story to tell, the most important thing is the story, not the form you use to shape it."

Patricia Smith

"It's not down on any map. True places never are."

Herman Melville

ARIA WOKE UP sitting at a table in a busy restaurant. Mari was sitting across from her reading a menu. Here inside a well-lit cafe she didn't even look all that supernatural. Still, she was stunningly beautiful with long red hair and indigo colored eyes. Bagpipes and drums could be heard outside steadily moving closer in what must be some sort of parade. Wait staff bustled customers to their tables amid the din of human voices.

Dumbfounded did not adequately describe Aria's reaction to her surroundings. Not only did she wake up sitting in a restaurant, she was clothed in completely different attire from what she had been wearing on her ride in the moon cart. She was dressed in similar clothes to those women she saw around her, including Mari, a black ankle length skirt, a white cotton blouse and a decorative apron embroidered with colorful designs. Little white Amish looking caps sat on their heads. None of this made a lick of sense so Aria knew that she was dreaming.

"You aren't dreaming, Child" Mari spoke without looking up from the menu.

Aria's belief that she was dreaming was confirmed because she had not spoken aloud.

However the young waiter who had arrived to take the order looked real enough.

Mari handed the menu to him and said, "baratxuri saltsa ahate". He jotted it down and rushed off to the kitchen.

"I ordered duck in garlic sauce for you. It's nearly lunchtime. You were given extra time to rest."

"Thank you. What is this place?"

"Sargardo Tegian. A Cider House. But I think you mean, where is this place? We are in the village of Prats de Mallo le Preste, in the Pyrenees. The celebration going on outside is for Bear Day."

"It surprises me that a chthonic deity would eat in a restaurant."

"I'm not eating. You are."

"Then you can't eat human food, can you?"

"Of course I can. It's just that I wanted the cow's tongue sandwich and they are out of it."

"Oh my gosh. That is my all time favorite food! It was my birthday dinner request all my years growing up. I used to chase my sister around the house with it still uncooked and make her scream." Aria laughed at the memory. "And now to discover that it is a favorite of a chthonic deity is amazing!"

"I wish you would not think of me as the chthonic deity. As you can see, I look like you, I talk like you and I eat like you. I can, and more normally do, appear as a rainbow or a tree or the wind. But it would be hard to converse with you like that. By the way, cow's tongue is a favorite of the Euskara speakers and my name is Mari. You can call me Mari.

The drummers were now outside the cafe marching noisily down the street with a bevy of bears in tow. Not real bears but men dressed up in rugged, rather organic looking costumes resembling bears. Once they had passed, the noise levels dropped several decibels and conversations resumed inside the restaurant. Once again, Aria had to wonder if the Council knew that putting her in a crowded, noisy, normal environment in which to meet a chthonic deity would make her less overwhelmed and uncomfortable. Because it did. She felt like she was out to lunch with Esclarmonde. Sans sorrow.

Aria's duck arrived with a tall cold glass of cider. It smelled wonderful and Aria dove in.

"Would you have ordered the tongue for me if it had been available?"

"Of course. If only as a tool to teach you this and other things that you have in common with these people."

"Are you talking about the bears?"

"Correct. This yearly festival, Journee de l'Ours, is a celebration of a private belief."

"I understand your husband is a bear."

Mari laughed and tossed her head and her red hair rippled on her shoulders. "I have no need of a husband. I have lovers and Bjorn is one of them. The bear is a form often assumed by the more-than-human. I prefer this term over deity. Modern age people have no comprehension of the more-than-human. It is why people here in Gascony write the story that you love so well. Stories are living time portals. In the story lives the memory of loving the bear."

"If these people left a story about something as difficult to accept as interspecies relationships and it's well loved, I'm sure I would have read it. Believe me, I haven't."

"Believe me, you have. And as a child, no less. It is called Beauty and the Beast."

"For heaven's sake! That is my favorite fairy tale. I love Belle because she is a reader, like me. Is the beast in the story originally a bear?"

"Yes, Child."

"And that story was written right here in this state. In Gascony?"

"Gascony is not a state. Basqueland, encompasses an area nearly the size of the American state of New Hampshire, and yet, you do not find it listed on any maps but their own."

"Why? Did France conquer it and swallow it up?"

"No one ever conquers the Basque. The Sumerians don't do it, the Egyptians don't do it, nor the Romans, or even the Franks, the French."

"I know about the Sumerians. They are those cradle of civilization folk. Certainly they were here before the Basque."

"You traveled to the village of the Magdalenians with Esclarmonde. The longest thread of civilization exists there. The difference between the Sumerians and the Basque is that the Basque don't write it down."

"Like the Picts!"

"Who are also Euskara speakers. These are almost a mythological people. In the Norse sagas it is said that Heimdall creates the three races of being, the Aesir, who are the more-than-human, the Jotun, who are the giants, and the Vanir. The Vikings call the Basque the Vanir."

"Then I have reached the Beginning of Things. These Basque people are the beginning."

"You do not seek a linear beginning of civilization. You seek the time when things as they affect your modern reality get their start. A path to follow is recommended from this start point. The seminal races, the Basque, the Scots, the Irish, the Welsh, the Scandinavian and Icelandic resist this path for hundreds, if not thousands, of years. Often that resistance is done at the point of a knife blade or the fires of the stake."

"You are talking about the Crusades, aren't you?"

"It is the High Church that puts up the road sign pointing to the path. When they realize that there are those who will not follow and succumb to their false beliefs, even under threat of death, they plot to weave original belief systems into their own dogma. For example, a hartz-kume, a little bear, is called a Martin in Gascony. Martins are venerated as heroic beings. The Church declares a St. Martin's Day in November to supplant it. Over long periods of time, these clever substitutions do take root, even here in Basqueland. But thinly at best. They call both the Mary of Bible and me by the same name, Lady Mary."

"Is a Vanir a bear?"

"The Vanir are the elves. The Albigens. They are most closely associated with weather and natural phenomena. They help humans but they also stand apart from them. The Aesir, a coven of the Sidhe, headed by Odin, are quite the opposite. The Aesir, rulers of humans, seek out their companionship. The Jotuns, hybrid giant offspring, have it in for the Aesir and wage constant war against them, while the Aesir subdue the peace loving Vanir into the shadows of existence."

"The Basque are a race of elves? Wouldn't we know that about them by my era?"

"These people are almost a secret civilization and they hide here in plain sight. Both the elves and the mother races share an Rh negative bloodtype. The Basque, being unconquered, remain nearly genetically unaltered while also maintaining their language isolate, a speech unrelated to all other languages on earth."

"Why do you call it a mother race and not a father race?"

"The mother race carries the mitochondrial DNA of the elf maidens. This is genetic evidence of maternal continuity since it is only passed through the mother."

"Is all DNA mitochondrial?"

"Not at all. DNA is an information storage system. The best in the world. It's actually a molecule, whereas mitochondrial DNA is called an endosymbiont. It too is an information system but it is also a living organism inside the body of another living organism. It is a living, sentient, separate life form from human beings."

"Basque are pure elven, huh?"

"They also share the R1b haplogroup of the Boat People, whom science calls the Bell Beakers. They arrive in Languedoc, en masse. The Bible calls them the Tribe of Dan."

"Then they conquered the Basque!"

"The neolithic Boat People are not the conquering type. They see their domains as the waters and not the land masses. They are peaceful souls who worship the moon."

"Are they human?"

"They don't look entirely human. They have elongated heads, large eyes, long earlobes, and very white skin. Traits still evident in the modern age Basque. The Basque embrace the symbol of the Boat People, the ball and cross."

"The sacred tribes! I know about that. St. Columba used that symbol and so did the Knights of the Garter. But why did the Boat People come here. It's a land mass."

"Survival probably. Languedoc is also called Douceur de Vivre, the Sweetness of Life. It is the single most ideal location on the entire European continent in which one can survive uninterrupted forever. Even in your modern age it is a land of agriculture, sunflowers, and four hour lunches."

"So they retired from being the Boat People?"

"The Basque are extraordinary sailors. It is a Basque man who is the first to circumnavigate the earth after Magellan dies on the voyage. The Vikings say that it is the Vanir, the Basque, they discover inhabiting every remote island they ever find."

"Are you Basque, Mari?"

"I am revered by the Basque because they still retain their knowledge of the moon. It pleases me to ride among them when the moon is full."

"And you probably enjoy your time in the fresh air."

"Your cosmology of the world is in error. There is as much fresh air in my world as in yours."

Aria's claustrophobia colored her remark. "I just don't envision air trapped inside the earth as fresh."

"The earth has no inside to it."

"Of course it does. It has a crust and a mantle and an inner core. And evidently there is some kind of black sun in the core."

"Have you traveled through the crust and the mantle to the core?"

"Well of course I haven't! But scientists have."

"That could be your assumption based on the veracity of their data.

In truth, no humans drill further than eight miles into the crust. The data could be speculation."

"Scientists don't speculate. Science is purely fact based."

"Then when facts are unattainable, are your scientists findings deemed infallible like the High Church Pope?"

"That's very different. The Pope doesn't base his beliefs on solvable experiments."

"What solvable experiment proved that the earth has a core?"

"Well I don't know! I'm not a geologist. But I'll bet you that the earth is not just eight miles deep."

"I don't say it is, Child. I said that is where the exploration stops. I understand that it is difficult to grasp such a radical change in thinking. Imagine how difficult it is when the cosmology is first changed from geocentric to heliocentric, when geocentric has held sway for thousands of years."

"When did it get changed?"

"Shortly before your European ancestors begin migrating to the American colonies."

"That seems like yesterday to me now. I met my American ancestors my first night of this trip. This is my sixth day here and I've been traveling back into the past further each day. Which sort of validates my point that none of you know anything about science. It hadn't been invented yet."

Mari laughed out loud at her comment. "I don't think it's on the itinerary, but would you like to converse with one of your Sumerian ancestors?" Noticing the embarrassed look on Aria's face, she moderated her tone. "Modern people are so confident in their own farsighted view while childishly unaware they are standing on the shoulders of giants. And also modern people are blissfully unaware of the history of giants in the first place."

"Well don't judge modern people by me. I certainly have discovered how unaware I am about history but I don't feel very blissful about it now. And I know less than nothing about the people who live here in Gascony."

"You knew less than nothing. Now you know a great deal."

"Only that they have my strange blood and speak a strange language that is attributed to a sun god in a fifth dimensional world under my feet but not in the dirt. And they are part bear and part elf."

"While all that speaks truth, they are in reality simply sailors and shepherds and witches."

"Witches? No no no no no! No witch talk. If we're talking the devil here then I want to go home right now."

"Did I say the devil? I am a witch, Child. I do not know this devil of whom you speak. Demonization is a ploy used by those in power. The pot calls the kettle black. That is a Basque proverb. If you can believe that I am evil, then you will not see the evil in the one who is calling me that. A gentler name for a witch is an herbalist or a midwife. She is summoned voluntarily when life gets too raw to handle. It is at these times that all else run away but she remains. She is as repulsed by the putrid wounds but she tends to them anyway. Her heart also pounds in her chest when extracting the breach child, where not one, but two lives, are held in her hands. Her heart breaks too as she holds the hands of the dying while they face their greatest fear alone. These are not acts of evil. The goat, the symbol of a happy home, is not a satanic icon. The raven, the phoenix of the elven kings, is not a sinister being, but rather the most intelligent of all the birds."

"Are all Basque women witches?"

"All Basque women are the heads of their households. They are matrilineal. The woman inherits through the woman's lineage. The etxy, the home, that they make is the sanctuary of the heart. There are no churches except for these. What home maker has no witch in her?"

"I've always known that proverb you used. I didn't know that it was Basque though."

"They have many. No pain, no gain. Time flies when you are among friends. A rolling stone gathers no moss. A bird in the hand is worth five in the tree. When the cat's away, the mice will play. Where there's a will, there's a way."

"Okay then. A very wise people, these Basque. Odd that they would reject Christianity."

"The only Christianity they reject is the one being forced on them. They know Jesus as Kixme. They revere Mary Magdalene who lives among them and they know both of them as Ambassadors of Love. In the belief system of the Basque people, there is a duality of existence. There are two worlds, Berezko, the natural world and Aideko, the supernatural one.

"The Roman church frowns on the supernatural, I guess. They would find that heretical, right?"

"There is plenty of the supernatural in Roman doctrine. An American president, Thomas Jefferson, creates his own bible by removing everything of the supernatural from the New Testament. It is one hundred three pages long."

"Then why do they care what the Basque believe?"

"Because one's beliefs create one's reality. They want to control that reality. They have no trouble changing their own beliefs when it serves that control. The Jesuits work to alter the cosmology of the earth for this purpose. If you believe in the heliocentric version then you are only the tiniest insignificant speck in a cold, endless universe that came into being when something called nothing popped. But if you believe in a geocentric world then it is obvious that it is created for you and encased under a dome. Someone put that there. Someone greater than yourself. In some belief systems, God is a more likely concept."

"You are called a god, or I guess goddess is the right term, but you didn't put it there, did you?"

"I am of the More-Then-Human, as I told you. And for the Basque, there are many more. I am associated with the moon. Whereas someone like Olentzaro, for instance, is a giant and a coal merchant and comes down from the snow covered mountains on Christmas Eve to deliver gifts."

"Santa Claus! That's who I first thought you were when I saw you flying in your moon cart." She failed to add that it had scared her half to death.

"Hold out your hand, Child, and I will leave you with a memory gift from us. You have spent a week now in Gascony and you will not return again."

"Oh, I haven't been here in Gascony the entire week. I've only spent three days here in France", Aria said as she stretched her arm across the table.

"The Basque use a lunar calendar. One week is three days long." Mari placed her hand palm down over the soft underside of Aria's wrist and said no more.

Aria suppressed a smile for she didn't want Mari to know she had already guessed that when she removed her hand, Aria would discover a ball and cross tattooed there in blue ink.

Extremely loud drumming started up right outside the door of the Cider House causing Aria to crane her neck to see the celebration marching down the street. When she returned her attention to their table, Mari removed her hand from Aria's wrist leaving her to gasp in awe. Instead of the expected tattoo, she found a natural looking birthmark where none had been before. It was a perfectly formed tiny pink heart. A small tear escaped from the corner of her eye.

"We love you, Child. Now look again at the parade passing by. Do you see that large white bear? Follow him to the Chapel of the Madeleine."

"A large white bear?" Aria asked as she struggled to see past the patrons in the cafe and the large throng of people watching the parade pass by outside. "Do you mean that person on the stilts?" But Mari did not answer her question because Mari was no longer in the Cider House.

Aria felt her panic in her rapidly pounding heart. This was exactly why she was afraid to come to France, she couldn't speak the language. And this wasn't even French that was being spoken all around her. She hoped that Mari had paid the bill because she did not hesitate to bound out the door and into the crowd without a word to anyone. If the bear-costumed man were not on stilts she would not have been able to see him at all in the crush of celebrants. It took nearly two blocks in which she was both able to catch up near to him and also to realize that she was scurrying through a modern town. She hadn't really noticed while sitting in the cafe that she was not in an old world environment. The store fronts were modern, the street was covered in asphalt. She was trying to process the idea that perhaps she could hail a cab to an airport and fly home.

Except she had no money. Except she didn't speak Euskara. Except it might be a little bit in the future or a little bit in the past and no way to straighten it out once she got home. So when she finally spotted the white bear at the end of an alleyway heading into dense forest, she figured her best bet was still to follow her guide.

Only minutes inside the forest and she knew that she was lost. She only knew how to be a desert person where one could see for miles. Now she couldn't even see her way back to the alley from whence she had come. She tried in vain to recognize a landmark but all she saw were trees. The forest was foreign to her. The tears began again.

"Noli temere", a deep male voice boomed from amid the trees as the white bear emerged into view. She was right about him being a man in a bear suit but she was wrong about the stilts. He was very very tall. "Sorry I gave you a fright. There is a nice path over there and I was trying to locate it when I lost you. I'm Ursus Beron, by the way. The Council asked me to accompany you to the chapel so I could tell you a little about the Merovingian kings."

"Are you a grandfather?"

"A distant cousin of yours through Dagobert II Merovingian. I have another name. It is Sigisbert IV, Prince Ursus, l'Ours. I am the last Count of Razes of Merovingian descent."

"Where is Razes?"

"It is another name for Rennes which is where our path leads, to Rennes le Chateau."

"To Solomon's treasure?"

"I doubt that it is there now. The Goths stash the Emerald Tablets there once. Our mutual grandfather, Dagobert II marries Giselle de Razes in the Chapel of the Madeleine."

"Jules Verne, the writer, knew the priest there, I was told. The priest gave him the maps to the center of the earth, Yet now, I've been told that there is no center of the earth."

"I've never heard of any maps there. But Dagobert's heart is buried there. It is his happy place and his personal chapel. He spends his youth hidden away in Ireland to be safe."

"Safe from what?"

"From being a Merovingian. They are the last bloodline kings, and Dagobert, the very last. The bloodline kings are called the Kings of the Franks. The High Church appointed kings are known as the Kings of France. The church is done with bloodline kings so they kill Dagobert."

"Isn't the crown normally passed to the blood heirs of the king?"

"Yes, but this term bloodline refers to your bloodline."

"Mine?"

"Those with Rh negative blood. They are the archons, the rulers. But the church puts an end to bloodline rule with their fake document they call the Donation of Constantine. Do you know who Constantine is?"

"The Holy Roman Emperor?"

"That's him. But the document isn't his. It is proven to be an obvious fake stating that the appointment of kings can only be granted by papal authority. Ignoring the proof, they use it anyway and still do in your age, I'll wager. Anyway, just as they plan, the Merovingian culture dies with Dagobert."

"What is the Merovingian culture?"

"It's the culture of the Elder Faith which is basically a recognition of interconnectedness.

That is the basic tenant, that nothing exists apart. We are all one."

"How is that threatening?"

"It is difficult to control people when it is their belief that creation and the Creator are part of themselves. Better to give God a name, call God Him and call Him vengeful. Then teach the followers to be god-fearing."

Aria fidgeted with her little cap that had become untied as they walked along the easy path toward Rennes. Prince Bear towered over her as he walked alongside. "I see", he said, "that you have a birthmark of an arrosa bihotza, a pink heart, on your wrist. The Merovingian kings are all born with a birthmark. Not a pink heart, but a red cross. It is either over their hearts or between their shoulder blades. Each one is proclaimed king on his twelfth birthday. They are all magicians. Their magic is in their long red hair. It is why they never cut it."

"That is like the story of Samson in the Bible. His strength was in his hair."

"Samson is a Spartan. But the Spartans do not use that name for themselves. They call themselves Danaans. They are of the Tribe of Dan."

"What kind of a king can you be at twelve years old?" Aria was picturing a twelve year old boy, complete with magic kit, cape, and top hat, trying out his magic tricks on the admiring neighbor kids.

"It might surprise you. Why, Sigibert III, at the age of ten, leads his own army into battle. When he loses the battle, he sits in his saddle and cries. And yet, the Merovingians are remembered as the Do Nothing Kings. They are priest kings more than heads of state. You might compare them to the Samaritan Magi. They are clairvoyant and telepathic. But more than anything, they are healers."

Aria thought about the Tribe of Dan and her own Rh negative blood and wondered if she had the ability to do magic too, especially if it meant healing people. Perhaps she could try it out once she got home again. If she got home again.

The path and the forest ended and the Chapel of the Madeleine could be seen from across an open field. A man stood outside the door with wine colored hair that fell to his knees.

"Dagobert?", Aria asked of the Bear Prince.

"That, Umea, is le Chevelu, Clovis the Great."

Oh dear oh dear, Aria thought. Not just a king but a magician who could read her thoughts. As Ursus turned to walk back into the woods she wanted to go with him. Funny how only just yesterday she was afraid of bears and now she preferred their company over magic kings. "What does le Chevelu mean?", she asked his retreating figure.

"Long hair."

Aria repeated over and over again as she crossed the field, don't think, don't think, don't think. She was able to read the inscription written on the wall before reaching the long haired king. "How horrible is this place", it read, "This is none other than the house of the Lord and this is the gate of heaven."

"It's from the Bible", he said once she was standing next to him. "Genesis, chapter eight. The account of Jacob and his pillow."

"That's the Stone of Scone!" I was just there yesterday. In Scone. But what does this verse mean?"

"The House of God is a reference to the stone. When Jacob wakes up from his dream, he anoints the stone with oil and names it Beth El, which means the House of God. He is expressing his fear over having just climbed to the top of a ladder and having met God Himself. And you were afraid to meet me!", he said and smiled.

"Why is this particular story in the Bible so significant?"

"Because knowledge is power. God can be met at the top of a ladder and heaven is just over our heads."

Aria wasn't sure what she should ask of this handsome grandfather with the amazing mane of red hair and felt tremendously self conscious. He smiled at something over her shoulder and she turned to see a family of deer exiting the forest. A mama and two babies. She gasped in delight, as she always did at such a sight. Deer sightings in her desert landscape were extremely rare. The trio broke into a run as they crossed the field and seemed to be headed exactly in their direction which shocked Aria even more. They were indeed running to, and not away from, her and Clovis. It reminded her of dogs racing to be close to their master. Aria could barely contain her glee when the little family approached them, completely fearless and nudged up against the two of them wanting to be pet. Aria scratched both babies behind the ears and they begged for more. Clovis stroked the mama's neck while she planted soft kisses on his chin. Both Aria and Clovis were giggling like children at such delight. And then, as suddenly as they had arrived, the deer turned and bounded back across the field and disappeared from view into the forest.

"Oh my gosh, I love your deer", Aria exclaimed.

"They aren't mine. Aren't they yours?", he responded in all seriousness.

She was pretty sure he was joking but it didn't matter because the interaction with the wild animals had dissipated much of her nervousness over contact with a magic king. She followed him into the chapel and took a seat next to him beneath a stained glass window. "Are you my grandfather?"

"I am that. Through Mariah on your mother's side and Nancy Ann on your father's."

"Is Merovingian your last name or a title?"

"It is from my grandfather's name, Merovee. It means Sea Egg. My great grandparents, Chlodio and Vaerica, are expecting a child when she goes for a swim in the sea. It is there that she is raped by the Quinataur, who is also called the Lord of the Deep Waters or Kronos."

"Isn't that the Greek god of time?"

"Yes it is. And his home is in Oceanus, the world encircling river, from whence comes the concept that time is a river."

"My little uncle who was born on the Mayflower was named Oceanus."

"Names are important. Your grandmother, Mariah, has a father named Enoch. Her father is a shoemaker. The Enoch of Mt. Moriah, is also a shoemaker. Enoch is renamed Moriah, the wind, after he is translated to heaven and becomes the angel in the whirlwind. Your great grandfather, Enoch, marries a woman named Phoebe Breeze. Words, like my hair, are a source of magic.

"Did your great grandma lose her baby when she got raped?"

"No. The baby gets an extra father."

"You do know, don't you, that you cannot get pregnant once you are already pregnant?"

"You do know, don't you, that you cannot step off your balcony in Southern California and into a castle in Scotland? It's best not to cling too tenaciously to your reality as being the only one. It will benefit you once you return home and begin to work that magic that you intend to try."

She blushed to realize that he had read her thoughts when she was still standing in the woods with Ursus. Uncomfortable with this thought, she raced on with her questions."Did your grandfather get DNA from both of his fathers?"

"Yes, but it is Vearica's DNA that is the prize. All Merovingian kings must marry Gothic princesses to obtain it. Albigensian blood is purer than our own Cimmerian ancestry. My own mother, Basina Thuringia, a Gothic princess, is already married to a man named Basanus when she seeks out my father and asks him to marry her."

"Was Dagobert's wife a Gothic princess?"

"Yes, Giselle de Razes. They are married right here in this chapel."

"I was told that the Goths brought something called the Emerald Tablets here."

"Rennes le Château has always been a place of hidden treasure. And by treasure, I talk of the supernatural, which is exceedingly rare. So rare, in fact, that it has never been added to. The few relics, hidden here for a time, are among that number."

"King Solomon had them all, huh?"

"He has a great many. But there are others. The Pharaoh, Imhotep, has his Impossible Things. On the American continent there are skulls carved of crystal that no modern age tools can replicate. These and others point to a higher intelligence than is currently understood in your modern programing. The purpose of this treasure is to make you wonder."

"Wonder what?"

"Just who is at the top of the ladder, the stairway to heaven."

"Why does all that treasure end up here?"

"Because before it is Septimania and before it is Languedoc, this place belongs to the Tribe of Dan. Like it says over the door, this is a gate, a portal. It is a good place to move treasure between dimensions."

A portal to where?, she wondered.

"To Arcadia", he spoke aloud, "ruled by the Spartans."

"Who call themselves the Danaan", she completed.

"And who wear their hair long like me as that is the source of their power. Their sign is the ball and cross."

"I am confused by all the names I've heard associated with the Lands Beneath. You call it Arcadia, but I've heard it called Eden, Hyperborea, Agartha, Avalon and AMOR. Which one is it?"

"Pay attention to words, Child. You answered your own question when you said the Lands Beneath. Lands. Plural. How many different lands exist on this plane. Flip it over. How many can you fit there?"

"Was Samson a god from Arcadia?"

"The term god is a misnomer because it becomes lumped in with the Creator. Pan is the protector in Arcadia."

"The goat man?"

"Yes, he is the protector of shepherds and is the primary deity of the elementals. Nature is his domain. Both the Basque and we Merovingians are called Shepherd Kings. Pan's worship, as such, is first established in Thrace by the Phyrgians and in Wales by the Cimmerians. The Greeks name their holy city of Amon Ra, Panopolis. Ra is the sun deity from Ak, the star of the gods."

"Is there a name for the sun on earth?"

"Sol."

"What is outside this existence with it's two suns?"

"The primal sea."

"Are you a Christian, Clovis?"

"A heretical one. I am an Arianist. My wife, Chlotilde, is a follower of the Roman church but all of her family are Arianists like me. It's frustrating for her. She insists that I be baptized into her faith. I do it because I love her but she knows that I remain an Arianist."

"Is Arianism the same as Catharism?"

"Similar. Again I can articulate the power of words. Names are sound images of things.

Look at the names for the gnostic followers of Catharism, and the Roman followers, the Catholics. Catharic and Catholic. Both contain the name of St. Catherine. However the 'ol' in Catholic means 'all', as it is self proclaimed as the Universal Church due to its being a blending of all the belief systems of the time. The 'ar' in Catharic signifies 'before' to indicate the gnostic beliefs, like Arianism, that exist before the Catholics impose their dogma."

"Who is St. Catherine?"

"She is the most popular saint of all time. She spins the wheel. The Roman church, hungry for converts, builds on her popularity. But later they ban her veneration. It is never their intention to elevate women."

"Why not?"

"In order to establish a patriarchal society. Women are powerful entities capable of creation and tuned into intuition. So the church overlays St. Catherine with Mary Magdelene and then proclaims Mary to be a harlot. Even the word mammon, or mother, becomes confused with money, also a much sought after, powerful, and demonized energy."

"But I thought we got the word money from the word mammon."

"The word money comes from a woman, Juno Moneta, the girlfriend of Cupid. Cupidity means greed for money."

"What about the star of the gods, Ak? What does that name mean?"

"In Egyptian it means light. In it's spelling 'oc' as in Occitan, it is the root of octo meaning eight, the symbol for infinity. Infinite Light. As the root of ocular, it means sight or vision. Enlightenment. The Eskimo word for illumination is Ang-ak-oc."

"I wonder if I have all this right", Aria ruminated. "Our world is a bubble in a vast primal sea, split in half, with Ak lighting up one hemisphere and Sol the other. That's a far cry from infinite space and spinning, spinning, spinning around the sun. How could humans come up with such a contrary idea in the first place?"

"Probably from the Emerald Tablets. The idea for heliocentricity is in it. Dark magic is a real thing and often employed by those in control."

"Why, if there is a ceiling over our heads and people knew about it for thousands of years, didn't someone go up and check it out?"

"Someone tried. His name is Nimrod. He builds what you know of as the Tower of Babel. Its real name is the Temple of the Seven Lights of the Earth. Nimrod builds it to climb up to meet God. Even King Kosingas of Thrace threatens his subjects that he will ascend to the firmament to complain about them to the Great Goddess, Hera."

"But I live in the age of rocket ships. Anyone could fly up and see the firmament if it were really there."

"Can anyone in the rocket age drive along one of your highways without a permission slip etched in plastic in their wallet? Do you personally know someone who builds their own rockets and is not within the scrutiny of the Moon Men?"

"And all of this information is just one big giant secret because, as you point out, I am not even free to drive down the highway without being monitored and controlled?"

"It is only a secret if you believe it is. That's the secret. The information being shared with you is public knowledge. It always will be. Your grandfather, Robert Dudley, lover of Queen Elizabeth I, will sire a son with her by the name of Francis Bacon. Their son is a member of what is known as the Invisible College, a cadre of souls who will keep all this information alive for countless generations. But these stories are best left for the train."

"The train? Where am I going?"

"Back to Scotland."

"I'm in France, Clovis! I can't get to Scotland on a train from here. There is water between."

"It's shallow. Noli Temere. Follow me now or you'll miss the connection."

A staircase led down only a flight or two revealing a bank of elevators with shiny copper doors. He led her to the last one and the doors slid open. "Does the train take me back to Scone?", she asked as she stepped inside.

"To Argyll."

"To Inverary?", she asked always hopeful that Inverary equalled home.

"To Aberfoyle."

She took one last look at her Shepherd King grandfather and wondered how the secrecy that ruled the world could ever cease to be. Just before the door closed again she heard him say, "The truth will set you free".

When she stepped out of the elevator she thought for a split second that she actually had returned home. Not to her Eden, certainly, but to her time period. For there before her wondering eyes was a modern high speed rail train with at least six cars that she could see behind the engine. If it weren't for the costume of the conductor, she would have been jumping for joy. He was dressed in kingly and regal clothing complete with the poofy pantaloons and leggings below his sash-bedecked coat.

Knowing she was still lost in time, regardless of the uplifting modern train, she walked over to where he stood by the door of the first car and shook his hand.

"Coel Hen", he said introducing himself. He was a well fed middle aged man puffing on an aromatic pipe. "Just like Clovis, I'm further back in linear history than those you are meeting here on the Storybook Train but the Council thinks this is the best opportunity for us to meet. And of course I am more than happy to oblige once I hear that they will be serving sky blue pumpkin soup for dinner in the dining car. What a treat! Can't remember the last time I've had it." He removed the pipe after a long inhale and puffed out what looked remarkably like a pumpkin shaped smoke cloud.

A Storybook Train and sky blue pumpkin soup? Now this sounded like fun! And Mr. Hen was very cheery. Aria happily followed him into the first car. And her happiness increased tenfold because it was a library. Beneath the windows on both sides of the car were shelves stuffed with leather bound books. The train might have appeared modern and sleek on the outside but inside was very different. Wooden planks made up the flooring but a thick persian rug dominated the center of the car upon which sat a wonderful overstuffed, over-fluffed, comfy chair and ottoman. A rosewood tea cart adorned with a soft lit lamp, a teapot, and a cup and saucer, was the only other piece of furniture in the car. Aria wanted nothing more than to curl up in the chair with one of the books and disappear into someone else's fairy tale. But they kept moving. She spied the old fashioned card catalog in the file by the door as they were leaving to enter the next car and hoped she would be given time to go through it.

The next car, she was told, would be where she would sleep tonight en-route to Scotland. It had a canopy bed and black-out curtains. The cheery Mr. Hen explained that Aria had three more grandparents waiting for her in the dining car and that they would all dine together once she was ready. But to her delight she was also told to take her time and enjoy the ride for a while as there would be scenery that she would not want to miss.

This news was music to her ears. She craved time alone. Especially time alone with books! Coel passed through into the next car leaving Aria, at long last, by herself. She raced right back into the library car, grabbed a book at random and plunged into the enveloping chair. The plaid tea cozy now covering the teapot reminded her that she was on her way back to Scotland. The tea was piping hot and there were scones dripping with butter on a thin china plate. She no longer bothered to wonder where all this came from.

The train moved out as quiet as an electric car and in moments had entered a dark lava tube. The soft lamp did not provide adequate light for reading so Aria poured and drank her tea and enjoyed her scones while the train raced through the tube. A wool tartan cloak, looking just like the one she had left in the carriage at Giggleswick, was draped across the ottoman. She pulled it up over her lap and nearly fell asleep from the rhythmic movement of the train, but became fully awake again when the train exited the tube and natural light filled the library car. Surprised that the train was on the surface when she could have sworn it was on a downward descent was confusing. Was she in France still? Or was this England? It couldn't be Scotland because she was slated to sleep on the train. Well, it was already twilight so it would be too dark to tell soon anyway.

But darkness did not arrive. The train sped along for mile after mile. Storybook towns were surrounded by storybook farms that merged into storybook landscapes. Aria was glued to the scene outside her windows. Every little farmhouse and every little fast glimpsed cobblestone lane and every Dickens-like roadside tavern tugged at her heartstrings. Could anything be so cute and still be real? She longed for the train to stop at a station so she could get off and stay forever. She would inquire as to where this place was as she definitely planned to make a return trip someday under brighter circumstances.

It was the scent of pumpkin soup that broke her revery. How long had she sat here in fascinated awe? It seemed like hours yet it still wasn't dark. But it must be dinner time since she could smell the soup so she left the book, still unopened, on the ottoman and headed out to find the dining car. As the library door closed behind her, Aria just missed seeing the herd of green horses, no bigger than spaniels, racing over a hill near the tracks.

The car beyond her sleeping car was empty. It was lined with stiff backed seats facing forward but no one was riding there. The car behind that one was the dining car and Aria smelled Thanksgiving the minute she opened the door. The soup was spiced with nutmeg and ginger, just like a pie, but just as Mr. Hen had proclaimed, it was sky blue and being served from the blue gourd it had grown in or one like it. There was also a cranberry sauce topped with thick cream and a basket overflowing with bread rolls. The scent of hot spiced cider wafted up out of little pottery cups.

"There you are, Child!", the man exclaimed as Aria walked in. "Quick, have a seat right here." Aria was pretty sure that he was anticipating his meal more than his time with her but at this point she wanted to dive into this beautiful soup as badly as he did. "Bertha will introduce everyone to you", he said as he splashed more soup into her bowl.

"Old Coel is especially fond of this soup", said the woman who must be Bertha. "You can only get sky blue pumpkins from the farms here in the Twilight Lands anymore. They used to be everywhere."

"The Twilight Lands?"

"We are traveling through the home of the elementals. They are masters at glamour, of fooling the eye. I hope they put on a good show for you out there."

"Fairies and gnomes? Those elementals?"

"Indeed. They don't have any need of shelter and such but they love to play at it. Like dress up. They especially like to mimic what you like or expect. Now enjoy your soup while its hot and I'll tell you who we are. I am Bertha Laon but better known as Bertha Goosefoot. This beauty here is Palastyne and that one over there is Alfhilder. Alfhilder, Coel and I are on your father's side through May of the Moon Men and Nancy Ann of the Virginia Company. Alfhilder is also ancestor to Wilson of the Silver Branch. Palastyne is also on your father's side through Newt of the Massachusetts Bay Colony and she is one of the triplet sisters of

Melusine, the Elf Queen. Alfhilder is the mother of Ragnar Lodbrock and I am the mother of Charlemagne."

"The Holy Roman Emperor?"

"So they say. But in reality, he isn't holy, nor Roman, nor an emperor. But that's him. And Old Coel is the great grandfather of Constantine the Great."

"Why do you refer to him as Old Coel? He doesn't look all that old to me." Coel looked at her when she made this remark and gave a thumbs up while spooning in another mouthful.

"His name, Coel Hen, means Old Coel."

"That's funny because if you were a king, you'd be Old King Cole", she said to the happy diner.

"I am a king", he said and reached for another roll to dip into his soup.

"You are? The Old King Cole I know about is a nursery rhyme for babies."

"Yeah. That's me!"

"Are you a merry old soul?"

"Don't believe everything you read about me!", he said and they both laughed.

"Why do you have a nursery rhyme written about you?" Coel shrugged when she asked as he clearly had no clue.

"The members of the Invisible College write about us", Bertha interjected.

"Sir Francis Bacon wrote Old King Cole?"

"Of course not, Child. The members of the College are as varied as the stories they tell."

"I don't remember a character in any book named Ragnar. Is there a story about him?"

"It's Ragnar's in-laws that people the Norse sagas. His wife, Aslaug Sigurdsdatter, also called Kraka, the Crow, is the daughter of Sigurd who slays Fafnir, the dragon. Fafnir is actually the dwarf prince who transforms into the dragon to guard the stolen gold of his father, the Dwarf King. He also guards a magic ring that belongs to Andvari, the dwarf who lives under the waterfall. Fafnir kills his father to obtain the ring that he demands in payment for building Valhalla."

"Why does a dwarf living under a waterfall have possession of a magic ring?"

"I think he kills his cousin for it."

"Who is Andvari?"

"Andvari is a sorcerer, Alberich the Sorcerer. He is the half brother of Merovee Merovingian", Alfhilder explained picking up the story. "My own father is Gandalf, son of Alf, the king of Alfheim. "The Scots call it Elphame and the Germanic call it Alfheim. It is the abode of the Elves."

"Wow! I love having storybook ancestors. Are you a storybook character too, Bertha?"

"I am Mother Goose."

"What?" Aria squealed with delight. "My grandmother is Mother Goose?"

"More will come after me. But it is Charlemagne who lives the fairy tale. Of all his many wives, the Elf Princess, Fastrada, is his undoing."

"Are all you guys mythological?"

"I'm not sure what you mean, Child, I'm just Bertha. My mother is Merovingian. Her name is Blanche Fleur, or White Flower. She is the daughter of Dagobert III and the sister of Makir ha David, king of Septimania."

"What does ha David mean?"

"Of the house of David. Of King David in the Bible."

"King Solomon's father? That must be why your son gets to be the emperor."

"Charlemagne only wants to be what he is, the king of the Franks and the Lombards."

"So he is a bloodline king, right?"

"Yes. He is hoodwinked into the emperor title."

"They conned him into it?"

"They don't even bother to do that. They sneak up behind him and slap the crown on his head."

"Figuratively?"

"Literally. They have that ridiculous Donation of Constantine document to appoint whoever they want."

"A lot of good that will do when they appoint a bloodline king. He won't be doing their bidding."

"You'd think!", Bertha snorted, "but he ends up doing whatever they want. And I'm ashamed to say that it is my own son who is famous for giving the followers of Odin the choice between "Christianity or immediate death"!"

"And let's not forget about what he does to the bears!", Alfhilder said with disgust.

Bertha clarified the reason for Alfhilder's agitation. "Alfhilder is sensitive to Charlemagne's mistreatment of the bears. A descendent of Ragnar's, and thus her own, is the father of Olaf the White. The Roman church is fiercely hostile to the bears and the bear cult. They have Charlemagne wage not one, but two crusades against the bears."

"He kills thousands and thousands of bears!", Alfhilder groaned contemptuously. "He deserves to get the ring!"

"The magic ring? The greater ring?"

"No. Well, yes it is magic but it isn't one of the greater rings. Charlemagne's tale is of the serpent and the ring", Bertha picked up the thread of her son's story. "It all starts at the wedding feast of Charlemagne and Fastrada. A serpent appears among the guests and drops an enchanted ring into Charlemagne's wine goblet. Charlemagne discovers the ring and places it on Fastrada's finger and is from then on hopelessly obsessed with her. When Fastrada dies, the power of the ring does not abate. Years after her death, he still can't bring himself to bury her. Bishop Turpin takes pity on him and removes the ring from the corpse one night while Charlemagne sleeps. Now Charlemagne is obsessed with Bishop Turpin. So Turpin tosses it into a forest pool. Now Charlemagne is obsessed with the forest pool. That's where he builds his grand palace, Aix le Chapelle, Chapel of the Waters. He proclaims it to be the capital of his realm and remains there the rest of his days."

"Robin Hood and I....er Robert and I, used a forest pool to get to a transport station."

"My sister's pool", Palastyne said. "The daleth. She and Raymond build Chateau de Lusignan by it."

"Are you a mermaid too?" Aria wanted to peek underneath the table.

"That is my sister's curse, not mine."

Aria was surprised by the term 'curse'. She had always thought that it would be fun and romantic to be a mermaid. Or was that Disney influence again? "Why is being a mermaid a curse?"

"Have you ever transformed from one being into another, Child? It is both painful and frightening."

"Who put a curse on her?"

"Our mother, who suffers from the same curse. They are only mermaids one day a week. But both Father and Raymond have to vow never to peek into their bath on Saturday and discover their curse if they want to marry these secretive women."

"Why don't they swim in the forest pool or the ocean?"

"Because the whole thing is a big secret. And like all secrets, it's hard to keep. When father finally peeks, then it's all over for us. Mother packs us up and hauls us off to Avalon to live."

"The one at Appleby?"

"Yes."

"So why did she curse your sister?"

"Oh she curses all of us. Melusine gets the worst of it because she is the oldest. We don't know that Father has taken a vow and we don't know he's broken it. Suddenly we are moved from Caledonia without any word as to why. Naturally we think Father is to blame since we are the ones who leave, so we conspire to get even. We imprison him in Brandebois Mountain. Mother is furious with us. She doesn't fault Father for breaking the vow but she does us for the revenge that we enact on Father, so she curses us."

"What was your curse?"

"I am sent to Mount Conigou, just north of Prats de Mallo le Preste in the Pyrenees, to guard my father's treasure. Our sister, Melior, is sent to Sparrowhawk Castle in Armenia in order to inspire love but never be free to enjoy it herself. I would say that Melior's punishment is the cruelest except that I have seen Melusine turn into the dragon."

"And Melusine was forced to go to Pictavia?"

"No. She is just anxious to get away from Mother. Melusine, being the oldest, is heir to the crown. Mother is the Elf Queen."

"And she meets Raymond in Pictavia?"

"He's a basket case because he has just accidentally killed his guardian in a hunting accident. He falls head over heels for Melusine and has no difficulty taking the No-Peeky-On-Saturday vow. They have ten boys before he breaks it. She is completely heartbroken over it too. She turns into the dragon and circles the Chateau wailing in sorrow."

"So she took her boys and left?"

"She has to leave but she doesn't take the boys. Geoffrey Big Tooth manages Father's lands in Argyll for a time and inherits Charteau de Lusignan."

"That's an odd name."

"Big Tooth, you mean? Yes, all the boys are a little off. Not mentally. They are all deformed in some way. One only has one ear, one has a blue eye and a red eye, and one even has a lion's paw growing out of his cheek."

"Your mother and you triplets lived in Caledonia but your father had lands in Argyll? Are you both Scot and Pict?"

"Yes. Father is Dal Riata and Mother is Pictish. Both are elven but Mother's clan is older. Father bears the title Gille Sidhean, or Elf Servant, because Mother is the Elf Queen. Father is descended from Lorne, son of Fergus who brings the Coronation Stone to Scotland. Lorne's people are chronicled in their own story called Lorna Doone."

"That's a cookie. And a lovely one to have with tea. I didn't know it was about some girl in Scotland."

"It isn't. Lorna Doone means the people of Lorne. The tale is about one of its citizens, Sir James Stewart, who after being imprisoned by Lord Blantyre, Scotland's treasurer, changes his name to Ensor Doone and takes to the woods and becomes an outlaw."

"Then that isn't a fairy tale, it's a true story."

"They are all true, Child", Bertha pointed out.

"Well not fairy tales. They might be based on some larger truths or a snippet of folklore, but essentially they are fiction."

"Are you familiar with the Dewey Decimal System?"

"Yes. I even noticed that you use that old card file system in your library car."

"Then you might want to take note that fairy tales are cataloged 398.2. Non fiction. The Dewey Decimal System comes out of the Victorian age, a time when Yeats, the acclaimed Irish poet, Senator, and Nobel Laureate, is meeting the Fairy Queen. The tales are disguised in parable form for those with ears to hear and eyes to see. The stories are about the elf maiden, the carrier of the mitochondrial DNA, who is put out of reach of the Grail Prince, who then must find her, release her, and perpetuate the dynasty. Never in these stories do you read of the gallant priest rescuing the damsel in distress. The church is the adversary."

"Why is it that these stories have the ability to last so long?"

"Because words have great power", Alfhilder said to her, "and stories, like memories, live on."

"I still don't fully grasp the ring thing. St. Valery has a ring, and St. Beaga has a ring, and Solomon has a ring, and Charlemagne has a ring, and Andvari too."

"Melusine has two rings", Palastyne added. "She gives both of them to Raymond when she leaves. One to protect him in battle and the other in court."

"But neither of those are the greater rings, are they?

"Only the Ring Lords have the greater of the rings. The Ring Lords are the portal guardians. Appleby is a portal and so is Rennes le Chateau. Solomon's Temple is one and so is Newgrange in Ireland. Tomorrow you will visit another one at Aberfoyle in Argyll"

"Will I meet a Ring Lord?"

"Uther Pendragon is there. He is one."

"That is who St. Columba crowned. Does St. Patrick do that too, crown pendragons?"

Coel answered her question. "St. Patrick is further back in linear history than Colomba.

Closer to my time", he added. "His sister is married to my wife's grandfather, Conan Meriodoc.

"Is Columba some sort of supernatural mentor to Uther, like Merlin is to Arthur?"

"Neither Columba nor Patrick are supernatural. But you are correct that Merlin is one such individual in Arthur's life, just as Odin is in Sigurd's life and even that of the Fairybear. As for me, all I have are three fiddlers!", he said laughing.

"You are related to Constantine the Great?"

"His mother, St. Helen of the Cross, is my granddaughter."

"Are you Roman?"

"Heck no! Helen's husband is Constantius Chlorus, the Roman ruler in Britain. It's in Britain that he meets Helen. Constantine doesn't grow up in England though. Yet he does come back to assist in his father's rule for about a year before Chlorus dies. Chlorus is buried in York. None of this matters a hill of beans as to why Constantine is made emperor. He marries Fausta. It's all matrilineal. Helen to Chlorus. Fausta to Constantine."

"What do you mean by Helen to Chlorus?"

"I mean that Chlorus needs matrilineal consent to rule Britain."

"Why is your granddaughter able to bestow such an honor?"

"Because of me. I'm a pendragon."

"You certainly are a King, aren't you? If these are matrilineal societies, why does your great grandson insist on establishing a patriarchal church?"

"He doesn't really do that. His mother is an Arianist. She's a follower of Lucien, the mentor of Arius. The Universal Church comes into being to serve Constantine's needs. He calls himself the Savior and the Messiah. He just wants to make sure that all gods are paid homage to so they won't take revenge on him after he dies in case he forgets one of them."

"Constantine believed in 'gods'?"

"He thinks he's one himself. He tells everyone how he is descended from Neptune. All this Catholic stuff comes after him. Probably by the bishops. I'm sure it must be the bishops who slap the Helen-of-the-Cross title onto his mother. They trot her off on vacation to the Holy Land and then claim she has found a piece of the True Cross. Now she is St. Helen of the Cross."

"Did she tell her son that he was descended from Neptune?"

"A belief in a pantheon of gods is perfectly common in our times. By making his church universal, Constantine can throw in anything he wants. The use of magic and spells is also common in our times. The Eucharist is a love spell already in use. The birthday of Jesus is overlaid with the pagan sun festival on the twenty-fifth of December. And yet no one ever seems to question why it is that the shepherds are out grazing their sheep in the wintertime. Tell the story long enough and it becomes dogma."

"Enter the Invisible College, huh? Thank goodness for books!"

"Even books burn", Bertha added. "Look at the Library of Alexandria, the foremost wonder of the ancient world. Purposefully burned. And consider the dark ages when all books are banned for a few generations. Even a priest is not allowed to read a bible."

"Then how is it that I know the stories?"

"Ireland", Coel Hen said simply. "Patrick, and then Columba, use the Irish monasteries to start up one university after another. The dark ages do not visit Ireland. Safe refuge, meals, and books are offered free of charge to both students and to scholars fleeing persecution by the church. They even bring their own books with them."

"Weren't the Romans ruling Ireland then?"

"No one ever rules Ireland but the Irish until your grandfathers, Richard Strongbow de Clare and Dermot macMurrchada, invite the Norman Invasion in. Patrick is in Ireland as the Roman empire is collapsing. He is there for thirty years recording the tales of pagan Ireland. So he is also the first apostle to be in direct conflict with the High Church."

"Was he sympathetic to the stories or in conflict with them?"

"He grows up with them. He and Dereca and another sister are kidnapped as children by the ancestors of Wilson of the Silver Branch, the O'Neills of Northern Ireland. His nickname kinda says it all. The Welsh call him Maenwyn, One Dedicated to the Moon."

Aria finished off her bowl of cranberry sauce with whipped cream while Alfhilder refilled her cider cup. "I still don't know who your son, Ragnar, is."

"A fierce warrior, proud of his descent from Odin. He and his sons are a force to be reckoned with. They are Viking invaders. His son, Beorne Ironside, your ancestor, is also the ancestor of Bjorn the Old, Olaf's father. Ragnar's son, Sigurd Snake-in-the-eye, also your ancestor, is married to the daughter of the man who kills Ragnar. And it is Ivar the Boneless, ancestor of Wilson of the Silver Branch, who plots the terrible revenge the boys will take for their father's murder."

"Who murdered Ragnar?"

"King Ella of Northumbria throws Ragnar into a snake pit."

"Oooooooh! I can't even imagine such a death. Can there be worse?"

"Possibly what the boys do to Ella. Ivar, the thinker of the bunch, comes up with the plan to perform the custom of the Blood Eagle on him. Hanging from his wrists, Ella's back is sliced open and his lungs are pulled out one at a time through the hole until, outside his body, they each face the opposite direction resembling the open wings of an eagle. It is a slow and torturous death and if you plan to go to Valhalla you cannot scream. Ella does not go to Valhalla."

"Oh geez! That is sickening. How on earth did that poor girl marry your grandson after he had killed her father like that?"

"Bleaja?", Alfhilder said softly, "she's a lovely girl."

No one else said anything so Aria assumed, once again, that some questions didn't have answers.

"Why are Ragnar's children called the Boneless and Snake-in-the-eye?"

"It's genetic through his wife's family. Ivar is called the Boneless because he only has cartilage in his legs and has to be carried on his shield. His grandfather, Sigurd, kills the dragon, Fafnir. But not only that, on Odin's advice, Sigurd also drinks the blood of the dragon. He acquires the Language of the Birds from doing this and also the dragon's qualities. He and Brunhilde pass these traits on. So Ragnar's Sigurd has a serpent's eye and Ivar has no bones in his legs."

"Who is Brunhilde?"

"Ragnar's mother-in-law, the Valkyrie."

"What is a valkyrie?"

"The valkyries are the twelve handmaidens of Odin. It is their responsibility to deliver dead warriors from the battlefield to Valhalla and serve them the sacred mead. In Valhalla the warriors prepare for the battle of Ragnarok. Brunhilde is one of these twelve but because she opposes Odin's choice of a winner in a battle, he condemns her to live as a mortal. Sigurd falls madly in love with her and even offers her the magic ring as an engagement ring. She wisely consents only to being his lover."

"When is the battle of Ragnarok?"

"It happens at the end of the world. A member of the Invisible College named Wagner writes an opera about it. Brunhilde is in the opera. In fact she is the last voice heard. That is why some jest is made of her saying that "it ain't over till the fat lady sings"."

"But this dinner and this conversation are over, Child, as it is time for you to take your rest", Bertha stated.

Aria excused herself and thanked everyone and returned to the sleeping car. Once in the nightgown provided for her use, she dashed back into the library car to retrieve the book she had left lying on the ottoman. Tonight she would fall asleep reading. Just like at home. Diving under the thick warm quilts and turning up the lamplight next to the bed, she finally saw what book she had chosen. Expecting Robin Hood or Rapunzel, she was surprised to find L Frank Baum's the Wizard of Oz. This was not a tome from the Invisible College. Oz was not real. It was populated with witches, dwarves, wizards and screaming flying monkeys. And a home that Dorothy didn't know how to get back to.

She read about Dorothy losing track of Kansas until her eyelids drooped. Turning out the lamp and sliding deeper under the covers she thought about home. It still felt too far away but for some inexplicable reason the Beginning of Things felt as if it might be drawing nearer. Content with that small comfort she closed her eyes. This world was not ending here and now and she could not hear the fat lady singing so she fell asleep to the soft chiming of the apple bells as the train sped north to Scotland.

Merovee Merovingian

Progenitor – Merovingian Line

Ancestor of Mariah of the Masons

Ancestor of Newt of the Massachusetts Bay Colony

Coel Hen

Pendragon

Old King Cole

*Ancestor of Nancy Ann of the Virginia Company
and May of the Moon Men*

Ancestor of May of the Moon Men

Bertha Laon
Mother Goose

mother of Charlemagne

Ancestor of Nancy Ann of the Virginia Company

EMPEROR

Charlemagne

Ancestor of Nancy Ann of the Virginia Company

CHAPTER SEVEN

Hic Sut Dracones - Here Be Dragons

"What's the use of being Irish if the
world doesn't break your heart?"

U.S. President John Fitzgerald Kennedy

"Whatever their origins, they were no evil emanation
of the devil, but rather a grand, fierce, gentle,
romantic, brotherly, wise and ancient folk."

Reverend Robert Kirk
October 16, 1688
Aberfoyle, Scotland

The Golden Apples of the Sun, the
Silver Apples of the Moon.

Song of Wandering Aengus
William Butler Yeats,
1923 Nobel Laureate for Literature

SHE OPENED HER eyes to darkness since the black-out curtains had been employed to block out the perpetual twilight. Relieved not to be waking up in a busy restaurant, her next realization was that the train was not moving, meaning they were already in Scotland. And a smile crossed her face. She was now in love with Scotland, but then she was also in love with France and Northern England. No, the thing that made Aria smile was the baseless belief that when she was in Scotland, she was close to going home.

She leaped from the bed and hurried into the new day's attire. Another lovely gown. No horseback riding today. She couldn't help but wonder who would be waiting for her in the dining car. But to her alarm, she discovered that the door leading to the back of the train was locked. She raised a curtain and from what she could see in the cavernous gloom outside her window, the remaining train cars were gone.

She was still granted access to the library car which was warmly lit by the little lamp on the tea cart. Hot tea was left for her in the pot under the plaid cozy and also warm scones and smoked salmon. Her guide was late but she assumed that was to give her time to eat so she sat down in the big soft chair and enjoyed her breakfast. But once it was gone and she had drained the little pot, her anxiety arrived. Where was her guide?

She stepped out of the library car onto the platform thinking someone might be waiting for her but all she saw was a very dim green light over an elevator door. She was debating whether she should take the elevator or continue waiting for her guide when she noticed that the train was moving. Now thoroughly panicked, not knowing what to do, she froze and the train sped away. That solved her dilemma, she would take the elevator because she didn't intend to spend one moment longer than she had to in the dark cavern underground all alone with her claustrophobia. But once standing before the elevator door, she could not detect where the button was located. Did they have buttons? How had her guides managed to open the doors? The dim green light was of no help in locating a hidden or recessed button in the cave wall surrounding the door. Her breath became labored as the claustrophobia exacerbated. She pounded in frustration along the walls but to no avail. And suddenly she screamed. Just like that first night when she saw Mariah standing on her balcony under the falling stars. It was involuntary and it didn't help anything. She slid to the floor with her back against the door and sobbed.

When the tears ran dry she noticed the sign laying out of place on the ground and she could just barely make out what was written there, Sidhean Sluaigh Station. In smaller letters beneath was written the English translation. The Fairy Hill of the Hosts, it read. That seemed more than a little incongruous considering that this was the first time that she had been left without one. Forced to wipe her nose and dry her eyes on the underlining of her gown, she collected herself mentally and thought about the fairy hosts. How would they open this danged door? If only she had magic at her fingertips too. And suddenly it dawned on her that she had just that, because the most magical thing she could imagine was hanging from her waist. She jumped up and pointed the Silver Branch at the elevator door and gave it a little shake. The little apple bells said "Ding" and the door slid open flooding the platform with light.

The quick ride to the surface was elating. Not only would she be re-entering fresh air and sunlight, but she had encountered an obstacle in her path and overcame it without assistance. And home felt a little closer. Perhaps the apple branch really was a passport that would guarantee her safe passage out of here. When the door opened to fresh air and sunlight, her heart took flight for there stood Ewen of Otter with his wonderful bird legs showing below his kilt.

Aria ran to him and hugged him tight. Like the scream, the hug was involuntary. "Ewen!", she exclaimed as she released him, 'I never expected to ever see any of you again and now here you are!"

"When I hear that you will be coming up at Sidhean Sluaigh I volunteer to be your guide again. Otter, my home, is only a wee distance away. They say I'm to take you to the Pendragon which means you must still be on schedule, which means you'll be going home tomorrow."

"Tomorrow? Are you sure, Ewen? Are you absolutely sure? I mean you could have heard it wrong", she stammered on in her shock and awe.

"It's what I hear. But we had best get into the carriage", he said indicating the same black coach with matching team that Aria had ridden in from Inverary with John Wilson.

"How far are we from Inverary now?"

"The castle? We aren't headed to the castle. You are almost at the Beginning of Things I'm told, and the only things that begin at Inverary Castle are a lot of Campbells."

The team raced to wherever it was that Aria was set to meet Uther Pendragon. Ewen had alleviated her constant fear that she wouldn't get home again so she was truly enjoying the ride. "Is there some reason why you didn't meet me at the train, Ewen?" Aria wondered if the elevator thing had been some sort of a test.

"Sorry, Lass. I'm known for being tardy."

"Oh." Aria compared this trait to the Emery of her Eden. "It must run in your DNA. But never mind that, you must tell me where the Beginning of Things is located."

"I have no idea. I've never been there. I don't even know anyone who has."

"Well that's unsettling. Am I the first? Why do I have to be the first?"

"I doubt that you are, Lass. You're just the first that I know of. Right now I heartily suggest that you take advantage of the scenery outside the window as it's some of the finest in the world. Your quest will end soon enough."

"I thought you said that I'm not on a quest."

"I didn't say that. You asked if you are on a quest to find the Holy Grail. Now I know that your quest is to reach the Beginning of Things so that you can go home. Your quest is to go home."

Well that statement was unsettling too. What kind of an adventurer was she, after all? Was it so obvious to everyone that leaving the adventure was foremost in her thoughts? Why couldn't she just enjoy the ride?

Ewen was right about the scenery. It truly was spectacular. She thought about what might take place between now and tomorrow. Maybe she was in fairyland now. It was beautiful enough to be just that. And her ancestors that inhabited these lands were professing to be bears and elves, dragons and mermaids, wizards and greenwood lords.

Yet here she was, feeling like the reluctant pioneer, instead of celebrating her great good fortune at getting to be one in the first place. Everything about her thinking seemed to be skewed toward fear. She would have to work on that.

"Are we still in Scotland, Ewen?"

"Yes, Argyll. The Trossachs."

"I'm really glad I got to see you again, Ewen. I guess if I'm going home tomorrow I should give you the Silver Branch. It belongs to your family, I understand."

"Don't do that!", he answered a bit too quickly and alarmed Aria. "You're not home yet."

Aria's pulse began to race at the warning in his voice. He knew something she didn't. The carriage was fast approaching a hill standing alone in the landscape and figures on horseback could be seen at its foot.

"That is Doon Hill, Lass. Uther's fort is at the top. We are in Aberfoyle."

"Who are those people on horseback?"

"The offspring of the Pendragon."

"Is one of them my grandparent?"

"All of them are your grandparents."

The carriage pulled up alongside the four riders and stopped. Aria got out and felt very small looking up at them seated on their fine mounts. And smaller still once Ewen and the carriage raced back into the Trossachs. Only one of the riders was a woman and she was the first to speak. "Welcome to Aberfoyle. I am your thirty-ninth-ago grandmother on the line of Joseph of the New England Company. My name is Morgause." She did not dismount from her horse but stretched out her hand to shake Aria's.

"I'm her brother, Smerviemore", the next man said. "I'm your thirty-sixth-ago on the line of May of the Moon Men. And my brother over here is Eochaid I, the Bruide of Argyll."

"It means I'm the magician", Eochaid clarified. "I'm your ancestor via Kenneth macAlpin so through the lines of Newt, Nancy Ann and May. And Wilson of the Silver Branch too."

Only the last rider dismounted from his horse. He handed his reins to his brother, Eochaid, and walked over to shake Aria's hand. "I am Arthur, king in Camelot. Welcome to our father's home. You are descended from me through both May and Newt. If you are up to it, you and I will climb this hill to Father's fort. My siblings will not be joining us."

Aria stared at him in stunned silence. This was King Arthur! He who pulled the sword from the stone. He who was betrayed by Lancelot and Guinevere. He who built the Round Table. This could not really be happening. All she could manage to do was nod that, yes, she was up for climbing the hill. Fortunately, the climb up the hill was an easy one on a well worn path.

With the exception of Mariah, every ancestor she met in the library of Inverary Castle was descended from this one Scottish family. From the Pendragon. Genealogically speaking, certainly this was the Beginning of Things. She would meet the Pendragon. She would spend the night in his castle. Tomorrow she would go home. "Is this the Beginning of Things?", she asked her famous grandfather.

"It is the threshold. My father is a door in the trunk of an ancient tree. It is deeper roots that you are here to discover."

"How can you be my grandfather when you and Guinevere didn't have any children?"

"I am a king. I have other wives. I have a son, Mordred, with my half sister, Morgan le Fay. You are descended from me through his daughter, Tortolina. She is the ancestress of the house of Cromarti. They use the bear's head in their coat of arms. Perhaps to honor me."

"How is that?"

"My name is Arthur. It means bear."

"Is Morgan le Fay a fairy?"

"She is a del Acqs, granddaughter of the Lady of the Lake and the bard, Taliesin. My wife, Gwendolen, is a half fairy and our daughter, Gyneth, has her half brother, Mordred's, disposition. Merlin is forced to put her into an enchanted sleep as punishment for her cruelty."

The path was steeper as they climbed so conversation ceased

as they made their way slowly upward. The massive fort of Uther Pendragon filled the top of the hill. Arthur pulled open heavy doors and led Aria inside. Uther was sitting in a high backed chair near the fireplace. A partially bald man in a floor length white robe sat conversing quietly with him as Aria and Arthur entered the room. Their conversation ceased but they only sat silently waiting for Aria to discover the other individual in the room. It was a woman standing by the window lost in some inward speculation, staring out at the landscape, with a face so exquisite, so perfect in its proportions, that Aria was stunned and stared unabashedly at her. The train of her shimmering, form-fitting gown puddled on the floor behind her and glistened like moonlight on water. When she turned that fabulous head and looked Aria in the eye, Aria knew once more that she was in the presence of the More-Than-Human. The little apple bells began to jingle with her trembling.

Arthur took a seat by his father and the robed man scurried across the room to rescue the star-struck Aria. "This vision of loveliness", he said to Aria, "is Viviane, the Elf Queen. She is your grandmother on the lines of Joseph of the New England Company, Newt of the Massachusetts Bay Colony and May of the Moon Men."

The woman bowed her head ever so slightly in acknowledgement.

"I am Crimthann", he continued shaking her hand, "Crimthann Fedlimid. I am not your grandfather but I am descended from Niall of the Nine Hostages like those of your Prince Emery's O'Neill clan. I am cousin to your grandfather, Aedan, and it is I who crown him the Pendragon."

"Oh my gosh, you are St. Columba! I've been to your church."

The man smiled at her remarks. "Columba is my monastic nickname. In the language of the church it means dove. Dov in Hebrew means bear. Columba in Old Norse means black bear."

Aedan stood up from his throne-like chair and walked over to shake Aria's hand. He was so imposing a figure that her trembling had her apple bells jingling again, much to her embarrassment. Not knowing what was expected, she bowed her head slightly like Viviane had done.

Columba rushed on with the introduction. "This is Aedan macGabran, now Uther and the eighteenth Pendragon of Britain, the Prince of Forth and the King of Manau Gododdin."

Viviane fairly glided across the room and took a seat along with the rest by the fireplace. Aria was a jingling nervous wreck but they were all gracious enough to ignore it. Here she sat with Arthur, king of Camelot, the Elf Queen, the Ring Lord, and the apostle of the Picts. It took all the control she could muster to ask a question. "Is this Camelot?"

It was Arthur who answered. "This is Aberfoyle in Scotland. Camelot is south of here in the vale of apples, in Avalon."

"I've been there too", she continued squeaking, "to Appleby."

"The veil is thin between realities there. It is where Viviane is queen."

"In Appleby?"

"In Avalon. Viviane is the Lady of the Lake."

Having passed through a daleth with Robin Hood in Poitiers, Aria now understood that not all lakes are wet. She peeked rapidly out of the corner of her eye at her elven grandmother and expected her to be wet, regardless.

"Is Avalon a portal?"

"You are at a portal now, Child." Uther interrupted his son's narration. "You have arrived at the entrance of Emain Ablach, the Plain of Apples, the abode of the Tuatha de Danaan. When they leave Mag Mell, the Plain Happy, and sail to this dimension, they make their home here at Doon Hill so that they can learn how to win in battle. It is their intention to defeat the Firbolgs for the control of Ireland. Later they return here as a conquered people."

"Who would be able to conquer magical people? Other magical people?"

"That would guarantee a fair fight. No, it is the humans who conquer the People of Peace. No one excels at war and conflict quite like a human."

"Is there a portal guardian of this place in my modern times?"

"Really no need. By your era the Tuatha de Danaan are reduced to myth and legend leaving scant few to even look for them. The Shining

Ones prefer it that way. They can make contact with whomever they choose, whenever they choose. The good reverend of Aberfoyle, Robert Kirk, is one such soul."

"'Why would they initiate contact with a minister?"

"Because he has an intense interest in them. His childhood years are spent here when this fort is gone and this small mountain is called the Fairy Hill. He seeks to make contact also with beings from a different reality. They open the door and invite him in. He leaves his journal before they take him for good."

"Take him where?"

"To the Otherworld, Emain Ablach."

"He wanted to go there for good?"

"Not at all. He tries to make arrangements to escape but it fails. You can read about it yourself in his book. I believe it is called the Secret Commonwealth."

Aria was terrified by his response. The Tuatha de Danaan kidnapped a Christian minister against his will. What earthly chance did she have? No one had told her that she would be visiting the Otherworld but she had a sinking feeling it was going to happen anyway. If only she could get her hands on the minister's book in the hopes of avoiding his fate. "What exactly are you guarding at this portal?"

"If you are curious as to whether I guard in order to keep things out or to keep things in, the answer is yes."

"How did this come to be your job? Because you are the Pendragon?"

"I am born here. The River Forth runs near. I am the Prince of Forth."

"Are all pendragons born on Doon Hill?"

"Only me. Yet we are all from this region. My mother's father is King Brychan II and is the sixteenth pendragon. He rules the neighboring kingdom of Manau Gododdin."

"Are all of you related?"

"Interrelated."

"How many of you are there?"

"There are twenty one in total. Coel Hen, whom you met already, is the eleventh. The first is Cymbelline, remembered by the Shakespeares. The final pendragon is Cadwalader, father of Makir ha David, king in Septimania."

"Bertha Goosefoot's family!"

"Yes, Child, kingship is kinship."

"Passing down the power."

Uther looked skeptical. "More like passing down the genes. It's all genetic. It's the primary concern of the elves since it is their responsibility to monitor and maintain them. Merlin makes sure that Arthur has the right parents."

"By doing what?"

"By putting the glamour on me so that Arthur's mother thinks that I am her husband, Gorlois, when I take her to bed. Gorlois is out of town battling my troops at the time."

"Well, that isn't exactly fair, is it?"

"Probably why I am called Aedan the Treacherous."

"Arthur's mother is my daughter", Viviane announced. "Ygraine will enact her revenge through her sister, Viviane II. Merlin falls in love with Viviane but Viviane harbors no such feelings for him. He is blinded by his passion for her. She takes advantage of this weakness and has him teach her all his magic. Then she uses his own magic against him and imprisons him in a tree in the Forest of Broceliande."

"Who is the father of your daughters?"

"Taliesin, the bard."

"I know his name. A great architect in my time, Frank Lloyd Wright, names one of his houses Taliesin."

"The word means Shining Brow. Taliesin is only one of his three names. This one he gains by drinking the awen."

"What is the awen?"

"The knowledge of true reality. His childhood name is Gwion-Bach. As Gwion-Bach, he is servant to the White Moon Fairy, Cerridwen. Her own son, Morfran, is born so ugly that she brews him a potion of the awen in her cauldron to make him wise and poetic. But the brewing of the potion is laborious and requires stirring. This task falls to Gwion-Bach. Three drops splash out of the cauldron and land on his thumb, burning him, so that he sticks his thumb into his mouth to kill the pain. Now he has obtained the awen and knows in an instant that his mistress will not be pleased. So he flees. She indeed pursues him. But he has the power of the awen so he shape shifts into a rabbit. She shifts into a dog. Then he shifts to a fish but she becomes an otter. So he becomes a bird and she becomes an eagle. Finally he turns himself into a kernel of corn but she becomes a hen and eats him becoming pregnant. She vows to kill him as soon as he is born but he is far too beautiful and she cannot bring herself to do it."

"He grows up with her?"

"No. She wants nothing to do with him so she sets him adrift in a small boat on the sea. It is Elphin, the Prince of Wales, who finds him and raises him. And it is Elphin who names him. He is so shocked by the whiteness of his brow that he names him Taliesin."

"And Prince Elphin trains him to be a bard?"

Viviane laughed and it startled Aria because it sounded like bells if bells could laugh. "He has swallowed the awen. He has no choice but to be a bard. By now I imagine you are thinking that my husband is an imaginary person and discounting what I am saying. But that is not the case. Even in your time, Taliesin is remembered as the greatest bard Britain ever has. Even Mr. Wright, the architect, pays homage to his name. My husband reads to the King of Gwynedd from the Book of Enoch and even foretells of King Maelgwn's death by the yellow plague."

"Where is Gwynedd?"

"The House of Gwynedd begins in Wales with Maelgwn's brother, Cunedda. He is dispatched from Manau Gododdin by Vortigern, the twelfth Pendragon, to vanquish the Irish. Those of Gwynedd are albigens, the same as we del Acqs, the dal Riata, the Picts and the Goths." There was not a shadow of a doubt that the woman speaking with a bell accent was one of them.

"You mentioned the Book of Enoch. Like Mary Magdelene, his name pops up often. Who is he?"

Columba spoke. "He is the bird man. He is a unique individual even in the pages of the Bible. Portions of his own book are included there, in Daniel, Ezekiel, Isaiah and Revelations. Within the Bible, Enoch stands apart from all men. The Bible speaks of only two people who walk with God, one is Abraham and the other, Enoch. It speaks of only two people who are pleasing to God, Jesus and Enoch. And it speaks of only two people who are translated to heaven, Elijah and Enoch. When translated to an angel, Enoch is the most powerful of all angels and renamed Moriah, the Angel in the Whirlwind."

"What is Taliesin's third name?"

"Owen, Archdruid and Prince Bard Desposyni."

"Wait a minute! That's the Holy Family. Is he related to the Holy Family like Lancelot?"

"Lancelot is my nephew", Viviane said, "my sister Elaine's son. Her husband, Ban, claims descent from James the Just. However my husband is descended from Josheph ha Rama Thea"

"Joseph of Arimathea?", Aria gasped. "Why I created all the stained glass windows for our little community church dedicated to Joseph of Arimathea! I can't believe this!" The seeming coincidence of this astounded Aria into stunned silence while she contemplated it.

"I did not say, Joseph of Arimathea. I said Joseph ha Rama Thea. It is a title. It means 'of Divine Highness'."

Now feeling a bit deflated Aria asked, "then who is Joseph of Arimathea?"

"I would not know", Viviane answered. "Where is this place Arimathea?"

"Isn't it in the Holy Land?"

"No."

"Sheesh! No Nazareth. Now no Arimathea either? Is history really that hard to record and preserve?"

"The recording of history is an intentional act and of vital importance in practicing the art of control. Your author, George Orwell, sums it up simply when he says that "the present can be controlled, and the future shaped, by secretly creating a past". It explains to someone like you, who seeks the truth, the importance of stories which suggest the idea that the past might not be what you are told."

"Is it the truth I am seeking?", Aria asked wistfully. "Isn't everyone doing that?"

"You might be saddened by just how many have no curiosity at all, Child. They are content to live in a fog of unknowing and are usually resentful when truth intrudes."

"Did your sister live at Bamberg Castle or in a lake like you?" Aria figured as long as she was weird enough to seek the truth, she might as well not be shy about it.

"My sister does not live at Bamberg, nor does she raise her own son. I do. He is my foster son and it is I who name him Lancelot du Lac. Of the Waters. Like myself, del Acqs, of the Waters."

"What water are you talking about, the ocean?"

"I speak of the Great Above. It is a Sumerian concept. I believe you know already who the Sumerians are. Heaven and Earth are the created objects of a primeval sea. Heaven is the sky. The space above the sky is called the Great Above. Earth is the surface and the space below is called the Great Below. It is in the Great Below that the chthonic deities live."

"Is that what you are, a chthonic deity?"

"No, I am a Fountain Fey, like Melusine and her mother, Pressina."

"Did you make Excalibur?"

"Arthur's sword is made by an Avalonian elf."

"Do you take it back when Arthur dies?"

"No. The gifts of the Eldritch World are rarely returned. The Fairy Flag of Dunvegan still hangs in the castle of the macLeods on the Isle of Skye into your era. Odin's banner hangs in the church where the Fairybear is laid to rest. Excalibur does not come back. Richard the Lion Heart gives it to Tancred, King of Scicily."

"Even the stories to protect the truth are faulty. How are we supposed to know what to believe?"

"You have only to be still, silent, and listen to your heart. Still and silent are not common states in the modern world, so your ability to hear what you heart has to say is greatly hampered. You perceive Merlin, for instance, to be imaginary, without considering that the Roman church goes to all the trouble to blacklist his Prophesies in their Council of Trent. Your heart will tell you, if you ask, that this action would be akin to taking Peter Pan to the High Church council to declare Neverland null and void."

"Well it's a good thing that the church is no longer the government, huh?" Aria was picturing Peter Pan on the hot seat in front of a roomful of High Hat Bishops.

Aedan laughed. Yet it wasn't a laugh reminiscent of bells but rather of hardened disdain.

"The church is so large in your era that it can no longer be seen."

"On no", Aria responded to him, "you'd be surprised how fast people are falling away from the church in my time."

"God is replaced with money in your time. Where do you think it is kept?"

Aria wasn't expecting him to question her but he sat there waiting for an answer so she knew she was about to embarrass herself once again. "Some of it is in Fort Knox, I guess."

"Money, the control mechanism of your present time, is controlled by a sovereign entity existing inside another sovereign entity. Called simply the City, it is fully surrounded by the City of London in the country of England, and even the modern queen cannot enter the City without permission."

"The money is inside London?"

"The money itself is elsewhere. It is only controlled within Britain. The money is located within a sovereign entity existing inside another sovereign entity called the Vatican in Rome in the country of Italy."

"That's a pretty big responsibility for a few Swiss Guards."

"The military arm that protects the money is controlled within a sovereign entity existing inside the sovereign entity that is the United States of America. It is called Washington D.C."

"Well that's our capital but it isn't where the military is located. The United States is a country. We have a military. All countries have a military."

"Your country in your time is two hundred and forty two years old. How many of those years will your country spend being at war?"

"I don't know", she said and bit her lip.

"Over two hundred thirty-four years. Just who are you defending yourselves from?"

He didn't seem to expect an answer from her but was rather expressing his disgust so she didn't answer. She looked at Columba instead. "Are you a Roman Catholic?"

"Yes, but Patrick and I are both deemed to be sorcerers by the church. Still, I am listed as a Catholic saint and credited with being one of the twelve apostles of Ireland. Patrick and I are the practitioners of the pre-Roman Nazarine principles called Enochian Judaism. It comes to be called the Celtic Church with it's beginnings on my isle of Iona as well as in Northern England, Wales and Ireland."

"I can only assume that Nazarine does not signify someone from Nazareth, right?"

"The created past puts Jesus into the non-existent Nazareth for a reason. By rights, he should be called Jesus of Bethlehem, not of Nazareth. So why? Because there is a prophesy before his time saying that Jesus will be a Nazarine."

"So what is a Nazarine?"

"It is a tribe of people. The word Nazarine means green. The root of this word, zara, means to scatter seed. Jesus comes to scatter the seed of truth."

"Is that the principle of the Nazarines, to scatter truth?"

"The Nazarines have only two principles. The first is the pursuit and dedication to the truth above all else. The second is the pursuit of wellness for everybody, not just the few. Their attributes set them apart from other people. They seek a world without temples, display unbridled generosity and would rather die than allow deceit."

"Yet you crown Aedan as the Pendragon. Didn't you know about his deceit against Arthur's mother?"

"First of all, I don't say that Aedan is a Nazarine. But more important, I don't want to crown him as Pendragon at all. I am told to do it."

"By whom?"

"By an angel."

Aria stole a quick glance at Aedan and wondered if she had misspoke. "Who did you want to be the Pendragon, Columba?"

"His brother, Eoganan. The angel tells me on three separate occasions that I am to support Aedan and three times I refuse. So he hits me with a scourge. What else can I do?"

"I didn't know that angels could be mean. Why did it have to be Aedan?"

"Genetics. It's always genetics. It is a an important union of the Rose Line of the dal Riata and the Apple Line of the del Acqs coming together in the person of Arthur. Aedan may be treacherous but Arthur is not and it is Arthur's story of Camelot that lives on."

"Clovis the Great said that I should pay attention to words. What does Camelot mean, Arthur?"

"Curved light. It's a principle of physics. It presents itself in the double slit experiment of modern scientists. When you curve light around an object, you render it invisible. When you stop looking at something, is it really there?"

"And you say that Camelot is in Appleby?"

"I said Avalon, but still, my headquarters are at Carlisle to the north."

"Maud Armstrong and David of Scotland lived there."

"And it is there that I am crowned king."

"By Columba?"

"By Merlin."

"But he isn't a Catholic bishop. He's a wizard, isn't he?"

"He is a holy man and a druid of the Elder Faith. Like Gwenhafer, he is of the Blue People.

"The Phrygians? The Thracians? The pixies? Who are they?"

"The Bee Line of the albigens. The Picts."

"Were you raised by Merlin?"

"I have a foster family who are elves in Brittany. I only pull the sword from the stone because my foster brother, Cai, has forgotten his own sword in the tent at the tournament. He is the next to compete. I need to get him a weapon, quick!"

"I have an ancestor in Scotland who also is fostered by elves. Angus, I think his name is."

"Foster care is common among us. Gwenhafer is fostered in the court of Cador. He is the military commander of Father's troops against Ygraine's husband, Gorlois, during my treacherous conception. Cador carried shame for his, albeit innocent, part in the deception that resulted in my birth. I feel bad for Cador. When I'm dying on the battlefield, I bequeath my kingdom to his son, Constantine."

"That was very nice of you."

"As a Grail king, I am entrusted to portray the embodiment of service and fighting for the good of humanity. I collect a band of warrior knights. Twelve of them. And I sit them at a Round Table to demonstrate that no one is to be valued above another."

"Is the grail the cup that Jesus drank out of at the last supper?"

Viviane's bell voice spoke the answer. "The mechanism of the Grail is the question. Lancelot's grandson, Galahad, finds the Grail Castle but fails to ask the question and so is denied entrance. He corrects this mistake on his second visit."

"Who hears the question?"

"The Fisher King. The one who is wounded by the Dolores Stroke thus causing the wasteland."

"Where is the Grail Castle?"

"It is the Castle of Eden in Northern England. Later it is called the Castle of Souls and later still, the Castle of Joy, or Joyous Garde."

"Bamberg Castle? I've been there too. Castle Corbenic. I met Mari and the Fairybear there."

"Near here, in Manau Gododdin, sits another castle, Castle Gloom, also called Dolores Garde", Arthur added. "It is where Mordred imprisons Gwenhafer for her affair with Lancelot."

"So what is this important question that needs to be asked?"

"Who am I?", Arthur said.

"Excuse me?"

"That is the question, Who Am I? The grail is the bloodline of the elves."

Ewen would be pleased that she had discovered the Holy Grail without even looking for it. Yet it was doubtful that she would ever see Ewen again. "I was told that I would be returning home tomorrow. Will I stay here tonight?"

"Tonight you will dine with the Irish", Aedan stated simply. "Tomorrow you will visit Emain Ablach."

This information felt treacherous. She wanted to cry at the thought of having to travel to Ireland today. She had no idea how late it was but a trip on the submarine and then a dinner with more ancestors seemed to be too much to cram into the rest of this day. Yet it was the mention of Emain Ablach that really shook her up. First of all, wasn't the portal here on Doon Hill? Did she have to travel back here tonight as well? And the biggest stressor of all was her absolute certainty that she did not want to visit the Otherworld but felt like it was going to be forced on her anyway. Reverend Kirk went there against his will and didn't come back. Something was going on here and she no longer felt safe. A tear slid down her cheek.

"Na biodh eagla ort, Child", Columba said to soothe her. "It is not as you imagine."

"What is Emain Ablach?", Aria asked knowing that she had better pay close attention.

"The Plain of Apples", Aedan explained. "Your Silver Branch is from there. It is ruled by Manannan macLir who gives the branch to your Emery's ancestor."

"Who?" Aria was distracted and not paying attention, and didn't really care if she got an answer. She was fast slipping into despair. She now felt very alone in a very foreign place.

"The man on whose submarine you ride, the Man of the Sea. His name, Manau, is used to signify my nearby kingdom, Manau Gododdin, The Stone of Manannan. The kingdom has a different name in your era but still it bears his name, Clackmanannanshire. A very long name for Britians's smallest county. The Wee County, it is called."

She perked up a bit at the mention of the submarine. Aria liked Manannan's submarine and thought that he might be in some way involved with her positive experiences in it. "Did the winners or the losers leave the history of this man? Is he a good guy or a bad guy?"

Aedan studied her for too long an interval before answering her questions and made her uncomfortable. "Winners and losers? Good guys and bad?" His voice was not grandfatherly and reassuring but cold and critical. "Is reality that simplistic to you?"

Aria did not answer his question.

"Which are you, Child?"

Again, she didn't know what to say and he was frightening her so she did not answer.

"Who among those who struggle for power are the good guys? We repeat to you over and over…of the Moon Men,…of the Masons,…of the Virginia Company, and so on to remind you over and over again of the powers behind your roots. You are descended from the invaders, the controllers, the spinners of myth. But that is just in your country and close to your time. These struggles are ancient. Would it surprise you to learn of Pict killing Pict? With nuclear bombs?"

Aria, feeling cornered by Aedan and his aggressive male belittling of her ignorance, struck back by correcting him. "The atomic bomb was invented right before I was born."

"Then what is it that vitrifies the ancient forts of Scotland?"

"I don't know that word."

"It means glassification. The glassification of stone is caused by extreme heat, usually caused by a nuclear detonation."

"Or maybe lightning", Aria guessed.

"Perhaps. If it strikes in one spot and lasts for ten minutes."

"If there was atomic weaponry in ancient times, I don't think we would all still be here." Aria didn't feel as confident in her argument as she was trying to sound.

"That possibility is considered at the time. That is the reason the truce is called."

"Between who?"

"Naturally between those with power and those seeking power. It happens in 432 AD."

Aria was brought up short by hearing an exact date. "What happened in 432?"

"Patrick is consecrated as bishop and Christmas is celebrated for the first time on December 25th, the date of the pagan sun festival."

"How does that prove that a truce took place?"

"You tell me, Child. It's time for you to answer your own question."

Aria sat dumbstruck. His words held so much weight and authority that she knew she could not wriggle out of giving an answer. "Well… let's see….um", she stammered while attempting to chance upon a suitable answer. "Both of these events center on religion so the truce must be between people with differing religious beliefs." Aedan made no indication of whether this was correct or not so she blundered on. "St. Patrick practiced the faith of the Celtic Church, and yet becomes enfolded into the flock of the Roman Church, who then dispatches him to a Celtic country where he functions as a member of the Invisible College for thirty years, recording and preserving the ancient tales of Celtic Ireland."

Proud of her powers of deduction, or was that blarney?, Aria was still dismayed that Aedan would give no indication of whether or not she was on the right track. She continued, "Christmas is the celebration of the birth of Jesus which we are told happened when the shepherds were outdoors tending their flocks. But that would happen in the springtime and not on December 25th when it's cold. I presume the practitioners of the sun festival used the icons of the fir tree, Santa Claus, and mistletoe. Therefore the birth of Jesus is an overlay allowing both holidays to be celebrated at the same time."

Aria was quite pleased with herself to have come up with this hypothesis, yet Aedan only stared at her with his poker face and his cold blue eyes. "From which faction do you have your descent?", he asked.

"Both?", she asked and squirmed at the thought of his reproval should she be wrong.

"And what is the opposite of love?"

Finally he had asked a question that she could answer without having to wonder if she was correct. "Hate."

"That is incorrect. Both hate and love are powerful emotions that attract and attach you to the object of that attention. No, Child, the opposite of love is indifference. Not caring at all. It's called apathy and apathy is the final symptom of a dying civilization. But who cares?"

The pun was not lost on her and his words left her silent again. In that silence, a tall man stood at the threshold of the door framed by a night landscape. Yet the window on the opposite side of the room looked out onto full daylight. What strange magic was at work here? And the man who had entered, backlit by moonlight, was stranger still. He had to be at least seven feet tall, if not more. Both his skin and his long straight hair were paper white. He stepped quietly into the room where the light of day revealed him to be both youthful and attractive, while his green/gold eyes said that he was perhaps ancient. He wore a simple white tunic and sandals adorned with gold.

Columba smiled when he saw the stranger and walked over to greet him. Aria knew, instinctively now, that this tall individual was her next guide to wherever it was that the Irish were waiting, so she followed Columba across the room. "This is Keynaymikalhighnapa", Columba was able to say without tripping over the name. "He is here to escort you to Emain Macha, the Iron Mountain, in Northern Ireland. You will dine with the Irish in the Hall of the Speckled Hen, and then Key will return to escort you to your sleeping quarters for the night. In the morning, you will be escorted to Emain Ablach."

The white man said nothing, turned and walked back out into the night and waited silently for Aria outside the door.

"That's Northern Ireland out in that night landscape, isn't it? Is this what you meant about it not being what I was imagining?"

"Reality is being manipulated for your benefit."

"And what about him? Which grandfather is he?" She looked at the huge pillar of a man practically glowing in the moonlight.

"He is not your grandfather at all. Key is no relation to you. Key is the man who guides Robert Kirk in his sojourns through this portal."

Aria probably turned as white as Key. Her knees wobbled but she would not allow herself to collapse in front of Aedan the Treacherous.

Pulling herself up and breathing deep, she gathered her courage to face her fate. But it wasn't too late yet. Maybe Arthur or Viviane would take pity on her, except that the looks on their faces did not attest to this hope. Her throat got tight, tears formed, yet having no other option Aria stepped out into the Northern Irish moonlight.

The towering, glowing, white man was easy to follow. He didn't speak to her at all for which she was extremely grateful since she was still swallowing down tears. He didn't rush. In fact, he ambled along as if he had all the time in the world. Disconcerting considering the circumstances. They moved steadily toward a large beehive shaped building which Aria assumed was the Hall of the Speckled Hen. When the chill air penetrated to her bones, Aria began to shiver. Key handed her a wool tartan cloak that he pulled from who knows where. She was sure that it was the one she had used on her carriage rides and was glad to be wrapped in its warmth once more.

The hall was further than it looked or the guide was walking so slowly that Aria had enough time to quell her fears about this being the Otherworld. She was told it was Northern Ireland. Tomorrow would be the Otherworld. Like some nightmare travel itinerary. Well, she would be like Scarlett O'Hara and think about that later. And as long as she was conjuring famous Irish characters she would picture Maureen O'Hara and John Wayne, fresh from the movie, the Quiet Man, as the grandparents who would greet her at the door of the Speckled Hen. She smiled weakly and decided to go with that thought since any other one was too terrifying to consider.

Keynaymikalhighnapa deposited Aria at the door of the Hall of the Speckled Hen and turned and walked away. She quietly opened the huge door and slid into the room. Maureen and John were not inside, just as she had feared. In their place sat the giant. He had one eye and it was closed giving the impression that he was asleep. He was so massive that he made the three bears, Siward, Bjorn and Ursus, seem like cubs. Having only one leg and one arm, he was seated on an enormous bench cut from granite and rested his back against the wall. His humongous head nearly touched the dome of the ceiling.

Aria, now knowing how to control involuntary screams, did not scream. Instead she backed slowly to the door she had just entered because the group of men busy with some activity in the floor of the center of the room, were not even aware of her entrance. She would slip back out and run like hell. But her hand never found the door handle because the door had disappeared. Her bells rang out to proclaim her position as she stood shaking against the doorless wall.

The four normal-sized men ceased their activity for a moment and looked in her direction. But not for long. They were just then pulling a large pig or boar-like animal out of a pit in the ground. The hot coals they had removed from over the top now sent streamers of smoke up to and out of a hole in the center of the beehive roof. The burly men heaved the aromatic pork onto a tarp and began cutting it up into chunks with wicked looking knives. The lion's share was being placed into a cauldron, probably for the giant. Smaller plates were also being filled and placed on a table nearby set for six. Since the giant wouldn't fit at the table, they must be expecting someone else. Two of the men lugged the heavy cauldron over to the still sleeping giant and placed it on his lap. The other two looked at Aria and pointed to her place at the table. She used the distraction of the giant balancing his bowl, for he was not asleep after all, to scurry across the room and take her place at the table.

The giant did not wait for the others to begin eating. He ate with a spoon the size of a shovel. Aria watched, marveling at how he could balance the cauldron on his one knee, and not knock it over with the giant spoon in his one hand, while not looking.

She could barely breathe. She thought she might be sick. There was a plate of the roasted pork in front of her, same as the others. The sixth setting had none. A large bowl in the center of the table contained cooked apples in a sauce smelling of cinnamon, nutmeg and cloves. When the long bearded man to her right plopped a large helping of the sweet apples onto her plate, the scent soothed her nerves, and her stomach, and hunger arrived. Realizing the giant couldn't cross the room if he wanted to, she decided to enjoy the amazing food. It may well be her last meal. Some sort of ale was being poured and swallowed down by the men faster than it could be re-poured. Aria felt safer from the giant surrounded by these lively men.

The man sitting across from her said, "I'm going to tell you who we are, Child, but you're going to have trouble with our names. Except for Balor over there against the wall, who is not your ancestor. He is on his best behavior tonight and will do you no harm. I am Conor macNessa, the king of Ulster, your fifty-fifth-ago grandfather from Joseph of the New England Company. I'm also called Conchobar. The man on your right is Cormac, the man on your left is Conall and this other man is Conair Mor. You can call Cormac, Longbeard, as everyone already does. Longbeard is the fifty-fifth-ago ancestor of your Prince Emery. Conair Mor is also your grandfather, from May, Newt, Nancy and even Wilson. Conall Cearnach is my nephew. My sister's son. He's a Red Branch hero, but we'll come back to that. All of us are kings, except for Conall. My other sister, Dectera, not Conall's mother Findchoem, is married to Balor's great grandson, Lugh. Balor is the King of the Fomorians."

Aria was tremendously relieved not to be descended from the giant, Balor. She timidly asked Conchobar what a Fomorian was.

"The Fomorians sail here from the Lands Beneath before the de Danaans. And I know that Balor over here looks imposing but he is powerless without his attendants to raise his eyelid. You don't want to be around when that happens. If looks could kill, right?"

Aria stole glances around the room as Conchobar talked, looking for the missing door. There were countless unidentifiable weapons hanging everywhere on the walls. More than likely, the Hall of the Speckled Hen was more of a war room than a dining room. "What is a red branch?', she asked of the only one who was not a king.

"This place, Emain Macha, is the seat of the Red Branch", Conall answered. "It is named for our mutual ancestor, Ross the Red."

Conchobar winked at his nephew and said, "And Conall is almost its greatest hero."

Conall laughed. "You can't shame me, Uncle. I'm not in competition with Cuchulainn. I would never expect the praise that he deserves."

"Cuchulainn is my other nephew, Dectera and Lugh's boy. The Branch's greatest commander is Finn macCool, Longbeard's son-in-law."

Suddenly Aria gasped in surprise because the door reappeared. A woman walked through rivaling Mari and Viviane in her otherworldliness. All the men, except Balor, rose to their feet as she crossed the room. She had hair the color of Clovis the Great that was caught up in braids on her head and she wore a crescent moon shaped crown of silver. Her dress was the same red as her hair and dotted with moonstones. Her blue/white skin emitted an actual soft glow like the moon itself. She sat down at the sixth setting. Although she was a small woman, even when seated you had the distinct impression that you were looking up at her.

Conchobar introduced her before sitting back down. "The Red Queen. Macha. Ruler of Emania, the Land of the Moon. Your sixty-ninth-ago grandmother through Joseph of the New England Company."

Aria was having dinner with mythological people. If she ever got to share this experience with her family and friends, they would not believe it. Even being bad at math, Aria could figure out that sixty-nine generations ago must be around two thousand years in the past. Near to when Jesus lived. But they were mythological. And this woman could shine. Then Aria remembered that Jesus could do that too.

Conchobar poured a goblet of mead for Macha and offered one to Aria as well. Conversation was non-existent because Aria was so tongue tied that she realized she had forgotten to ask a question. "You are the Red Queen because you rule the Red Branch?"

"I rule the Land of the Moon, Emania. The moon is associated with the color red. Maga, the daughter of Aengus Og, is married to Ross the Red. It is his name that is given to the Branch."

"Who is Aengus Og? Isn't that my grandfather in Scotland who commands the troops of Robert the Bruce?"

"Your grandfather was no doubt named for the Aengus of which I speak. Aengus Og is the god of Love and Dreams, the Prince of the Tuatha de Danaan. The abode of Aengus Og is in the south, in County Meath. It is called the Brugh na Boinne. In your age it is called Newgrange. The de Danaan do not build it. It is why they come to

Ireland. They must challenge the Firbolgs and the Fomorians in order to possess it. My sons have colonized a place on the River Forth in Scotland and it is here that the de Danaan reside while they train for battle."

"They fought their war at Newgrange?"

"No. The Battle of Moytura, against the Firbolgs and Fomorians, is fought near a village called Cong."

"I saw the Fairy Tree in Cong! The one with the little curtain over the door. My sister and I have been there." Aria was amazed by this coincidence. And how odd that the village of Cong should be talked about in this gathering since it is around the village of Cong that Maureen O'Hara and John Wayne film the movie, the Quiet Man.

"Cong is a place of great power to the Tuatha de Danaan. Although they win the Battle of Moytura, their loss is great. Their king, Nuada, loses his hand in the battle and a blemished king cannot reign. Balor's grandson, Bres, replaces Nuada. Bres is of both Fomorian and Sidhe descent. And he is a vicious tyrant. His reign is disgraceful. He has the Royal Sidhe performing manual labor. He pays his wages in nuts, of all things. You still make note of this act in your modern time when you refer to being forced to work for peanuts."

"ENOUGH WOMAN!", the giant roared making all their cups rattle against the table from the booming bass notes of his voice. Balor had joined the conversation. "The Sidhe take our land. They deserve what they get at the hands of Bres. We are here first."

"You come here from Mr. Herman. You would fight for it too if you found it inhabited", Macha snapped back.

"Mt. Herman? Where is that?"

Although the question was directed to Macha, it was Balor who responded. "Phoenicia.33.33 degrees north, 33.33 degrees east. Entry point of the Watchers."

Unavoidably conversing with an irritated giant, Aria squeaked out, "Are you a Watcher?"

"Are you blind, Child?" His voice was so loud and so deep that ripples formed in their cups.

"A Watcher is not a man?", she asked trembling.

"Of course not. They call themselves the sons of God. But some of them are disobedient sons. And a higher authority judges them. And judges them harshly. The sinners transport Enoch to speak on their behalf to this authority at the headquarters at Brugh na Boinne."

"Enoch is a Watcher?"

"Of course not", he grumbled "Enoch is a man who becomes an angel."

"Did he get their sins absolved for them?"

"No. They are not forgiven. Their sins are too egregious. They have taught the art of war and how to use metals."

"Are there good Watchers and bad Watchers?"

"Humph! Good and bad. Life is not like that", Balor said reminding her of Aedan.

Aria addressed her next question to Conchobar in the hopes that the giant would stop talking to her. "Are you all descended from the Tuatha de Danaan?"

"Only Conair Mor has a Tuatha de Danaan parent. He can tell you."

"My real father is Nemglan, the Tuatha de Danaan bird god. My mother is the daughter of Etain, the fairy woman, and her husband, Cormac, brother of Nessa. Nessa is Conchobar's mother. After Etain gives birth to my mother, she leaves the baby with Cormac to raise and returns to fairyland. Cormac is so distraught over Etain's abandonment of him that he cannot even bear to lay eyes on the child. He orders his attendants to kill the baby. But my mother is so cute that they cannot bring themselves to do it so they give her to the cowherds to raise. That is how she gets her name, Mes Buchalla, fosterling of the cowherds. But even the cowherds fear that Cormac will discover her and kill her so they build a house for her with no windows in which to shelter her. However, the little house has a skylight and it is this window through which my father flies and then transforming into a man, impregnates my mother with me. Soon after, she is found by Eterscel, the High King of Ireland, who marries her, never realizing that her child is not his."

"Are you a High King of Ireland too then?"

"Yes, but High Kingship is not kinship. It is determined by the prophesy of the Bull Feast. And it is prophesied that the next High King will arrive walking and naked. The prophesy is relayed to me by the bird men while I am on a hunting expedition. So naturally, I take off my clothes and walk back. Now I'm the High King."

"Ask Balor about Bres's prophesy coming true, Child", Conchobar said with glee.

"They push us out", Balor bellowed as if bellowing was his only volume. "I leave after the defeat and they track us down or it never would have happened."

"Track you down? You only go to Tory Island, Balor. It's a stone's throw from here. And then you steal their damn cow and as much as invite them over."

"Excuse me", Aria said, "what are you talking about?"

"I'm talking about the prophesy that Bres, the tyrant, will be killed by his own grandson. Balor is responsible for fulfilling the prophesy when he steals the blue cow from the Tuatha de Danaan."

Balor reacted to Conchobar's words by pounding his mighty fist on the stone bench causing the building to shake. But he didn't deny the accusation.

So Conchobar happily told the tale. "Bres lives on Tory Island too. When he is told the prophesy, he locks up his only daughter, Eithne, in a tower. Her handmaidens are entrusted with keeping her away from men and men away from her, thus insuring no grandchildren. Enter Balor, the cattle thief. Naturally, Cian, of the de Danaan, comes looking for his cow. But what he spies is Eithne in the tower and is smitten. Disguising himself as a handmaiden too, he enters the tower and leaves Eithne with child. Or rather, with children. Eithne dies giving birth to triplets. Boys. Bres has the grandsons tossed into the whirlpool but the Morrigan flys in and rescues one of them, Lugh, who grows up and marries my sister. He is fostered by the Tuatha de Danaan and at the age of twenty-one kills his grandfather, Bres, in the second Battle of Moytura, fulfilling the prophesy."

"Why don't you tell the child how you die, macNessa?", Balor retaliated.

"Conall kills me."

"Uncle! Why do you slander me like that? She doesn't know that you are teasing. Let me tell the story." Turning to Aria he said, "It is true that it is the brain ball made by me that kills Uncle Conor. But I didn't do the slinging."

"What is a brain ball?"

"It is a weapon shot from a sling. I kill the King of Leinster and crush up his brains and marinate them in lime. That is what the ball is made of. But Cet macMaga takes the ball without my knowing and it is Cet who shoots Uncle Conor with it."

"Who is Cet?"

"His mother is Maga, wife of Ross the Red, and daughter of Aengus Og, Prince of the Tuatha de Danaan."

"What is a brain ball death like, Conchobar?"

"Well it's not instantaneous. The darned thing just lodges in my head. I live for seven more years before it bursts and kills me."

"Aedan said that Picts killed Picts. Is that what this is about? Aren't you all related?"

Conair Mor explained. "The Red Branch members are the Fenians. The Fenians are the Picts. My Fenian descendants are the dal Riata, the offspring of Conaire II and Conn's daughter, Saraid."

"Conn of the Hundred Battles? The Conn who had the Stone of Scone roar for him?"

"Yes. Conn is aligned with the Fenians. His dal Riata descendants migrate to Scotland and take the stone with them."

"My descendants", added Conall, "are the Fenians who oppose the dal Riata. We are the Dalaradia Picts. The Dalaradia migrate with my son, Lugaid Loisech, south to Leinster and are called the Laigin, the people of the Raven. The Laigin are the overlords of the Deisi of Leinster and it is their king who I kill to make the brain ball. The Deisi is the tribe of your grandfather, Dermot macMurchada, who invites the Norman Invasion in with Strongbow de Clare."

"Conn must have been favored if the Stone roared for him, don't you think?"

"Conn is my grandfather", Longbeard announced. "And he is descended from one of Conchobar's wives, Clothru, and her triplet brothers, the Finns. The White Ones of Emain Macha."

"Conn is a giant, like me!", Balor added.

"The Stone roars for giants?"

"The Stone roars for the rightful heir, regardless. It roars especially for giants", the giant remarked.

"Conn was a Fomorian?"

"No", Longbeard answered. "Giants are usually hybrids. Conn's mother is Maeve Lethderg, the Kingmaker. Her origins are unknown. Maeve is the wife or lover of nine successive kings. One of them is Conn's father, Fedlimid. I marry her too."

"I marry her too", Conchobar said.

"Did you produce any giants with her, Longbeard?"

"No. But my commander, Finn macCool is a giant, you know."

"I thought the Red Branch consists of Picts. Picts aren't giants."

"Finn is not a Pict. They are his troops. His father, Cool, is captain of the Fenians when he marries Finn's mother, Muirne of the White Neck. Muirne is Tuatha de Danaan. Her father is not pleased that she chooses to marry a mortal."

"Shouldn't you be a giant too, Conair?"

"I'm not a hybrid. My mother is of de Danaan descent as well as being the granddaughter of Fand the Fairy Queen. Father is the bird god."

"Why did your grandmother leave her husband and your newborn mother behind and return to fairyland?"

"The Etain that returns is the reborn Etain. The original Etain is married to Eochaid Airem, the uncle of Clothru and the three Finns. But she is kidnapped by Midhir, King of the Fairies. He loves her and woos her to his crystal mountain, Bri Leith. Eochaid follows to rescue her but Midhir has disguised every fairy there to look just like Etain."

"He doesn't just leave her there, does he?"

"What else can he do? Aengus Og volunteers to rescue her by turning her into a butterfly."

"And she flies home?"

"And she flies into a tankard of ale that the woman, Etar, drinks and becomes pregnant with the new Etain."

This was not the outcome that Aria was hoping for. Did one have to be reborn in order to escape from Fairyland? Right now, living her whole life over from the beginning seemed very tiring. She was not a young person like Etain or Gwion-Bach. It's so very hard to be young and not know anything. Was she brave enough to do that all over again?

"Do you and the Kingmaker have giant children, Conchobar?"

"No. But my stepfather, Factna, is a giant. I'm the result of an affair between my mother, Nessa, and the great druid, Cathbad."

"Who is the woman who marries her three brothers?"

"Clothru? She is one of my wives. But she doesn't marry the Finns. They are her brothers. She brings them here to Emain Macha and talks me into helping her incite them into rebellion against their father. Knowing that none of the three have any heirs, she takes each one to bed the night before the battle against their father, hoping to conceive."

"Don't tell me! She gets pregnant with triplets!"

"The Finns are captured and decapitated in the rebellion. Their father dies of grief. And Clothru gives birth to Lewy of the Red Circles. The child is born with a red circle around his neck and a red circle low on his torso. He is part of each father, Bres, Nar and Lothar. One triplet from the neck up, one in the torso and one from the torso down. Lewy is fostered by Conall's cousin, Cuchulainn, the real Red Branch hero", he smiled again at Conall who grimaced, "and comes to power when Conair Mor is killed by pirates at the Hostel of de Derga. But the stone won't roar for Lewy and it makes Cuchulainn so angry that he splits the stone with his sword in anger."

Macha, who had sat silent through the tales of the men, looked at Longbeard and said, "You should tell her about your Silver Branch."

"This belongs to you?", Aria pointed to her waist.

"I'm ashamed to say that it does. I beg Manannan for it and offer my wife and kids in trade to possess it. I'm sorry right away. He gives the family back to me though. Our kin are known to have a weakness for otherworldly gifts. It's not a proper excuse, but there you go. My Uncle Connla disappears permanently into the Lands Beneath when a fairy woman offers him an apple to ride with her in her crystal boat. My father is devastated by the disappearance of his brother and is now called Art the Solitary because of it."

Macha issued a sudden command that Aria could not understand. "Fanacht le Solas!"

All of the men, including the one-closed-eyed Balor, turned their faces up toward the smoke hole in the center of the roof. Longbeard leaned close to Aria and whispered, "She said to wait upon the light." At that precise moment the full moon was framed perfectly by the smoke hole as it passed over the Hall of the Speckled Hen. A hushed reverence filled the room until the moon and its light had passed.

"We are moon people", Macha said. "Do you know how to say the word moon in Gaelic, Child?"

"No."

"Gaelach. My husband, Nemed, is also of a moon clan called the Yamnaya. They are remembered as the Bell Beaker people of Languedoc in France. Our time together is at an end now, mo grah, as you require your rest. A place is prepared for you near here and Key is waiting for you at the door to show you the way."

All of the men, except Balor, stood as Macha rose to her feet and left the room. Aria walked out moments later but saw no trace of her moon glow grandmother. Key was waiting as Macha had said. He turned slightly and pointed at a cottage only yards away shining in the moonlight. Aria put her cape back on and quickly crossed the short expanse to her night's refuge. The tall white man did not accompany her.

The cottage was framed in climbing white roses that looked like little moons. Candles flickered in each of the windows making the diamond shaped panes shimmer with movement. The wooden door with the half moon window was slightly ajar and Aria could see the glow of a fireplace within. The small house could have been transported from the landscape of the Twilight Land through which she had recently passed.

She closed the door and blew out all the candles. The small room was warm from the fire and its golden glow let her see that no nightgown had been left for her use. She untied the Branch, removed her slippers, cloak, and gown and crawled under the inviting bed covers, placing the Silver Branch on one of her pillows just to keep it close. Just in case. It was her guaranty of a safe passage home and she was never less sure of that eventuality than she was right now on the eve of her return.

Home. Tomorrow she was supposed to go home. Too many doubts spoiled any consideration of celebrating early. The good Reverend Kirk had never returned home and neither had Longbeard's Uncle Connla. Etain had to live her life over again in order to return. What would be her own fate? Had she been too trusting all along? Would she step off her balcony under the falling stars if she could do it over again? She wasn't so sure now. Maybe, like Longbeard, she had paid too high a price to have this magic tied to her waist. Had she lost her Eden for good?

Macha was right about her needing rest but sleep did not come easy this night. She stared at the moon until it set behind the horizon. By then she had formulated her plan to tell the tall white man that she had decided not to visit Emain Ablach after all and then have him show her how to activate the Branch enabling her to leave. No doubt it was something very simple. So simple that she should have thought of it all along. Beneath the covers, Aria clicked her heels together three times and said, "There's no place like home." Disappointed to still be in Northern Ireland, she rolled over on her side and finally fell asleep.

Ancestor of May of the Moon Men

Saint Columba

Apostle of the Picts

Ancestor of Wilson of the Silver Branch

CHAPTER EIGHT

The road to hell is broad and straight
The road to heaven is thick with briars
The road to Faery is a winding path through the ferns

> Thomas the Rhymer
> Scottish nobleman who met the
> Queen of Elphame

"They are surely there, the divine people, for only we who have neither simplicity nor wisdom have denied them, and the simple of all times and the wise men of ancient times have seen them and even spoken to them."

> William Butler Yeats

"A safe fairyland is unknown in all worlds."

> J.R.R. Tolkien

"God doesn't make the material, he just makes the patternings."

> Salina Adams Martin
> Age 3

> God is light. In Him there is no darkness at all.
>
> 1 John 1:5

ARIA FELL ASLEEP on Iron Mountain but she woke up in an apple orchard. Trees heavy with fruit surrounded her thatched roof cottage. But it was summer air that moved dream-like across the room where she lay. Autumn is apple season, not summer. The breeze had pushed open a window and apples hung just outside within reach. She moved naked across the room and plucked one. It was unlike any apple Aria had ever eaten in her life so she reached for a second one to devour as well. It was then that she saw the man watching from a distance.

Surprised at first to be seen naked, she was even more surprised that she had completely forgotten about this being the day she would return home. She stepped back near the bed and slipped into her gown from the day before and tied on the apple branch. Before she could slip into her shoes she heard a soft tap on the door. It amazed her how quickly these people could move.

Answering the door, she was again perplexed to discover that her guide was not the tall white man after all. He was far more normal looking except for his extreme good looks which immediately made her like him. He was dressed in green with a peacock feather in his Robin Hood style hat. He wore a gold torc around his neck and more gold jewelry on his bare arms and ankles.

"I'm Midhir, King of the Fairies. I'm here to escort you to the Council."

Aria sucked in her breath and hoped her proclamation would be effective. "Actually, I've decided not to go to Emain Ablach."

"Too late!", he proclaimed while looking around at the apple orchard surrounding the cottage. He looked and sounded annoyed with her and suddenly he didn't seem quite so likable.

"Is it you who kidnapped an ancestor of mine named Etain?" Aria put more force into this statement than the last. She was determined to let him know that she knew who he was and would not be letting him manipulate her.

His words were cold. "I believe that the word you heard is "wooed". Kidnapping is not necessary when your supposed victim follows you like a puppy dog. Etain is the object of my affection, whereas you are an assignment."

Aria felt her ego deflate and as had happened so many other times on the journey, she also felt shame for her ridiculous assumptions. Why would the Fairy King, and for heaven's sake, anyone this incredibly handsome, even consider "wooing" someone as old and ordinary as Aria anywhere? He turned sharply and walked away. She left her shoes behind on the stone floor and followed after him without a second thought. A bit like a puppy dog.

They walked for a fair distance through the endless orchard without any conversation between them. This man was not her grandfather and judging by his demeanor, probably hadn't a care in the world whether Aria made it home today or not. All she could do now was hope that someone on the Council was going to take pity on her and allow her to return to a home that she missed more than she ever could have imagined.

After a time they arrived at a tall hedge that formed a wall through the orchard where only a chest high metal gate afforded a view beyond. The view beyond appeared to be more endless orchard.

"You must pass through this gate to reach your destination", he said while stepping back from it.

Aria examined it and discovered that it had neither latch nor hinges. The gate appeared to be welded to the gateposts with no way to open it. A two foot length of three inch diameter pipe was also welded to the top of the gate perpendicular to the ground looking like a telescope so Aria peered through. The scene through the pipe was different from the one looking over the gate. Startled, she looked back at Midhir. "This gate doesn't open."

"You must pass through the keyhole."

"What keyhole?"

"The pipe you just peered through."

"I don't understand. It's three inches wide."

He turned around and picked up a garden statue that was nearly concealed within the overgrown hedge. It was of an angel carved in stone that stood nearly three feet high with retracted wings and long wavy hair. The muscles of his bare arms flexed with the weight of the statue as he raised it up level with the top of the gate. Then he did the impossible and fed the stone statue through the pipe as if feeding sausage into a casing. A moment later it reappeared on the other side in its original bulk and now stood just beyond the gate staring back at them. Suddenly Midhir approached her and touched her hand. The sensation was so foreign and disturbing that she did not notice her own journey through the pipe with Midhir.

Speechless, Aria found herself beyond the gate looking out over Emain Ablach. There was no orchard here. Her view was of a vast plain of green grass as far as the eye could see. In the center of this plain was an apple tree so large that the climate zone in the topmost branches was different than the one at the trunk. A wind passed over the plain and the heavy laden tree played its apples orchestra style. Beautiful music filled the air and all of Aria's senses until she realized she had forgotten to breathe. She clutched the head of the angel for support and stared in disbelief at the behemoth chiming in the open field. Now she noticed something standing alongside the tree. A tower, tall and thin and apparently made of glass or something, maybe crystal, because the tree could been seen through it.

"Aluminum", Midhir said reading her thoughts. "Transparent aluminum."

"I don't want to go there", she said feeling suddenly apprehensive.

"Too late!", he pointed out again and now they were standing on the grass gazing up at the see-through tower. Thunder cracked and made Aria jump as the bright sunny day darkened beneath rain-heavy black clouds that had appeared directly over the tree and the tower.

Midhir touched her lightly on the wrist and delivered her instantly into the space at the top of the tower where the Council awaited her arrival. The storm boomed as loudly within the transparent walls as it had without and the slender tower swayed dangerously toward the apple tree playing its thunderous bells. If she wasn't so frightened she might have recognized the tune as Night on Bald Mountain.

The rain began to fall with such ferocity that the deafening roar of it lashing against the aluminum walls drowned out the chiming symphony altogether. The needle shaped structure was surely about to snap in the unrelenting hurricane of a wind. Aria was forgetting to breathe again only this time from terror.

There were eight or nine individuals in the transparent tower top room and it seemed as if Midhir was making introductions but Aria didn't hear a word of it. Her mind had shut down. Insanity had made its appearance just as she suspected it would all along. Whatever words Midhir was speaking were not reaching her rational mind. She had tucked that safely inside of herself where she was currently hiding and neither of them would be emerging any time soon. Was that a bear over there?

Three birds were now in the room with Aria and the others. Tall birds. Probably cranes. Moments later all three had hopped atop Midhir's shoulders and outstretched arm. She noticed that he had stopped talking and his expression was still one of annoyance with her. And yet he spoke to her and she heard his words. "These are my birds. Denial, Despair and Churlishness." The three birds stared at her and even they seemed annoyed with her.

"What is churlishness?"

"Ill natured and rude."

Aria couldn't deny the despair she was feeling over having been wooed to fairyland. Pretend to be someone's grandparent and they'll follow you anywhere evidently. What an idiot she had been. What a gullible fool. Robert Kirk was probably here feeling just as foolish. None of it mattered now. She was never going home again and that thought alone was more than she could bear. Gone was her Eden and the life that she loved. She had traded it away, and just like her Emery's ancestor, Longbeard, she regretted it. But wait! Maybe she still had a chance. "Is one of you Manannan macLir?"

"I am he", a tall man with sea-weedy looking hair answered.

"I regret giving up my home for this Silver Branch and I would like to trade it back."

"I have no further use of it. You are welcome to keep it."

"Well I want to go home. I need to go home." That being said, she began to cry.

The rain stopped as her tears began. The dark ominous clouds were gone. The summer sun was shining in the cloudless blue sky and the tree playing its melodious tune could once again be heard. Even Midhir and his churlishness had left the building.

"Untie the Branch and you will be home", said the Man of the Sea.

Without a moment's hesitation Aria grabbed the silver ribbon and tugged. The knot only barely loosened before Aria found herself standing once again in her glass tower room. The tea cup and the toast were lying on the floor. The sun was shining but all else was the same. So shocked, so startled was she to be finally where she thought she would never be again, that her hand jerked involuntarily pulling the knot tight and thus depositing her once again before the Council in the top of the transparent tower. She gasped and pulled to loosen the knot again. And again she transported effortlessly to her Eden's tower. Relief rained down like the storm she had just experienced. It was finally over. She was home. All manner of things were well. She went to remove the Silver Branch from her waist when an emotion tugged at her and stilled her hands. They had not lied and wooed her to fairyland after all because she was home. The passport had worked, just as promised. No harm had come to her. They had merely answered her questions and fed her. She was certain that she probably only had this one last opportunity in life to act very very brave and if she did, she would know from that point on that she was not ordinary, for an ordinary person would not do what she was about to do. Aria pulled the knot tight again and looked confidently into the eyes of the Council who had assembled to meet her.

"You can only do that one more time and only one way", Manannan told her.

Aria took her seat before the Council. Four men, five women and a bear sat across from her in the circular room. She was staring at them like they were specimens at the Reptile Gardens in South Dakota. The bear sat in a large chair that looked as if it had been carved from a massive tree trunk. The bear sat upright and crossed its legs. There was a tiny blue skinned woman glowing like a night light and a paper white woman who resembled Key. The white woman also appeared to be glowing. In fact they all had a bit of a shine to them that was pleasant to behold.

Manannan introduced them. "I am your uncle, Child. And I am the ruler here in Emain Ablach. Linus, he pointed out, is also your uncle and Arianrhod over there is your aunt. All else are your grandparents. First I will introduce the Primal Mothers. Danu of the Tuatha de Danaan, Waters of Heaven" he said indicating the tall white woman. "Mathonwy, the Bear of the Ash Grove", he nodded toward the bear. "Circe of the Agathrsi, Ruler of the Stars", this said of the blue glowing woman. "Freya, Disir of the Vanir, and wife to Odin." There was one other woman sitting with the group but she was not introduced. Nor did she glow. "Freya's husband, Odin", he indicated of the man with the broad brimmed hat covering half his face, "god of War and Wisdom, who is the great grandson of the Primal Father, the giant Ymir. Next to Odin is Beli Mawr, Mathonwy's son-in-law and my brother's boy. Beli Mawr is the father of your aunt, Arianrhod, Goddess of the Moon. Your uncle Linus, Mathonwy's great great grandson, is the first bishop of Rome. Linus is the first Pope. And last, but very far from least, is Mary Magdalene, Stella Maris, Mistress of the Waters." Indicating, the blue woman again he said, "Circe, the most ancient of us, is your seventy-fifth-ago ancestor and the remainder of us range from your fifty-eighth-ago to your sixty-sixth-ago. We are the Council."

Aria was speechless. She wasn't at all surprised to find all these mythological types here in fairyland, but Mary Magdelene? On the Council in fairyland? She had always assumed that the mythological beings lived eons ago, so far into the annuls of time that there would be no conceivable way to determine just when. But here they were contemporaries of Mary and therefore contemporaries of Jesus. This was the mythological age? Then this was the Beginning of Things. It had to be because she was on her way home. Her quest complete.

"Did you travel here two thousand years ago from the Lands Beneath?"

Danu nodded.

"What is your home called?"

"It is called the Green Diamond. Its center is shaped like a heart and called the Glen of Precious Stones. The four cities sit at the four points. They are called Falias, place of the Stone of Destiny, Murias, place of the Cauldron of Regeneration, Gorias, place of the Sword of Light and Fanias, place of the Spear of Destiny. The heart-shaped center of the Green Diamond glows red like a ruby yet contains all gems within it. It is in this Glen of Precious Stones that we refresh our long lives."

"Is that where we are now, in the Green Diamond?"

"This is Elphame. It is a region in Southern Scotland that is prepared for us by the sons of Macha and Nemed."

"Why did you leave the Green Diamond to come here?"

"It is in decline. Its citizens are debased. The Fomorians and the Fir Bolgs migrate first to this dimension."

"I thought the Lands Beneath was a perfect world. A kind of paradise. How can it fall into decline?"

"It is an assumption of yours that perfection exists. All things strive toward perfection. Your own world included. All conditions exist in all realities. We in the Lands Beneath strive for perfection and sometimes fail. The Watchers enlist the influence of the Royal Sidhe to counter balance the violence and debauchery escalating here on earth.."

"Aren't you the Watchers?"

"No. And neither are we gods or goddesses. The Roman Church wants to add us to their lexicon of saints, but the Irish adamantly oppose. We are not saints either. We are a different type of being from an inter-dimensional reality that you refer to as magical invaders."

"Do you know who God is?"

"We know of the spark of God in this place. We call it Ak."

"The sun in the Lands Beneath?" Aria looked unconvinced.

"Would you prefer a man with a long white beard?"

Not wanting to argue with a magical invader, Aria still could not let this go. "We are told that man is created in God's image."

"There are geneticists acting as gods on earth. It is they who say "let us make man in our image"."

"The Bible does not mention more than one God."

"But it does, Child. Adon and El Shaddai."

"Well that is what Esclarmonde was saying, there is a good creator God of light and an evil god of the dark material world. So Ak is the good Creator God?"

"God is light and Ak is that spark on this world, an energy force that is somehow connected to everything. We all possess that light. There is a spark in each of us giving us all the ability to be like God the Creator and to create."

"She speaks of our concept of the All One", Odin interjected. "It is an interconnectedness that permeates all that is. Our symbol for that is Odin's Cross."

Freya punched her husband lightly in the arm. "Do you have to make everything your own?" She looked at Aria and explained. "You hear it called the ball and cross. The Creator's Cross."

Odin smiled and winked at his wife. 'I'll get away with it when I can, Woman." But to Aria he said, "She speaks truth. It isn't mine alone. The Spartans use it and the Nemedians, the North and South Americans, the Egyptians and Babylonians and countless others as well."

"What does it symbolize to you?"

"Love and light. The Creator."

"But you are a god of war, aren't you?", Aria asked wondering about the dichotomy.

Odin didn't seem to take her remark as an insult at all when he replied. "The cosmos is pluralistic, Child. Religion, on the other hand, is starkly dualistic, black or white, all or nothing. You are for me or against me. Primordial unity is not divided into two opposing sides. You correctly label me a god of war because I am one. I am called

Terrible One. But I am also Allfather because seven out of eight Anglo Saxon genealogies start with me. The principal of universal order, Child, is that in One is All. Creation is not labeled good or bad, it just is!"

Aria wondered why Odin wore his hat pulled down so far over his face. It was difficult to make out his expressions but his words sounded kind, god of war or not. The gargantuan apple tree was playing an uplifting refrain making Aria happy with her decision to return.

"What kind of an influence did the Watchers expect you to have on the world, Danu?"

"Genetic. My son, the Dagda, and the earthen river goddess, Boanne, produce my grandson, Aengus Og. Her river, the Boyne, runs right by Watcher Headquarters."

"Mt. Herman in Phoenicia?"

"No. Uamh Greine, the Cave of the Sun, in Ireland. Newgrange. Brugh na Boinne. Aengus uses words to trick the Dagda out of it. It is the place where Enoch pleads for clemency for the sinning Watchers."

"But I thought you went to Cong."

"We battle at Cong for the right to control the Brugh na Boinne. The clock."

"What clock?"

"Newgrange is the clock. A Venus clock. Until the invention of the atomic clock, it is the most accurate clock in the world. It measures sacred time."

"Why is measuring time important?"

"It is the control mechanism of this dimension. Time is the illusion that operates this reality. You are time bound. How do you measure time, Child?"

"By the stars?"

"Yes, Child, by the stars. And when they move over your head they make music. The Music of the Spheres. Your dance of life is created by this symphony of sound. We, of the Sidhe, know how to manipulate this magic."

"How can time be other than what it is?"

"Real time is one infinite moment called the now. People on earth spend the least amount of their lives there. The past and future live only in people's regrets and expectations which then become the focus of their thoughts. A thought is energy and since energy flows where attention goes, their energy is forever sent off into the nowhere. A people with no energy are easy to control."

"How do we live in the now?"

"Be like God. Create. It is impossible to even think about the past or the future when one is lost in the godlike endeavor of creating. Ask an artist, a baker, a mother giving birth, the mathematician seeking the solution. Power resides in the now. By distractions with past and future, that power is lost."

"And you use the moon to move the stars?"

"The Chaldeans say that the lights of the stars are imbedded in nested, inverted, crystal bowls called the Firmament."

"These bowls are moved independently by star angels", little blue Circe said, "of which I am one."

"I am one too" added Arianrhod. "And St. Catherine."

"Do you all live at Newgrange?"

"I live at Caer Sidi", Arianrhod answered, "a revolving island at the North Pole, directly beneath the Stella Maris, the Star of the Sea."

Odin expounded. "That is the North Star, Child. It is the light that looks down on the top of the World Tree that transverses both worlds. It is the center around which all the lights of heaven revolve. The moon is brought in to move them."

"Brought in by whom?"

"Mani, the moon mother. She pulls Buri, the moon, into place behind her chariot. Then she kidnaps two children, Jakka and Bil, from Middle Earth, the surface world, and puts them to work on Buri."

"Two children?"

Arianrhod answered. "Jack and Jill. Jakka means to increase and Bil means to dissolve. Waxing and waning."

"Oh, I see now, it's allegorical."

Odin took the conversation back. "No it isn't allegorical. The wolf,

Hati, is going to devour Buri at the Battle of Ragnarok. And the wolf, Fenrir, of the North Pole, will be loosed to devour the sun."

"The Valkyries have something to do with that battle, right?"

"I am like a Valkyrie", Arianrhod said, "but called a Swan Maiden. I escort fallen warriors to Emania, the Land of the Moon, to prepare for Ragnarok."

"You must be very busy, Arianrhod. You spin the moon to spin the stars to give us time and seasons but then you also carry fallen warriors to the moon?"

"Not to the moon. To Emania, the Land of the Moon. These are family obligations. My father's brother, Cassibellanus, is also a servant of the moon."

Beli Mawr grinned at his daughter with pride but spoke to Mathonwy. "Tell the Child how to read the seasons in your portrait."

Aria was surprised by the soft feminine voice being uttered by the bear. "In the stars I am represented as Ursus Major. Do you know of this constellation?"

"I think it's the Big Dipper."

"Correct, the Big Dipper that endlessly circles the Stella Maris marking out the seasons. It also points out which star is the Stella Maris, the North Star, also called Arcturus, the bear guardian. Locate the handle of Ursus Major and follow the arc to Arcturus. The handle pointing east means spring, pointing south is summer, west is autumn and north is winter."

Aria was pleased that she felt no fear as her bear grandmother explained about the stars. And her next question was for the Terrible One, who also did not scare her. "What happens in the Battle of Ragnarok?", she asked Odin.

"The world is destroyed, only to be rebuilt as Okoiner, Land of Warmth, where the red brick walls and the golden roof of the Hall of Sindri appear"

"So it's a happy ending then."

Odin laughed heartily at her remark. "If we win, Child, only if we win!"

Two small blue men entered the tower room pushing a cart as tall as themselves. On the cart were glasses of blackberry wine and goblets of mead arranged around a bowl of golden apples.

"Join us in a refreshment, Child", Odin said as all nine of the Council members rose from their seats to shuffle over to the drink cart.

Aria picked up a glass of wine and then offered it to Odin standing next to her. Freya, holding her own glass of wine, told Aria, "He can't drink the wine. His diet consists of mead and these apples only. But you should drink the wine, Child, you'll find it most delicious."

Odin picked up a goblet of mead for himself and handed one to Mathonwy.

"You look very healthy for a man who lives on honey wine and apples", Aria said.

"It's not by choice. I'm not immortal, even in the Otherworld. Here it is even harder to maintain my youthful countenance so I stick with drinking just the sacred mead and eating only the Apples of Idun."

"What is it with you people and apples?"

"Apples are a treasure of the Otherworld. The rest of the supernatural treasures feed the mind and the soul and the quest for power and riches. Naturally, those remain always in the hands of a few. Apples are a fifth dimensional treasure available to all that feeds the physical self. An apple is of the rose family and like the rose, vibrates with the same frequency as love." Odin bent over to pet one of the two wolves who sat passively at his feet. "This is Geri. And that one is Freki. They are my friends. I am of the wolf line."

"What is the wolf line?"

"The Albigens. I am Goth and of the wolf line. You met the del Acqs and the High Kings of Ireland who are of the apple line. The Picts and the Merovingians are of the bee line. Dal Riata are the rose line."

"You are the Elves!"

"Not according to my wife", he laughed. He glanced over at Freya sipping her wine.

She gave him a momentary contemptuous scowl. "A real elf is a lover of peace, Old Man."

"I won't deny you that, Woman."

"Because you can't", she bantered back, "having drunk from the Cauldron."

"Freya speaks of the Cauldron of the Well of Wisdom", he said. "I earned my one drink fair and square by allowing myself to be impaled on the World Tree, the Ash, for nine days and nine nights."

Freya clucked her tongue and added, "And he gives up one eye for it too!"

"Whoa! Was it worth it?"

"Absolutely!"

Odin was smiling with pride and Freya was looking like the critical wife, her words a bit venomous. "Quick to boast of your exploits, Langobarden? Why don't you tell the child about your part in vanquishing the peace loving Vanir?"

"I can't deny you that either, Woman. I said I was sorry. How many times do you want me to say it?"

"Have you said it to Frey even once?"

"Who is Frey?", Aria asked.

"My brother in Alfheim", Freya said. "He is Lord of the Light Elves and god of rain and sunshine. The storm we enjoyed when you arrived is his. Odin here, enters this reality through Alfheim, our home of the gentle folk. We have no need or knowledge of violence so you can just picture how effortless it is to vanquish us. Odin erases our history from his stories and proclaims himself as Elf King. He covets our magic and forces me to teach it to him. He already tortured our sorceress, Gullveig, so naturally I'm thrilled to comply." Sarcasm dripped from her words.

"Why did you marry him?", Aria asked. She recognized the critical banter that most wives direct toward their husbands in social settings when it is least possible for them to defend themselves.

"Genetics, Child. Odin and I are the parents of Skjold, Yngvi and Tiu."

"What was that other name you called him?"

"Langobarden. Longbeard."

"You are the only one who calls me that, Freya, and don't think I don't know why. You'll never cease the taunting for having outwitted me over the Winilli."

"You deserve whatever taunting you get. I'll tell the story. The Winilli are a Scandinavian tribe. Your sixty-fifth-ago grandmother, Gambara, is their leader. They overpopulate and experience a forced exodus to Scoringia, ruled by the Vandals. A battle is set to ensue between the Winilli and the Vandals. The night before the battle, the leader of the Vandals meets with Odin to see if he can tell him who will win. Odin announces that the first troops he sees in the morning will be declared the winners. Well, your grandmother Gambara comes to consult with me in search of the same information. I know that the Winilli are smaller in troop size so I advise her to have the wives of the warriors tie their long hair in front of their faces like beards and join their husbands on the battlefield. At dawn Odin says to me, "Who are these long beards?" I make him honor his oath and declare the Winilli the winners. They change their name to Langobarden and later, Lombard, and practice a cult of Odin. Charlegmagne is at one time their king."

"Charlemagne doesn't deserve to be anyone's king, bloodline or papal", Mathonwy growled, her voice no longer soft. "He forfeits his soul, if you ask me, when he slaughters the bears."

Beli Mawr and Linus each took a goblet of mead and Beli handed another one to Mathonwy, his mother-in-law, who had already drained her cup.

"Are you two related?", Aria asked of Beli and Linus.

"Yes." Beli answered. "I'm married to Mathonwy's daughter, Don, and Linus is our descendant through our son, Llud Llaw Ereint. Llud rules Camulod."

"So you are the first pope of Rome, Linus? Didn't you feel awkward accepting the Bishop of Rome job knowing that the Apostles had chosen James the Just?"

"Not really. The Judaism that Paul espouses follows the traditions of Moses. The Apostles are inspired by the older Enochian Judaism. My appointment as Bishop of Rome is perfectly legitimate. I'm installed by

Paul himself. It's written up in the Apostolic Constitutionality, Book One, Chapter 46."

Beli laughed and slapped him on the back good naturally. "Yet look at the staff he carries. It's made from the sacred ash tree. The Romans aren't going to risk an affront to Enochian ways if they can help it."

Linus felt compelled to come to the defense of his church. "Those old traditions don't change over night. It is a gradual transference. For instance, Peter and Paul's High Church switches family awareness to a cult of saints. Folk songs are replaced with Bible readings and praise for the greenwood changes to stories of the desert. Change is the only constant. It is the time of change."

"But Peter is an Apostle. Why would he switch religious sects?"

Mary Magdelene picked up her glass of wine and answered Aria's question. "Because of what Linus just said about it being a time of change. The matriarchal, which expresses a reverence for women, is changing to the patriarchal, expressing a reverence for men. Peter and Paul do not revere women and so are good candidates to usher in this change. Peter does not even believe that women are worthy of life."

"What made it the time of change?"

"The Music of the Spheres. The Procession of the Equinox. A new epoch begins. The earth moves into the time of Pisces, the fish. This epoch winds down in your modern era."

"They label you a harlot to denigrate you! That must be so discouraging to you."

"Not at all, Child. The shoemaker is still making his shoes. My ancestor and yours, Enoch, is the shoemaker. When he is translated into an angel it becomes his purpose to unify spiritual energies in order to reveal their common connection to the divine. Much like sewing shoes together. He is still sewing."

"You guys lived two thousand years ago. Even he must be getting discouraged by now."

"Oh never! Work is achievement. The time spent at the work is immaterial. If the work continues, the result eventually arrives. There is a mountain in your state of South Dakota that is being shaped into a Native American hero by the name of Crazy Horse. When one lone individual, the sculptor, chinks away the first rocks in that transformative process, he knows that he will never see the end result. But he is not discouraged. He can see in his mind's eye the finished sculpture, regardless of its magnitude. His wife and children continue to chip away at his dream, now theirs, after he dies. Slowly, Crazy Horse emerges from the mountain. Legions of people pick up the dream and continue the work. It does not stop. The day is coming when all of those who contribute to the work will see the largest manmade monument on earth be made manifest by their hands."

"You have to wonder where someone like that sculptor came up with such a grandiose plan in the first place."

"The Irishman, William Butler Yeats, says that it comes from a daimon."

"A demon?"

"No. It is pronounced 'Die Moan'. It is a guardian spirit who guides and protects the ones it watches over. It loans us its enormous energy or keeps it from us, depending on our choices in life. Do we go after the big picture or are we happy with the small? The sculptor of the mountain chooses the very big picture. There is no size limit on dreams. The daimon is bored by our petty trivial pursuits and sickened by us when we choose in favor of them over the grand passion that is our life's work. We are most loved by this guardian spirit when we take on the impossible and dare to believe we can achieve it."

"Why are you here, Mary, in Emain Ablach serving on the Council with all the mythological people?"

"This Council is your family. I am your family. It is our way to teach you about the All One. About the interconnectedness of all things."

"But did you actually know these people when you were alive on earth?"

"Of course. My daughter is married to the grandson of Beli Mawr and Don. Mathonwy and I share descendants. We all share descendants and only want the best for them as you do for yours."

"I classify Beli and his wife as mythological. Certainly your daughter didn't marry a mythological type."

"Yes, she marries a giant. His name is Bran and he is also an Archdruid. Bran the Blessed, we all call him. We are very proud of him. The sweet dear is decapitated but even then his head continues to live and prophesize."

"Is this allegorical?"

"Not at all. Bran is quite historical. His head is buried at the Tower of London."

"Is Bran a Fomorian, like Balor in Ireland?"

"Mathonwy's family is in Wales", the little blue woman said reaching for her glass of wine "Don't you just love this blackberry wine? Danu and her people brought it here from the Green Diamond."

"Is that your home too?"

"Agartha is my home in Hyperborea. The blue people are the first group to migrate out of Hyperborea. The Fomorians sail here from Bereshia near the Green Diamond."

"How is it possible to sail a boat from another dimension in an upside down world?"

"The North Pole is not a block of ice. It's an ocean. And in the ocean is a hole. The hole is an entrance to the Lands Beneath. There are books written by people, who whether by chance or design, are able to transverse these realities by either sailing or flying through."

"Wouldn't passenger planes see this hole when they fly over the pole?"

"Planes do not fly over the pole. That secretive route is left to Admiral Byrd and his fellow Masons to discover."

"The Hyperboreans take this route", Beli said. "They are the descendants of Boreas, who migrate to the British Isles. I am of this line. The mother of Boreas is EOS, the Shining Dawn, sister to Selene, the Moon. Their descendants in this world are known for their Rh negative blood and being born with white hair."

"I was born with Rh negative blood and white hair!", Aria said with awe and a bit of pride.

"We know this, Child. That is why you are here."

"Is Selene the moon in Hyperborea?"

"There is no moon in Hyperborea. There is no night. There is no sleep."

"But sleep is nice."

"Selene thinks so too. She even seduces Endymion so that he chooses to stay asleep always just to be in her presence."

"Who is Endymion?"

"The Man in the Moon."

"I can't help but notice that you people all shine like the moon. Why is that?"

Beli glowed a little brighter by her words. "We are the Shining Ones. We are self aware that we are a spark of the All One whom we call Love and Light and so we don't hide it. I have another name, Belanus, which means the Shining One. The word elf means to shine. The el in Gabriel, Raphael and Michael means to shine. Eloh in Elohim means to shine."

"Who are the Elohim?"

Mary Magdalene set her glass back on the cart. "The Elohim are exiled here to watch over the Gate of the Elder Gods, not to practice genetic manipulation on the populace as they end up doing. Their gene slicing takes on a life of its own when the side effects are a wider than normal range of emotions, the strongest being love. With love comes creativity, an unstoppable force like the love engine that drives it. The opposite spectrum of greed and power also become present. But this does not make humans an experiment to be watched. Humans are a wonderment. The more adverse the conditions, the more creative the response to them."

Aria set her wine glass down too and noticed that the room was beginning to thin out. The Council members were talking among themselves and laughing softly in bell sounds. The meeting was at an end and it was finally time for Aria to return home. Goodbyes had not been a part of her experience here in this time squished world. Now that she felt assured that she would be leaving for good, her emotions were about to have her clinging to the door jambs. She was going to miss these people who had gone to such lengths to teach her something. Her throat constricted and once again she found herself struggling to fight back tears. A side effect of being human, she figured.

Mathonwy padded over near to Aria. "Don't cry, Child. We forced you to experience exile by frightening you with Frey's storm today and having Midhir, the kidnapper, guide you here. But we are the ones in exile. You are going home. We never will. Remember our plight, take heart and send us your love."

"How could I not?', Aria sniffed and put her arms around the soft furry neck of Mathonwy and gave her a hug.

"It pleases me, Child, that you have lost your fear of bears. You have only to look up and I'm there. Find the Stella Maris. I'm the second star to the right."

"And straight on till morning!", Aria quoted Peter Pan. "Those are the directions to Neverland." It amused her that Peter Pan hadn't turned out to be one of her ancestors after all.

Mathonwy walked away and Circe was the next grandmother to approach Aria. She lightly touched the Silver Branch at Aria's waist and pointed out that as an elf maiden Aria was also the Guardian of Starlight. Then she reached up on tip toe and whispered something in Aria's ear and she too walked away.

Danu approached next with a package in her hands tied up with silver ribbon. "Please give this gift to your sister, the Queen Ma Suit, and take with you six things to remember. The first three are the fairy elements and they are the three esteemed above all else. They are Fire, Water and Light. Fire is God's touch, Water is the mother of life and Light is God Himself. The last three, as important as these, are the hazel, the sun, and the plough. The hazel is the tree of knowledge, the sun, our sun, is the creator of our world and the plough is Ursus Major, the Big Dipper, that we hide in plain sight to remind you that you are living in a loop of endless seasons." Danu also gave Aria quiet instructions as to the gift for her sister and she too walked away.

Mary Magdalene not only approached Aria, she put her arms around her and hugged her in a loving mother's embrace. The sensation of human touch, the scent of human skin and the love in the embrace turned Aria to mush and she cried like a baby. Mary kept hugging her until the tears stopped. Then holding her out at arm's length and staring into Aria's red rimmed eyes, she asked, "Do you know what Jesus calls me?"

"No", Aria sniffled.

"Woman Who Knows All. And what I know right now is that you have one more question that was never answered."

"I do? What is it?"

"You want to know who the Watchers are."

"Oh my gosh", Aria exclaimed, "I really do!"

"They are the birds."

"The birds?"

"Yes, Child. Think about it. What other creature in the world speaks your language?"

"You're right. My friend owns birds. She told me once how one of them hid under the covers of the bed. When she finally discovered where he was and lifted the covers up, he looked up at her and said "Peek a Boo!"."

Mary laughed at her story. "And think of the people you have meet here or have been told of who speak the Language of the Birds. People are so used to seeing birds all around them that they don't even notice them. But those who study birds know that it is in their nature to eavesdrop. Birds are also here to evolve into an understanding of love and creativity. They have, in fact, changed from cold blooded to warm as love and affection grows in them. They are recognized as royalty in the fairy realm. King Oak is Robin Redbreast, King Holly is King Wren, or Father Christmas, and Queen Ash is Jenny Wren, beloved Queen of the Fairies."

Freya walked up to Aria with two blue/black ravens perched on each shoulder. Mary lovingly touched Aria's cheek before walking away.

"These two", Freya said, "are Hugin and Munin. Thought and Memory. They are the companions of Odin. They ask me to convey to you that there are reminders of us still in your world. They exist in your names for the days of the week. How you mark time. Sunday and Monday are, of course, named for the Sun and the Moon. Tuesday is named for our son, Tiu. Wednesday is Woden's Day. That is Odin's Saxon name. Friday is my day, Freya's Day. And Saturday is Saturn's Day. Saturn is another name for Chronos, Time, the existence in which you find yourselves."

This information pleased Aria and she expected Freya to walk away also but she remained in place. Suddenly, to Aria's great surprise, the bird Munin began to speak. It was not human speech and yet for some inexplicable reason, Aria could understand it. "A state of zero polarity can be reached", Munin said, but it was Hugin that finished the sentence, "by following the Golden Rule and doing all things in moderation." Then Munin spoke again saying, "Remember this…you think the gods are dead." Again Hugin completed the thought, "But they think you are!"

Freya and Odin's ravens left then leaving Aria alone in the transparent tower top room with Manannan macLir, Man of the Sea, Ruler of Emain Ablach. "Thank you for inviting me and giving me this opportunity", she said to him. "And especially thank you for loaning me the Silver Branch."

"I am known for my gifts. As I said before, the Branch is yours to keep. I have a feeling you will be giving it away yourself very soon. Did you know that I give the Cauldron of Regeneration to the Dagda, Danu's son, when they move into the Brugh na Boinne?"

"It surprises me that a matriarchal people would have men as their rulers."

"Your modern author, John Crowley, will wisely say, "the hardest thing in any civilization is to find something for the men to do!" Don't you love it?", he laughed. "Before I came here I ruled the Green Diamond jointly with Tethra, the Fomorian king. Notice how we screwed that one up too!" And he laughed some more.

"Manannan? If it is true that there is no outer space beyond our bubble world, what is out there?"

"Water. The Waters of Life. The Primordial Sea", said the Man of the Sea. "Now I have one last gift to give away and it is for your brother, Prince Hazno." Manannan reached inside the pocket of his tunic and pulled out nothing and handed it to Aria. He explained its significance and new purpose while she stared, amazed, at the nothing in her hands. Then imagining her brother with such a gift she broke out laughing and Manannan joined in. And so with the laughter of the ruler of the Plain of Apples ringing in her ears, Aria loosed the Branch and went home for good.

EPILOGUE

Morongo Valley, Southern California

"There's no place like home."

    Dorothy
    L. Frank Baum, The Wizard of Oz

ARIA WASN'T EXPECTING surprises when she returned home so she was surprised when they showed up. They appeared to her as realizations. Three of them.

The first realization was that home is not bathed in some magical veneer. On the contrary, it appeared almost faded, as if her memory of it had not been entirely true. This effect, although unsettling, passed over time until Aria could once again only discern the harmonious heartbeat of her Eden.

The second realization was that home is not a physical place. Home is something carried inside of one's being and hers had undergone a serious remodel. Like all remodels, once completed, the previous condition of the environment is all but forgotten.

The final surprise was the realization that even though she knew that she was NOT ordinary, it did not serve as a source of self pride. No one, she had discovered is ordinary. All are uniquely individual and All are One. Her own descent from so many unique individuals only left her with a deep sense of noblesse oblige…to whom much is given, much is required. The tiny heart-shaped birthmark on her wrist would forever serve as her reminder.

Once Aria had sufficiently processed these realizations, she threw a dinner party for Queen Ma Suit, Prince Hazno and Little Prince Emery. She set a table for four in her glass tower room with her mother's dishes and her grandmother's silverware. She served blackberry wine, mead and apple cider, white pumpkin soup dyed sky blue, salmon, oatcakes, baked apples in a cinnamon, clove, and nutmeg sauce, scones, split tailed mermaid cookies and Starbucks coffee.

By the time the sun had set behind Mt. San Gorgonio and the stars had come out, she had shared the tales of her adventure with their ancestors. Naturally, they didn't believe a single word she had said. She had always been different. Now was no exception. They loved her anyway.

"I brought memory gifts for each of you. The first one is for you, Ma Suit, from Danu of the Tuatha de Danaan. She calls you the Lady of the Plaids and said only to let you keep your gift if you can name the tartan design it is woven in."

"What?", Ma Suit said aghast. "Don't even give it to me then. I don't know the names of tartan designs."

"You might be surprised", Aria said handing her the package tied up with silver ribbon.

Even before Ma Suit had completely removed the cloak that had kept Aria warm on her adventure, she was laughing with relief. "Why, it's argyll! The diamond design. Everyone knows what argyll is." She was impressed that Aria had gone to such lengths to connect her gift with the fantastical story. But it also had her worried for her sister's sanity.

Aria rambled on as Ma Suit examined her gift. "Clan Campbell's argyll tartan is actually blue. Did you know that blue in Old German means shining? But I'll bet the Council made the cloak green for a reason."

"I love my green diamond cloak!", Ma Suit said as she stroked the soft wool.

"The next gift is for you, Brother. But you won't be able to see it."

Hazno, misunderstanding and feeling slighted, frowned and folded his arms over his chest. Aria thought that he reminded her of Odin with his long grey braided beard. Ignoring his disappointment she said, "Your gift is called Feth Fiada. It is the Cloak of Invisibility belonging to Manannan macLir. It was worn by Lugh, brother in law of King Conchobar, in the second Battle of Moytura against his Fomorian ancestors where he kills his grandfather, Bres, and fulfills the prophesy. Manannan requests a new use for his cloak and so he specifically needs it to belong to you."

"What new use would that be?", Hazno asked now more than mildly intrigued while remaining steadfastly skeptical.

"Mirth. A sense of humor. Sillyness. Do you know where that word silly comes from? Selene the Moon. People get silly when the moon is full." Then she placed what looked like nothing onto her brother's lap beneath the table. Hazno took a quick peek and smiled impishly but said nothing.

"Your gift, Emery, is the Silver Branch that Manannan knew I would be giving to you because it was given to me by your Grandma Rose's Grandpa Wilson." She stood up and collected the Branch from out of a drawer in her dresser. As soon as the three dinner guests heard the otherworldly chimes of the living apple bells, they all had to rethink their insanity evaluation of Aria. She handed the Silver Branch to her Emery and whispered something in his ear. After lowering the lights in the room, Aria sat back down at her place at the table and said to Emery, "Now, mo grah, could you get the lights?"

Emery waved the magical apple branch of his clan, per instructions, at the night sky outside the glass tower windows and the stars began to fall. Every single one of them.

In the twinkling starlight filling the room, Prince Hazno could be seen grinning. He threw the Feth Fiada over his head and disappeared from view. Ma Suit and Emery stared wide eyed in silent disbelief at the spot where Hazno had just been sitting. Aria, knowing her brother well, smiled in anticipation of the surprise she knew would be coming.

Suddenly a long grey braided beard popped into view, held by the miniature toy plastic hand that Prince Hazno always carried in his pants pocket. You never know when you'll need one. The tiny hand twirled the beard braid round and round and round like the pastie on a strippers breast. And they laughed and they laughed and they laughed.

As their laughter rang out over Aria's starlit Eden, two little sparrows sat on their nest in the eaves of the glass tower room. A small crack in the slats afforded the birds a view of the family in the room below. A view that had been enjoyed by countless clan of their nesting kind where now and forever they watched.

THE END

Pope Linus

First Bishop of Rome

Ancestor of Nancy Ann of the Virginia Company

Enygeus ha Rama Thea, wife of Bran the Blessed

Ancestor of Mariah of the Masons and Joseph of the New England Company

Mary Magdelen

Ancestor of Mariah of the Masons and Joseph of the New England Company

ACKNOWLEDGEMENTS

I OWE THIS book to a leprechaun I photographed in a tree in Cong, Ireland. I am pretty certain that he is the true author of this story. He is the muse that sat on my shoulder for eight long years and cracked a constant whip to keep me working. He yelled his name in my head, AENGUS OG, from which I discovered the Sidhe. He now lives inside the pages of this book and I think my readers shouldn't be surprised when magic appears in their lives.

I want to thank my grandmother, Irma Armstrong Carnahan, for giving this book its name, and also for inspiring me to write in the first place by giving me her mother, Elizabeth Ebright Armstrong's hand written journal of their covered wagon trip from Salmon City, Idaho to Homestead, Oregon.

I want to thank my daughter, Salina Adams Martin, for receiving the dream about the Green Diamond and I want to thank the fairy woman and Scottish writer, Fiona MacLeod, for revealing its identity.

I want to thank my sister, Susan Carnahan Podell, and my brother, Shawn Carnahan, for helping me to form my questions based on their character of both wise and skeptical investigation as well as an attitude of humor. Aria is an amalgamation of the three of us.

I want to thank my dad's sister, Dolly Carnahan Schultz, for being the catalyst for looking into our genealogy in the first place. And for her passionate love of history and her stewardship in keeping safe all the family information left in her care by her mother, Irma. And I especially want to thank her for her oft pondered idea that, "There's something odd about the Basque!"

I want to thank my mom's sister, Verda Whitcanack Parmelee, for being the giant upon whose shoulders I stood to find this genealogy in the first place. And at under five feet tall, no less. Thank you for all those summers you spent in Cantril, Iowa researching our roots, long before there was such a thing as the internet, and for finding those roots in Plimouth Plantation.

I want to thank my husband Don's relative, who mailed us the hand written, old school researched genealogy of the McEuen clan all the way from Rose McEuen's pioneering of Palm Springs, California with her husband Oliver McKinney, back to Otter and Castle McEuen in Argyll, Scotland.

I want to thank my angelic Valentina Society friends, Kimi and Christina Hicks, for sharing tea party with me every month for seven years where I was fortunate enough to have the light bulb come on over my head illuminating the idea that books and genealogy are a good legacy to pass down to those we love. Where would this book be if we hadn't stopped for tea?

I want to thank Father David Bergdorf for explaining to me what the opposite of love is. And for being an Ambassador of Love himself!

The years I spent writing The Silver Branch contained some of the darkest moments in my long life. And so I especially want to thank my grandson, Hunter Bruce Adams, and my son-in-law, Michael Stenblom, for surviving their ordeals against all odds and teaching every single one of us that Heroes still exist and walk the earth.

I want to thank my friend, Will Nies, for having the courage not to take the End of Life pill when his suffering became too great, and instead allowing Christopher Robin, an unknown stranger, to treat him with his magical oil. And then upon returning to health, to share the oil with his daughter, Kimberly Nies, who passed it to her mother, Lori Altman, with the instructions, "Give this to Dayle, it might just save her life."

I want to thank Christopher, for being the world's best microbiologist, and a faithful friend over the decades to our friend, Seth Tolson, and for saving my life with his magic oil when the dragon of sarcoidosis swallowed me whole.

I want to thank my nephew, Sheridan Carnahan and my daughter-in-law, Michelle Gebhardt Adams for assisting with the computer work that is so foreign to me so that I would have a way to share the Silver Branch by having it published. I want to thank my neighbors, Carla Harrower and Maria Pritchard, for reading the book and then convincing me by their very enthusiasm that the story is indeed not for my family alone but should be shared with all. I want to thank my Aunt Mary Louise Whitcanack, our wonderful friend, Christian Brodine, and heart of my heart, my friend Lori Altman, for providing the generous means to make the sharing a reality. Thank you to all the wonderful people at Archway Publishing, especially you, Teddy Wilhelm, for making the daunting experience of publishing a book such a joyous one. It is a very big deal to get to hold one's Big Picture Dream in one's own hands. My gratitude is to the moon and back.

I want to thank my daughter, Brenna Adams Stemblom, for her remarkable creation of the cover art for the book. And to my son, Kyle Eli Adams, for his surprise creation of the beautiful Silver Branch that Brenna used in the photograph. And I want to thank Brenna Chanel Lee, a fellow author, who modeled for the cover and made Aria look so good!

I want to thank my dogs, Chico and Lewis, and often times even Bo Bo Kitty, for their dogged insistence that we start and end every day with a walk down to the cottonwood grove and back. I don't believe that it is even possible to write a story about a visit to Fairyland if one does not have one's feet daily making contact with Mother Earth.

I want to thank my husband, Don, for cheering me on, year after year, even though I should have been helping to earn a living. And for the laughter and the tears he shed as I read the book to him out loud, not once but twice. And for his infectious humor when he tells people that he might have accidentally married his sister!

And last of all I want to thank a remarkable family which is my own. My primary intention was to leave this story as a legacy for all the descendants of Mariah, Joseph, Nancy Ann, Newt, May and Wilson.

I was surprised to learn how attached I became to all the ancestors as I researched their lives. And I want to thank those ancestors for that morning, when sitting in the sunshine, crying with gratitude that they had come into my life and enriched it beyond comprehension, they gave me yet another gift by having a temporary tiny pink heart appear on the soft underside of my wrist. Love is magic!

IN MEMORIAM

In memory of those who passed from this world while I wrote this book

Dolly Carnahan Schultz

Mary Louise Whitcanack

Cheryl Parmelee

Larry Whitcanack

Bob Armstrong

Kathy Stenblom

Doug Harrower

Rick Stratton

Timothy Shelley

Jane Crase

Joni Popovich

Glenn Podell

Will Nies

Chico and Lewis

Bo Bo Kitty

AFTERWORD

THE CASTLE OF Spirits, where my tale begins is Ashford Castle, once owned by the Guinness Family, on Loch Corrib (named for Manannan macLir) near the village of Cong, Ireland. George V, King of England, once went to visit Ashford Castle for a couple of days and loved it so much that he stayed for a couple of months. On the morning of February 6, 1952, when King George took his last breath in this world, I took my first in the delivery room of the brand new Desert Hospital in Palm Springs, California. My grandmother, Irma, standing at the nursery window, took one look at my wild stand-up white hair and said to her son, "Oh Brownie, No!"